UNFAMILIAR
TERRITORY

BOOKS BY ROBERT SILVERBERG

ROBERT SILVERBERG

UNFAMILIAR TERRITORY

CHARLES SCRIBNER'S SONS

NEW YORK

1 3 5 7 9 11 13 15 17 19   C/C   20 18 16 14 12 10 8 6 4 2

Printed in the United States of America
Library of Congress Catalog Card Number 73–3914
SBN 684–13432–2 (cloth)

ACKNOWLEDGMENTS

"Now + n, Now − n" originally appeared in Nova 2. Copyright © 1972
Harry Harrison.

"Some Notes on the Predynastic Epoch" originally appeared in Bad Moon
Rising. Copyright © 1973 Thomas M. Disch.

"Many Mansions" orginally appeared in Universe 3. Copyright © 1973
Random House, Inc.

"Good News from the Vatican" originally appeared in Universe 1. Copyright © 1971 Terry Carr.

CONTENTS

UNFAMILIAR
TERRITORY

1

CAUGHT IN THE ORGAN DRAFT

Look there, Kate, down by the promenade. Two splendid seniors, walking side by side near the water's edge. They radiate power, authority, wealth, assurance. He's a judge, a senator, a corporation president, no doubt, and she's—what?—a professor emeritus of international law, let's say. There they go toward the plaza, moving serenely, smiling, nodding graciously to passersby. How the sunlight gleams in their white hair! I can barely stand the brilliance of that reflected aura: it blinds me, it stings my eyes. What are they, eighty, ninety, a hundred years old? At this distance they seem much younger—they hold themselves upright, their backs are straight, they might pass for being only fifty or sixty. But I can tell. Their confidence, their poise, mark them for what they are. And when they were nearer I could see their withered cheeks, their sunken eyes. No cosmetics can hide that. These two are old enough to be our great-grandparents. They were well past sixty before we were even born, Kate. How superbly their bodies function! But why not? We can guess at their medical histories. She's had at least three hearts, he's working on his fourth set of lungs, they apply for new kidneys every five years, their brittle bones are reinforced with hundreds of skeletal snips from the arms and legs of hapless younger folk, their dimming sensory apparatus is aided by countless nerve-grafts obtained the same way, their ancient arteries are freshly sheathed with sleek teflon. Ambulatory assemblages of second-hand human parts, spiced here and there with synthetic or mechanical organ-substitutes, that's all they are. And what am I, then, or you?

Nineteen years old and vulnerable. In their eyes I'm nothing but a ready stockpile of healthy organs, waiting to serve their needs. Come here, son. What a fine strapping young man you are! Can you spare a kidney for me? A lung? A choice little segment of intestine? Ten centimeters of your ulnar nerve? I need a few pieces of you, lad. You won't deny a distinguished elder leader like me what I ask, will you? *Will you?*

*   *   *

Today my draft notice, a small crisp document, very official-looking, came shooting out of the data slot when I punched for my morning mail. I've been expecting it all spring: no surprise, no shock, actually rather an anticlimax now that it's finally here. In six weeks I am to report to Transplant House for my final physical exam—only a formality, they wouldn't have drafted me if I didn't already rate top marks as organ-reservoir potential—and then I go on call. The average call time is about two months. By autumn they'll be carving me up. Eat, drink, and be merry, for soon comes the surgeon to my door.

*   *   *

A straggly band of senior citizens is picketing the central headquarters of the League for Bodily Sanctity. It's a counter-demonstration, an anti-anti-transplant protest, the worst kind of political statement, feeding on the ugliest of negative emotions. The demonstrators carry glowing signs that say:

BODILY SANCTITY—OR BODILY SELFISHNESS?

And:

YOU OWE YOUR LEADERS YOUR VERY LIVES

And:

LISTEN TO THE VOICE OF EXPERIENCE

The picketers are low-echelon seniors, barely across the qualifying line, the ones who can't really be sure of getting transplants. No wonder they're edgy about the League. Some of them are in wheelchairs and some are encased right up to the eyebrows in portable life-support systems. They croak and shout bitter invective and shake their fists.

Watching the show from an upper window of the League building, I shiver with fear and dismay. These people don't just want my kidneys or my lungs. They'd take my eyes, my liver, my pancreas, my heart, anything they might happen to need.

*   *   *

I talked it over with my father. He's forty-five years old—too old to have been personally affected by the organ draft, too young to have needed any transplants yet. That puts him in a neutral position, so to speak, except for one minor factor: his transplant status is 5-G. That's quite high on the eligibility list, not the top-priority class but close enough. If he fell ill tomorrow and the Transplant Board ruled that his life would be endangered if he didn't get a new heart or lung or kidney, he'd be given one practically immediately. Status like that simply has to influence his objectivity on the whole organ issue. Anyway, I told him I was planning to appeal and maybe even to resist. "Be reasonable," he said, "be rational, don't let your emotions run away with you. Is it worth jeopardizing your whole future over a thing like this? After all, not everybody who's drafted loses vital organs."

"Show me the statistics," I said. "Show me."

He didn't know the statistics. It was his impression that only about a quarter or a fifth of the draftees actually got an organ call. That tells you how closely the older generation keeps in touch with the situation—and my father's an educated man, articulate, well-informed. Nobody over the age of thirty-five that I talked to could show me any statistics. So I showed them. Out of a League brochure, it's true, but based on certified National Institute of Health reports. Nobody escapes. They always clip you, once you qualify. The need for young organs inexorably expands to match the pool of available organpower. In the long run they'll get us all and chop us to bits. That's probably what they want, anyway. To rid themselves of the younger members of the species, always so troublesome, by cannibalizing us for spare parts, and recycling us, lung by lung, pancreas by pancreas, through their own deteriorating bodies.

*   *   *

Fig. 4. On March 23, 1964, this dog's own liver was removed and replaced with the liver of a non-related mongrel donor. The animal was treated with azathioprine for 4 months and all therapy then stopped. He remains in perfect health 6⅔ years after transplantation.

*   *   *

The war goes on. This is, I think, its fourteenth year. Of course they're beyond the business of killing now. They haven't had any field engagements since '93 or so, certainly none since the organ-draft legislation went into effect. The old ones can't afford to waste precious young bodies on the battlefield. So robots wage our territorial struggles for us, butting heads with a great metallic clank, laying land mines and twitching their sensors at the enemy's mines, digging tunnels beneath his screens, et cetera, et cetera. Plus, of course, the quasi-military activity—economic sanctions, third-power blockades, propaganda telecasts beamed as overrides from merciless orbital satellites, and stuff like that. It's a subtler war than the kind they used to wage: nobody dies. Still, it drains national resources. Taxes are going up again this year, the fifth or sixth year in a row, and they've just slapped a special Peace Surcharge on all metal-containing goods, on account of the copper shortage. There once was a time when we could hope that our crazy old leaders would die off or at least retire for reasons of health, stumbling away to their country villas with ulcers or shingles or scabies or scruples and allowing new young peacemakers to take office. But now they just go on and on, immortal and insane, our senators, our cabinet members, our generals, our planners. And their war goes on and on too, their absurd, incomprehensible, diabolical, self-gratifying war.

*   *   *

I know people my age or a little older who have taken asylum in Belgium or Sweden or Paraguay or one of the other countries where Bodily Sanctity laws have been passed. There are about twenty such countries, half of them the most progressive nations in the world and half of them the most reactionary. But what's the sense of running away? I don't want to live in exile. I'll stay here and fight.

*   *   *

Naturally they don't ask a draftee to give up his heart or his liver or some other organ essential to life, say his medulla oblongata. We haven't yet reached that stage of political enlightenment at which the government feels capable of legislating fatal conscription. Kidneys and lungs, the paired organs, the dispensable organs, are the chief targets so far. But if you study the history of conscription over the ages you see that it can always be projected on a curve rising from rational necessity to absolute lunacy. Give them a fingertip, they'll take an arm. Give them an inch of bowel, they'll take your guts. In another fifty years they'll be drafting hearts and stomachs and maybe even brains, mark my words; let them get the technology of brain transplants together and nobody's skull will be safe. It'll be human sacrifice all over again. The only difference between us and the Aztecs is one of method: we have anesthesia, we have antisepsis and asepsis, we use scalpels instead of obsidian blades to cut out the hearts of our victims.

*   *   *

MEANS OF OVERCOMING THE HOMOGRAFT REACTION

The pathway that has led from the demonstration of the immunological nature of the homograft reaction and its universality to the development of relatively effective but by no means completely satisfactory means of overcoming it for therapeutic purposes is an interesting one that can only be touched upon very briefly. The year 1950 ushered in a new era in transplantation immunobiology in which the discovery of various means of weakening or abrogating a host's response to a homograft—such as sublethal whole body x-irradiation, or treatment with certain adrenal cortico-steroid hormones, notably cortisone—began to influence the direction of the mainstream of research and engender confidence that a workable clinical solution might not be too far off. By the end of the decade powerful immunosuppressive drugs, such as 6-mercaptopurine, had been shown to be capable of holding in abeyance the reactivity of dogs to renal homografts, and soon afterwards this principle was successfully extended to man.

*   *   *

Is my resistance to the draft based on an ingrained abstract distaste for tyranny in all forms or rather on the mere desire to keep my body intact? Could it be both, maybe? Do I need an idealistic rationalization at all? Don't I have an inalienable right to go through my life wearing my own native-born kidneys?

*　　*　　*

The law was put through by an administration of old men. You can be sure that all laws affecting the welfare of the young are the work of doddering moribund ancients afflicted with angina pectoris, atherosclerosis, prolapses of the infundibulum, fulminating ventricles, and dilated viaducts. The problem was this: not enough healthy young people were dying of highway accidents, successful suicide attempts, diving-board miscalculations, electrocutions, and football injuries; therefore there was a shortage of transplantable organs. An effort to restore the death penalty for the sake of creating a steady supply of state-controlled cadavers lost out in the courts. Volunteer programs of organ donation weren't working out too well, since most of the volunteers were criminals who signed up in order to gain early release from prison: a lung reduced your sentence by five years, a kidney got you three years off, and so on. The exodus of convicts from the jails under this clause wasn't so popular among suburban voters. Meanwhile there was an urgent and mounting need for organs; a lot of important seniors might in fact die if something didn't get done fast. So a coalition of senators from all four parties rammed the organ-draft measure through the upper chamber in the face of a filibuster threat from a few youth-oriented members. It had a much easier time in the House of Representatives, since nobody in the House ever pays much attention to the text of a bill up for a vote, and word had been circulated on this one that if it passed, everybody over 65 who had any political pull at all could count on living twenty or thirty extra years, which to a Representative means a crack at ten to fifteen extra terms of office. Naturally there have been court challenges, but what's the use? The average age of the eleven Justices of the Supreme Court is 78. They're human and mortal. They need our flesh. If they throw out the organ draft now, they're signing their own death warrants.

*   *   *

For a year and a half I was the chairman of the anti-draft campaign on
our campus. We were the sixth or seventh local chapter of the League
for Bodily Sanctity to be organized in this country, and we were real
activists. Mainly we would march up and down in front of the draft
board offices carrying signs proclaiming things like:

KIDNEY POWER

And:

A MAN'S BODY IS HIS CASTLE

And:

THE POWER TO CONSCRIPT ORGANS
IS THE POWER TO DESTROY LIVES

We never went in for the rough stuff, though, like bombing
organ-transplant centers or hijacking refrigeration trucks. Peaceful
agitation, that was our motto. When a couple of our members tried to
swing us to a more violent policy, I delivered an extemporaneous
two-hour speech arguing for moderation. Naturally I was drafted the
moment I became eligible.

*   *   *

"I can understand your hostility to the draft," my college advisor said.
"It's certainly normal to feel queasy about surrendering important
organs of your body. But you ought to consider the countervailing
advantages. Once you've given an organ you get a 6-A classification,
Preferred Recipient, and you remain forever on the 6-A roster. Surely
you realize that this means that if you ever need a transplant yourself,
you'll automatically be eligible for one, even if your other personal and
professional qualifications don't lift you to the optimum level. Suppose
your career plans don't work out and you become a manual laborer, for
instance. Ordinarily you wouldn't rate even a first look if you developed
heart disease, but your Preferred Recipient status would save you.
You'd get a new lease on life, my boy."

I pointed out the fallacy inherent in this. Which is that as the
number of draftees increases, it will come to encompass a majority or

even a totality of the population, and eventually everybody will have 6-A Preferred Recipient status by virtue of having donated, and the term Preferred Recipient will cease to have any meaning. A shortage of transplantable organs would eventually develop as each past donor stakes his claim to a transplant when his health fails, and in time they'd have to arrange the Preferred Recipients by order of personal and professional achievement anyway, for the sake of arriving at some kind of priorities within the 6-A class, and we'd be right back where we are now.

*   *   *

Fig. 7. The course of a patient who received antilymphocyte globulin (ALG) before and for the first 4 months after renal homotransplantation. The donor was an older brother. There was no early rejection. Prednisone therapy was started 40 days postoperatively. Note the insidious onset of late rejection after cessation of globulin therapy. This was treated by a moderate increase in the maintenance doses of steroids. This delayed complication occurred in only 2 of the first 20 recipients of intrafamilial homografts who were treated with ALG. It has been seen with about the same low frequency in subsequent cases. (By permission of Surg. Gynec. Obstet. *126 (1968): p. 1023.)*

*   *   *

So I went down to Transplant House today, right on schedule, to take my physical. A couple of my friends thought I was making a tactical mistake by reporting at all; if you're going to resist, they said, resist at every point along the line. Make them drag you in for the physical. In purely idealistic (and ideological) terms I suppose they're right. But there's no need yet for me to start kicking up a fuss. Wait till they actually say, We need your kidney, young man. Then I can resist, if resistance is the course I ultimately choose. (Why am I wavering? Am I afraid of the damage to my career plans that resisting might do? Am I not entirely convinced of the injustice of the entire organ-draft system? I don't know. I'm not even sure that I *am* wavering. Reporting for your physical isn't really a sellout to the system.) I went, anyway. They tapped this and x-rayed that and peered into the other thing. Yawn, please. Bend over, please. Cough, please. Hold out your left arm, please. They marched me in front of a battery of diagnostat machines and I stood there hoping for the red light to flash—*tilt*, get out of here!—but I was, as expected, in perfect physical shape, and I qualified for call. Afterward I met Kate and we walked in the park and held hands and watched the glories of the sunset and discussed what I'll do, when and if the call comes. *If?* Wishful thinking, boy!

* * *

If your number is called you become exempt from military service, and they credit you with a special $750 tax deduction every year. Big deal.

* * *

Another thing they're very proud of is the program of voluntary donation of unpaired organs. This has nothing to do with the draft, which—thus far, at least—requisitions only paired organs, organs that can be spared without loss of life. For the last twelve years it's been possible to walk into any hospital in the United States and sign a simple release form allowing the surgeons to slice you up. Eyes lungs heart intestines pancreas liver anything, you give it all to them. This process used to be known as suicide in a simpler era and it was socially disapproved, especially in times of labor shortages. Now we have a labor surplus, because even though our population growth has been fairly slow since the middle of the century, the growth of labor-eliminating mechanical devices and processes has been quite rapid, even exponential. Therefore to volunteer for this kind of total donation is considered a deed of the highest social utility, removing as it does a healthy young body from the overcrowded labor force and at the same time providing some elder statesman with the assurance that the supply of vital organs will not unduly diminish. Of course you have to be crazy to volunteer, but there's never been any shortage of lunatics in our society.

* * *

If you're not drafted by the age of 21, through some lucky fluke, you're safe. And a few of us do slip through the net, I'm told. So far there are more of us in the total draft pool than there are patients in need of transplants. But the ratios are changing rapidly. The draft legislation is still relatively new. Before long they'll have drained the pool of eligible draftees, and then what? Birth rates nowadays are low; the supply of potential draftees is finite. But death rates are even lower; the demand for organs is essentially infinite. I can give you only one of my kidneys, if I am to survive; but you, as you live on and on, may require more than one kidney transplant. Some recipients may need five or six sets of kidneys or lungs before they finally get beyond hope of repair at age one-seventy or so. As those who've given organs come to requisition organs later on in life, the pressure on the under-21 group will get even greater. Those in need of transplants will come to outnumber those who can donate organs, and everybody in the pool will get clipped. And then? Well, they could lower the draft age to 17 or 16 or even 14. But even that's only a short-term solution. Sooner or later, there won't be enough spare organs to go around.

*   *   *

Will I stay? Will I flee? Will I go to court? Time's running out. My call is sure to come up in another few weeks. I feel a tickling sensation in my back, now and then, as though somebody's quietly sawing at my kidneys.

*   *   *

Cannibalism. At Chou-kou-tien, Dragon Bone Hill, 25 miles southwest of Peking, paleontologists excavating a cave early in the twentieth century discovered the fossil skulls of Peking Man, *Pithecanthropus pekinensis.* The skulls had been broken away at the base, which led Franz Weidenreich, the director of the Dragon Bone Hill digs, to speculate that Peking Man was a cannibal who had killed his own kind, extracted the brains of his victims through openings in the base of their skulls, cooked and feasted on the cerebral meat—there were hearths and fragments of charcoal at the site—and left the skulls behind in the cave as trophies. To eat your enemy's flesh: to absorb his skills, his strengths, his knowledge, his achievements, his virtues. It took mankind five hundred thousand years to struggle upward from cannibalism. But we never lost the old craving, did we? There's still easy comfort to gain by devouring those who are younger, stronger, more agile than you. We've improved the techniques, is all. And so now they eat us raw, the old ones, they gobble us up, organ by throbbing organ. Is that really an improvement? At least Peking Man cooked his meat.

*   *   *

Our brave new society, where all share equally in the triumphs of medicine, and the deserving senior citizens need not feel that their merits and prestige will be rewarded only by a cold grave—we sing its praises all the time. How pleased everyone is about the organ draft! Except, of course, a few disgruntled draftees.

*   *   *

The ticklish question of priorities. Who gets the stockpiled organs? They have an elaborate system by which hierarchies are defined. Supposedly a big computer drew it up, thus assuring absolute godlike impartiality. You earn salvation through good works: accomplishments in career and benevolence in daily life win you points that nudge you up the ladder until you reach one of the high-priority classifications, 4-G or better. No doubt the classification system is impartial and is administered justly. But is it rational? Whose needs does it serve? In 1943, during World War II, there was a shortage of the newly discovered drug penicillin among the American military forces in North Africa. Two groups of soldiers were most in need of its benefits: those who were suffering from infected battle wounds and those who had contracted venereal disease. A junior medical officer, working from self-evident moral principles, ruled that the wounded heroes were more deserving of treatment than the self-indulgent syphilitics. He was overruled by the medical officer in charge, who observed that the VD cases could be restored to active duty more quickly, if treated; besides, if they remained untreated they served as vectors of further infection. Therefore he gave them the penicillin and left the wounded groaning on their beds of pain. The logic of the battlefield, incontrovertible, unassailable.

*   *   *

The great chain of life. Little creatures in the plankton are eaten by larger ones, and the greater plankton falls prey to little fishes, and little fishes to bigger fishes, and so on up to the tuna and the dolphin and the shark. I eat the flesh of the tuna and I thrive and flourish and grow fat, and store up energy in my vital organs. And am eaten in turn by the shriveled wizened seniors. All life is linked. I see my destiny.

*   *   *

In the early days rejection of the transplanted organ was the big problem. Such a waste! The body failed to distinguish between a beneficial though alien organ and an intrusive, hostile microorganism. The mechanism known as the immune response was mobilized to drive out the invader. At the point of invasion enzymes came into play, a brush-fire war designed to rip down and dissolve the foreign substances. White corpuscles poured in via the circulatory system, vigilant phagocytes on the march. Through the lymphatic network came antibodies, high-powered protein missiles. Before any technology of organ grafts could be developed, methods had to be devised to suppress the immune response. Drugs, radiation treatment, metabolic shock—one way and another, the organ-rejection problem was long ago conquered. I can't conquer my draft-rejection problem. Aged and rapacious legislators, I reject you and your legislation.

*   *   *

My call notice came today. They'll need one of my kidneys. The usual request. "You're lucky," somebody said at lunchtime. "They might have wanted a lung."

*   *   *

Kate and I walk into the green glistening hills and stand among the blossoming oleanders and corianders and frangipani and whatever. How good it is to be alive, to breathe this fragrance, to show our bodies to the bright sun! Her skin is tawny and glowing. Her beauty makes me weep. She will not be spared. None of us will be spared. I go first, then she, or is it she ahead of me? Where will they make the incision? Here, on her smooth rounded back? Here, on the flat taut belly? I can see the high priest standing over the altar. At the first blaze of dawn his shadow falls across her. The obsidian knife that is clutched in his upraised hand has a terrible fiery sparkle. The choir offers up a discordant hymn to the god of blood. The knife descends.

*   *   *

My last chance to escape across the border. I've been up all night, weighing the options. There's no hope of appeal. Running away leaves a bad taste in my mouth. Father, friends, even Kate, all say stay, stay, stay, face the music. The hour of decision. Do I really have a choice? I have no choice. When the time comes, I'll surrender peacefully.

*   *   *

I report to Transplant House for conscriptive donative surgery in three hours.

*   *   *

After all, he said coolly, what's a kidney? I'll still have another one, you know. And if that one malfunctions, I can always get a replacement. I'll have Preferred Recipient status, 6-A, for what that's worth. But I won't settle for my automatic 6-A. I know what's going to happen to the priority system; I'd better protect myself. I'll go into politics. I'll climb. I'll attain upward mobility out of enlightened self-interest, right? Right. I'll become so important that society will owe me a thousand transplants. And one of these years I'll get that kidney back. Three or four kidneys, fifty kidneys, as many as I need. A heart or two. A few lungs. A pancreas, a spleen, a liver. They won't be able to refuse me anything. I'll show them. I'll show them. I'll out-senior the seniors. There's your Bodily Sanctity activist for you, eh? I suppose I'll have to resign from the League. Goodbye, idealism. Goodbye, moral superiority. Goodbye, kidney. Goodbye, goodbye, goodbye.

*   *   *

It's done. I've paid my debt to society. I've given up unto the powers that be my humble pound of flesh. When I leave the hospital in a couple of days, I'll carry a card testifying to my new 6-A status.

Top priority for the rest of my life.

Why, I might live for a thousand years.

2

$$\left\{ \begin{array}{l} \text{NOW} + n \\ \text{NOW} - n \end{array} \right\}$$

All had been so simple, so elegant, so profitable for ourselves. And then we met the lovely Selene and nearly were undone. She came into our lives during our regular transmission hour on Wednesday, October 7, 1987, between six and seven P.M. Central European Time. The moneymaking hour. I was in satisfactory contact with myself and also with myself. (Now $- n$) was due on the line first, and then I would hear from (now $+ n$).

I was primed for some kind of trouble. I knew trouble was coming, because on Monday, while I was receiving messages from the me of Wednesday, there came an inexplicable and unexplained break in communications. As a result I did not get data from (now $+ n$) concerning the prices of the stocks in our carryover portfolio from last week, and I was unable to take action. Two days have passed, and I am the me of Wednesday who failed to send the news to me of Monday, and I have no idea what will happen to interrupt contact. Least of all do I anticipate Selene.

In such dealings as ours no distractions are needed, sexual, otherwise. We must concentrate wholly. At any time there is steady low-level contact among ourselves; we feel one another's reassuring presence. But transmission of data from self to self requires close attention.

I tell you my method. Then maybe you understand my trouble.

My business is investments. I do all my work at this same hour. At this hour it is midday in New York; the Big Board is still open. I can put through quick calls to my brokers when my time comes to buy or sell.

My office at the moment is the cocktail lounge known as the Celestial Room in the Henry VIII Hotel, south of the Thames. My office may be anywhere. All I need is a telephone. The Celestial Room is aptly named. The room orbits endlessly on a silent oiled track. Twittering sculptures in the so-called galactic mode drift through the air, scattering cascades of polychromed light upon those who sip drinks. Beyond the great picture windows of this supreme room lies the foggy darkness of the London evening, which I ignore. It is all the same to me, wherever I am: London, Nairobi, Karachi, Istanbul, Pittsburgh. I look only for an adequately comfortable environment, air that is safe to admit to one's lungs, service in the style I demand, and a telephone line. The individual characteristics of an individual place do not move me. I am like the ten planets of our solar family: a perpetual traveler, but not a sightseer.

Myself who is (now − n) is ready to receive transmission from myself who is (now). "Go ahead, (now + n)," he tells me. ((To him I am (now + n). To myself I am (now). Everything is relative; n is exactly 48 hours these days.))

"Here we go, (now − n)," I say to him.

*   *   *

I summon my strength by sipping at my drink. Chateau d'Yquem '79 in a sleek Czech goblet. Sickly–sweet stuff; the waiter was aghast when I ordered it *before dinner*. Horreur! Quel aperitif! But the wine makes transmission easier. It greases the conduit, somehow. I am ready.

My table is a single elegant block of glittering irradiated crystal, iridescent, cunningly emitting shifting moire patterns. On the table, unfolded, lies today's European edition of the *Herald-Tribune*. I lean forward. I take from my breast pocket a sheet of paper, the printout listing the securities I bought on Monday afternoon. Now I allow my eyes to roam the close-packed type of the market quotations in my newspaper. I linger for a long moment on the heading, so there will be no mistake: *Closing New York Prices, Tuesday, October 6*. To me they are yesterday's prices. To (now − n) they are tomorrow's prices. (Now − n) acknowledges that he is receiving a sharp image.

I am about to transmit these prices to the me of Monday. You follow the machination, now?

I scan and I select.

I search only for the stocks that move 5% or more in a single day. Whether they move up or move down is immaterial; motion is the only criterion, and we go short or long as the case demands. We need fast action because our maximum survey span is only 96 hours at present, counting the relay from (now + n) back to (now − n) by way of (now). We cannot afford to wait for leisurely capital gains to mature; we must cut our risks by going for the quick, violent swings, seizing our profits as they emerge. The swings have to be violent. Otherwise brokerage costs will eat up our gross.

I have no difficulty choosing the stocks whose prices I will transmit to Monday's me. They are the stocks on the broker's printout, the ones we have already bought; obviously (now − n) would not have bought them unless Wednesday's me had told him about them, and now that I am Wednesday's me, I must follow through. So I send:

Arizona Agrochemical, 79¼, + 6¾
Canadian Transmutation, 116, + 4¼
Commonwealth Dispersals, 12, − 1¾
Eastern Electric Energy, 41, + 2
Great Lakes Bionics, 66, + 3½

And so on through *Western Offshore Corp., 99, − 8*. Now I have transmitted to (now − n) a list of Tuesday's top twenty high-percentage swingers. From his vantage-point in Monday, (now − n) will begin to place orders, taking positions in all twenty stocks on Monday afternoon. I know that he has been successful, because the printout from my broker gives confirmations of all twenty purchases at what now are highly favorable prices.

(Now − n) then signs off for a while and (now + n) comes on. He is transmitting from Friday, October 9. He gives me Thursday's closing prices on the same twenty stocks, from Arizona Agrochemical to Western Offshore. He already knows which of the twenty I will have chosen to sell today, but he pays me the compliment of not telling me;

he merely gives me the prices. He signs off, and, in my role as (now), I make my decisions. I sell Canadian Transmutation, Great Lakes Bionics, and five others; I cover our short sale on Commonwealth Dispersals. The rest of the positions I leave undisturbed for the time being, since they will sell at better prices tomorrow, according to the word from (now + n). I can handle those when I am Friday's me.

Today's sequence is over.

In any given sequence—and we have been running about three a week—we commit no more than five or six million dollars. We wish to stay inconspicuous. Our pre-tax profit runs at about 9% a week. Despite our network of tax havens in Ghana, Fiji, Grand Cayman, Liechtenstein, and Bolivia, through which our profits are funneled, we can bring down to net only about 5% a week on our entire capital. This keeps all three of us in a decent style and compounds prettily. Starting with $5,000 six years ago at the age of 25, I have become one of the world's wealthiest men, with no other advantages than intelligence, persistence, and extrasensory access to tomorrow's stock prices.

It is time to deal with the next sequence. I must transmit to (now − n) the Tuesday prices of the stocks in the portfolio carried over from last week, so that he can make his decisions on what to sell. I know what he has sold, but it would spoil his sport to tip my hand. We treat ourselves fairly. After I have finished sending (now − n) those prices, (now + n) will come on line again and will transmit to me an entirely new list of stocks in which I must take positions before Thursday morning's New York opening. He will be able to realize profits in those on Friday. Thus we go from day to day, playing our shifting roles.

But this was the day on which Selene intersected our lives.

*   *   *

I had emptied my glass. I looked up to signal the waiter, and at that moment a slender, dark-haired girl, alone, entered the Celestial Room. She was tall, graceful, glorious. She was expensively clad in a clinging monomolecular wrap that shuttled through a complex program of wavelength-shifts, including a microsecond sweep of total transparency that dazzled the eye while still maintaining a degree of modesty. Her features were a match for her garment: wide-set glossy eyes, delicate nose, firm lips lightly outlined in green. Her skin was extraordinarily pale. I could see no jewelry on her (why gild refined gold, why paint the lily?) but on her lovely left cheekbone I observed a small decorative band of ultraviolet paint, obviously chosen for visibility in the high-spectrum lighting of this unique room.

She conquered me. There was a mingling of traits in her that I found instantly irresistible: she seemed both shy and steel-strong, passionate and vulnerable, confident and ill at ease. She scanned the room, evidently looking for someone, not finding him. Her eyes met mine and lingered.

Somewhere in my cerebrum (now $-$ n) said shrilly, as I had said on Monday, "I don't read you, (now $+$ n). I don't read you!"

I paid no heed. I rose. I smiled to the girl, and beckoned her toward the empty chair at my table. I swept my *Herald-Tribune* to the floor. At certain times there are more important things than compounding one's capital at 5% per week. She glowed gratefully at me, nodding, accepting my invitation.

When she was about twenty feet from me, I lost all contact with (now $-$ n) and (now $+$ n).

I don't mean simply that there was an interruption in the transmission of words and data among us. I mean that I lost all sense of the presence of my earlier and later selves. That warm, wordless companionship, that ourselvesness, that harmony that I had known constantly since we had established our linkage five years ago, vanished as if switched off. On Monday, when contact with (now $+$ n) broke, I still had had (now $-$ n). Now I had no one.

I was terrifyingly alone, even as ordinary men are alone, but more alone than that, for I had known a fellowship beyond the reach of other mortals. The shock of separation was intense.

Then Selene was sitting beside me, and the nearness of her made me forget my new solitude entirely.

She said, "I don't know where he is and I don't care. He's been late once too often. Finito for him. Hello, you. I'm Selene Hughes."

"Aram Kevorkian. What do you drink?"

"Chartreuse on the rocks. Green. I knew you were Armenian from halfway across the room."

I am Bulgarian, thirteen generations. It suits me to wear an Armenian name. I did not correct her. The waiter hurried over; I ordered chartreuse for her, a sake martini for self. I trembled like an adolescent. Her beauty was disturbing, overwhelming, astonishing. As we raised glasses I reached out experimentally for (now − n) or (now + n). Silence. Silence. But there was Selene.

I said, "You're not from London."

"I travel a lot. I stay here a while, there a while. Originally Dallas. You must be able to hear the Texas in my voice. Most recent port of call, Lima. For the July skiing. Now London."

"And the next stop?"

"Who knows? What do you do, Aram?"

"I invest."

"For a living?"

"So to speak. I struggle along. Free for dinner?"

"Of course. Shall we eat in the hotel?"

"There's the beastly fog outside," I said.

"Exactly."

Simpatico. Perfectly. I guessed her for 24, 25 at most. Perhaps a brief marriage three or four years in the past. A private income, not colossal, but nice. An experienced woman of the world, and yet also somehow still retaining a core of innocence, a magical softness of the soul. I loved her instantly. She did not care for a second cocktail. "I'll make dinner reservations," I said, as she went off to the powder room. I watched her walk away. A supple walk, flawless posture, supreme shoulderblades. When she was about twenty feet from me I felt my other selves suddenly return. "What's happening?" (now − n) demanded furiously. "Where did you go? Why aren't you sending?"

"I don't know yet."

"Where the hell are the Tuesday prices on last week's carryover stocks?"

"Later," I told him.

"*Now.* Before you blank out again."

"The prices can wait," I said, and shut him off. To (now + *n*) I said, "All right. What do you know that I ought to know?"

Myself of 48 hours hence said, "We have fallen in love."

"I'm aware of that. But what blanked us out?"

"She did. She's psi-suppressant. She absorbs all the transmission energy we put out."

"Impossible! I've never heard of any such thing."

"No?" said (now + *n*). "Brother, this past hour has been the first chance I've had to get through to you since Wednesday, when we got into this mess. It's no coincidence that I've been with her just about 100% of the time since Wednesday evening, except for a few two-minute breaks, and then I couldn't reach you because *you* must have been with her in your time-sequence. And so—"

"How can this be?" I cried. "What'll happen to us if? No. No, you bastard, you're rolling me over. I don't believe you. There's no way that she could be causing it."

"I think I know how she does it," said (now + *n*). "There's a—"

At that moment Selene returned, looking even more radiantly beautiful, and silence descended once more.

*   *   *

We dined well. Chilled Mombasa oysters, salade niçoise, filet of Kobe beef rare, washed down by Richebourg '77. Occasionally I tried to reach myselves. Nothing. I worried a little about how I was going to get the Tuesday prices to (now − *n*) on the carryover stuff, and decided to forget about it. Obviously I hadn't managed to get them to him, since I hadn't received any printout on sales out of that portfolio this evening, and if I hadn't reached him, there was no sense in fretting about reaching him. The wonderful thing about this telepathy across time is the sense of stability it gives you: *whatever has been, must be,* and so forth.

After dinner we went down one level to the casino for our brandies and a bit of gamblerage. "Two thousand pounds' worth," I said to the robot cashier, and put my thumb to his charge-plate, and the chips came skittering out of the slot in his chest. I gave half the stake to Selene. She played high-grav-low-grav, and I played roulette; we shifted from one table to the other according to whim and the run of our luck. In two hours she tripled her stake and I lost all of mine. I never was good at games of chance. I even used to get hurt in the market before the market ceased being a game of chance for me. Naturally, I let her thumb her winnings into her own account, and when she offered to return the original stake I just laughed.

Where next? Too early for bed.

"The swimming pool?" she suggested.

"Fine idea," I said. But the hotel has two, as usual. "Nude pool or suit pool?"

"Who owns a suit?" she asked, and we laughed, and took the dropshaft to the pool.

There were separate dressing rooms, M and W. No one frets about showing flesh, but shedding clothes still has lingering taboos. I peeled fast and waited for her by the pool. During this interval I felt the familiar presence of another self impinge on me: (now $- n$). He wasn't transmitting, but I knew he was there. I couldn't feel (now $+ n$) at all. Grudgingly I began to admit that Selene must be responsible for my communications problem. Whenever she went more than twenty feet away, I could get through to myselves. How did she do it, though? And could it be stopped? Mao help me, would I have to choose between my livelihood and my new beloved?

The pool was a vast octagon with a trampoline diving-web and a set of underwater psych-lights making rippling patterns of color. Maybe fifty people were swimming and a few dozen more were lounging beside the pool, improving their tans. No one person can possibly stand out in such a mass of flesh, and yet when Selene emerged from the women's dressing room and began the long saunter across the tiles toward me, the heads began to turn by the dozens. Her figure was not notably lush, yet she had the automatic magnetism that only true beauty exercises. She was definitely slender, but everything was in perfect proportion, as though she had been shaped by the hand of Phidias himself. Long legs, long arms, narrow wrists, narrow waist, small high breasts, miraculously outcurving hips. The *Primavera* of Botticelli. The *Leda* of Leonardo. She carried herself with ultimate grace. My heart thundered.

Between her breasts she wore some sort of amulet: a disk of red metal in which geometrical symbols were engraved. I hadn't noticed it when she was clothed.

"My good-luck piece," she explained. "I'm never without it." And she sprinted laughing to the trampoline, and bounded, and hovered, and soared, and cut magnificently through the surface of the water. I followed her in. We raced from angle to angle of the pool, testing each other, searching for limits and not finding them. We dived and met far below, and locked hands, and bobbed happily upward. Then we lay under the warm quartz lamps. Then we tried the sauna. Then we dressed.

We went to her room.

She kept the amulet on even when we made love. I felt it cold against my chest as I embraced her.

＊　　＊　　＊

But what of the making of money? What of the compounding of capital? What of my sweaty little secret, the joker in the Wall Street pack, the messages from beyond by which I milked the market of millions? On Thursday no contact with my other selves was scheduled, but I could not have made it even if it had been. It was amply clear: Selene blanked my psi field. The critical range was twenty feet. When we were farther apart than that, I could get through; otherwise, not. How did it happen? How? How? How? An accidental incompatibility of psionic vibrations? A tragic canceling out of my powers through proximity to her splendid self? No. No. No. No.

On Thursday we roared through London like a conflagration, doing the galleries, the boutiques, the museums, the sniffer palaces, the pubs, the sparkle houses. I had never been so much in love. For hours at a time I forgot my dilemma. The absence of myself from myself, the separation that had seemed so shattering in its first instant, seemed trivial. What did I need *them* for, when I had *her?*

I needed them for the moneymaking. The moneymaking was a disease that love might alleviate but could not cure. And if I did not resume contact soon, there would be calamities in store.

Late Thursday afternoon, as we came reeling giddily out of a sniffer palace on High Holborn, our nostrils quivering, I felt contact again.

(Now + n) broke through briefly, during a moment when I waited for a traffic light and Selene plunged wildly across to the far side of the street.

"—the amulet's what does it," he said. "That's the word I get from—"

Selene rushed back to my side of the street. "Come *on*, silly! Why'd you wait?"

Two hours later, as she lay in my arms, I swept my hand up from her satiny haunch to her silken breast, and caught the plaque of red metal between two fingers. "Love, won't you take this off?" I said innocently. "I hate the feel of a piece of cold slithery metal coming between us when—"

There was terror in her dark eyes. "I couldn't, Aram! I *couldn't!*"

"For me, love?"

"Please. Let me have my little superstition." Her lips found mine. Cleverly she changed the subject. I wondered at her tremor of shock, her frightened refusal.

Later we strolled along the Thames, and watched Friday coming to life in fogbound dawn. Today I would have to escape from her for at least an hour, I knew. The laws of time dictated it. For on Wednesday, between six and seven P.M. Central European Time, I had accepted a transmission from myself of (now + n), speaking out of Friday, and Friday had come, and I was that very same (now + n), who must reach out at the proper time toward his counterpart at (now − n) on Wednesday. What would happen if I failed to make my rendezvous with time in time, I did not know. Nor wanted to discover. The universe, I suspected, would continue regardless. But my own sanity— my grasp on that universe—might not.

*   *   *

It was a narrowness. All glorious Friday I had to plot how to separate myself from radiant Selene during the cocktail hour, when she would certainly want to be with me. But in the end it was simplicity. I told the concierge, "At seven minutes after six send a message to me in the Celestial Room. I am wanted on urgent business, must come instantly to computer room for intercontinental data patch, person-to-person. So?" Concierge replied, "We can give you the patch right at your table in the Celestial Room." I shook head firmly. "Do it as I say. Please." I put thumb to gratuity account of concierge and signalled an account-transfer of five pounds. Concierge smiled.

Seven minutes after six, message-robot scuttles into Celestial Room, comes homing in on table where I sit with Selene. "Intercontinental data patch, Mr. Kevorkian," says robot. "Wanted immediately. Computer room." I turn to Selene. "Forgive me, love. Desolated, but must go. Urgent business. Just a few minutes."

She grasps my arm fondly. "Darling, no! Let the call wait. It's our *anniversary* now. Forty-eight hours since we met!"

Gently I pull arm free. I extend arm, show jewelled timepiece. "Not yet, not yet! We didn't meet until half past six Wednesday. I'll be back in time to celebrate." I kiss tip of supreme nose. "Don't smile at strangers while I'm gone," I say, and rush off with robot.

I do not go to computer room. I hurriedly buy a Friday *Herald-Tribune* in lobby and lock myself in men's washroom cubicle. Contact now is made on schedule with (now − n), living in Wednesday, all innocent of what will befall him that miraculous evening. I read stock prices, twenty securities, from Arizona Agrochemical to Western Offshore Corp. I sign off and study my watch. (Now − n) is currently closing out seven long positions and the short sale on Commonwealth Dispersals. During the interval I seek to make contact with (now + n) ahead of me on Sunday evening. No response. Nothing.

Presently I lose contact also with (now − n). As expected; for this is the moment when the me of Wednesday has for the first time come within Selene's psi-suppressant field. I wait patiently. In a while (Selene − n) goes to powder room. Contact returns.

(Now − n) says to me, "All right. What do you know that I ought to know?"

"We have fallen in love," I say.

Rest of conversation follows as per. What has been, must be. I debate slipping in the tidbit I have received from (now + n) concerning the alleged powers of Selene's amulet. Should I say it quickly, before

contact breaks? Impossible. It was not said to me. The conversation
proceeds until at the proper moment I am able to say, "I think I know
how she does it. There's a—"

Wall of silence descends. (Selene − *n*) has returned to the table of
(now − *n*). Therefore I (now) will return to the table of Selene (now). I
rush back to the Celestial Room. Selene, looking glum, sits alone,
sipping drink. She brightens as I approach.

"See?" I cry. "Back just in time. Happy anniversary, darling. Happy,
happy, happy, happy!"

*   *   *

When we woke Saturday morning we decided to share the same room
thereafter. Selene showered while I went downstairs to arrange the
transfer. I could have arranged everything by telephone without getting
out of bed, but I chose to go in person to the desk, leaving Selene
behind. You understand why.

In the lobby I received a transmission from (now + *n*), speaking out
of Monday, October 12. "It's definitely the amulet," he said. "I can't
tell you how it works, but it's some kind of mechanical psi-suppressant
device. God knows why she wears it, but if I could only manage to have
her lose it we'd be all right. It's the amulet. Pass it on."

I was reminded, by this, of the flash of contact I had received on
Thursday outside the sniffer palace on High Holborn. I realized that I
had another message to send, a rendezvous to keep with him who has
become (now − *n*).

Late Saturday afternoon, I made contact with (now − *n*) once more,
only momentarily. Again I resorted to a ruse in order to fulfill the
necessary unfolding of destiny. Selene and I stood in the hallway,
waiting for a dropshaft. There were other people. The dropshaft gate
irised open and Selene went in, followed by others. With an excess of
chivalry I let all the others enter before me, and "accidentally" missed
the closing of the gate. The dropshaft descended, with Selene. I
remained alone in the hall. My timing was good; after a moment I felt
the inner warmth that told me of proximity to the mind of (now − *n*).

"—the amulet's what does it," I said. "That's the word I get from—"
Aloneness intervened.

*   *   *

During the week beginning Monday, October 12, I received no advance information on the fluctuations of the stock market at all. Not in five years had I been so deprived of data. My linkings with (now − n) and (now + n) were fleeting and unsatisfactory. We exchanged a sentence here, a blurt of hasty words there, no more. Of course, there were moments every day when I was apart from the fair Selene long enough to get a message out. Though we were utterly consumed by our passion for one another, nevertheless I did get opportunities to elude the twenty-foot radius of her psi-suppressant field. The trouble was that my opportunities to send did not always coincide with the opportunities of (now − n) or (now + n) to receive. We remained linked in a 48-hour spacing, and to alter that spacing would require extensive discipline and infinitely careful coordination, which none of ourselves were able to provide in such a time. So any contact with myselves had to depend on a coincidence of apartnesses from Selene.

I regretted this keenly. Yet there was Selene to comfort me. We reveled all day and reveled all night. When fatigue overcame us we grabbed a two-hour deepsleep wire and caught up with ourselves, and then we started over. I plumbed the limits of ecstasy. I believe it was like that for her.

Though lacking my unique advantage, I also played the market that week. Partly it was compulsion: my plungings had become obsessive. Partly, too, it was at Selene's urgings. "Don't you neglect your work for me," she purred. "I don't want to stand in the way of making *money.*"

Money, I was discovering, fascinated her nearly as intensely as it did me. Another evidence of compatibility. She knew a good deal about the market herself, and looked on, an excited spectator, as I each day shuffled my portfolio.

The market was closed Monday: Columbus Day. Tuesday, queasily operating in the dark, I sold Arizona Agrochemical, Consolidated Luna, Eastern Electric Energy, and Western Offshore, reinvesting the proceeds in large blocks of Meccano Leasing and Holoscan Dynamics. Wednesday's *Tribune*, to my chagrin, brought me the news that Consolidated Luna had received the Copernicus franchise and had risen 9¾ points in the final hour of Tuesday's trading. Meccano Leasing, though, had been rebuffed in the Robomation takeover bid and was off 4½ since I had bought it. I got through to my broker in a hurry and sold Meccano, which was down even further that morning. My loss was $125,000—plus $250,000 more that I had dropped by selling Consolidated Luna too soon. After the market closed on Wednesday, the directors of Meccano Leasing unexpectedly declared a five-for-two split and a special dividend in the form of a one-for-ten distribution of cumulative participating high-depreciation warrants. Meccano regained its entire Tuesday–Wednesday loss and tacked on 5 points beyond.

I concealed the details of this from Selene. She saw only the glamor of my speculations: the telephone calls, the quick computations, the movements of hundreds of thousands of dollars. I hid the hideous botch from her, knowing it might damage my prestige.

On Thursday, feeling battered and looking for the safety of a utility, I picked up 10,000 Southwest Power and Fusion at 38, only hours before the explosion of SPF's magnetohydrodynamic generating station in Las Cruces, which destroyed half a county and neatly peeled $90,000 off the value of my investment when the stock finally traded, after a delayed opening, on Friday. I sold. Later came news that SPF's insurance would cover everything. SPF recovered, whereas Holoscan Dynamics plummeted 11½, costing me $140,000 more. I had not known that Holoscan's insurance subsidiary was the chief underwriter for SPF's disaster coverage.

All told, that week I shed more than $500,000. My brokers were stunned. I had a reputation for infallibility among them. Most of them had become wealthy simply by duplicating my own transactions for their own accounts.

"Sweetheart, what *happened?*" they asked me.

My losses the following week came to $1,250,000. Still no news from (now + n). My brokers felt I needed a vacation. Even Selene knew I was losing heavily, by now. Curiously, my run of bad luck seemed to intensify her passion for me. Perhaps it made me look tragic and Byronic to be getting hit so hard.

We spent wild days and wilder nights. I lived in a throbbing haze of sensuality. Wherever we went we were the center of all attention. We had that burnished sheen that only great lovers have. We radiated a glow of delight all up and down the spectrum.

I was losing millions.

The more I lost, the more reckless my plunges became, and the deeper my losses became.

I was in real danger of being wiped out, if this went on.

I had to get away from her.

*   *   *

Monday, October 26. Selene has taken the deepsleep wire and in the next two hours will flush away the fatigues of three riotous days and nights without rest. I have only pretended to take the wire. When she goes under, I rise. I dress. I pack. I scrawl a note for her. *"Business trip. Back soon. Love, love, love, love."* I catch noon rocket for Istanbul.

Minarets, mosques, Byzantine temples. Shunning the sleep wire, I spend next day and a half in bed in ordinary repose. I wake and it is 48 hours since parting from Selene. Desolation! Bitter solitude! But I feel (now + n) invading my mind.

"Take this down," he says brusquely. "Buy 5000 FSP, 800 CCG, 150 LC, 200 T, 1000 TXN, 100 BVI. Go short 200 BA, 500 UCM, 200 LOC. Clear? Read back to me."

I read back. Then I phone in my orders. I hardly care what the ticker symbols stand for. If (now + n) says to do, I do.

An hour and a half later the switchboard tells me, "A Miss Hughes to see you, sir."

She has traced me! Calamitas calamitatum! "Tell her I'm not here, I say." I flee to the roofport. By copter I get away. Commercial jet shortly brings me to Tel Aviv. I take a room at the Hilton and give absolute instructions am not to be disturbed. Meals only to room, also *Herald-Trib* every day, otherwise no interruptions.

I study the market action. On Friday I am able to reach (now − n). "Take this down," I say brusquely. "Buy 5000 FSP, 800 CCG, 150 LC, 200 T—"

Then I call brokers. I close out Wednesday's longs and cover Wednesday's shorts. My profit is over a million. I am recouping. But I miss her terribly.

I spend agonizing weekend of loneliness in hotel room.

Monday. Comes voice of (now + n) out of Wednesday, with new instructions. I obey. At lunchtime, under lid of my barley soup, floats note from her. "Darling, why are you running away from me? I love you to the ninth power. S."

I get out of hotel disguised as bellhop and take El Al jet to Cairo. Tense, jittery, I join tourist group sightseeing Pyramids, much out of character. Tour is conducted in Hebrew; serves me right. I lock self in hotel. *Herald-Tribune* available. On Wednesday I send instructions to me of Monday, (now − n). I await instructions from me of Friday, (now + n). Instead I get muddled transmissions, noise, confusions. What is wrong? Where to flee now? Brasilia, McMurdo Sound, Anchorage, Irkutsk, Maograd? She will find me. She has her resources. There are few secrets to one who has the will to surmount them. How does she find me?

She finds me.

Note comes: "I am at Abu Simbel to wait for you. Meet me there on Friday afternoon or I throw myself from Rameses' leftmost head at sundown. Love. Desperate. S."

I am defeated. She will bankrupt me, but I must have her.

On Friday I go to Abu Simbel.

＊　　＊　　＊

She stood atop the monument, luscious in windswept white cotton.

"I knew you'd come," she said.

"What else could I do?"

We kissed. Her suppleness inflamed me. The sun blazed toward a descent into the western desert.

"Why have you been running away from me?" she asked. "What did I do wrong? Why did you stop loving me?"

"I never stopped loving you," I said.

"Then—*why?*"

"I will tell you," I said, "a secret I have shared with no human being other than myselves."

Words tumbled out. I told all. The discovery of my gift, the early chaos of sensory bombardment from other times, the bafflement of living one hour ahead of time and one hour behind time as well as in the present. The months of discipline needed to develop my gift. The fierce struggle to extend the range of extrasensory perception to five hours, ten, twenty-four, forty-eight. The joy of playing the market and never losing. The intricate systems of speculation; the self-imposed limits to keep me from ending up with all the assets in the world; the pleasures of immense wealth. The loneliness, too. And the supremacy of the night when I met her.

Then I said, "When I'm with you, it doesn't work. I can't communicate with myselves. I lost millions in the last couple of weeks, playing the market the regular way. You were breaking me."

"The amulet," she said. "It does it. It absorbs psionic energy. It suppresses the psi field."

"I thought it was that. But who ever heard of such a thing? Where did you get it, Selene? Why do you wear it?"

"I got it far, far from here," said Selene. "I wear it to protect myself."

"Against *what?*"

"Against my own gift. My terrible gift, my nightmare gift, my curse of a gift. But if I must choose between my amulet and my love, it is no choice. I love you, Aram, I love you, I love you!"

She seized the metal disk, ripped it from the chain around her neck, hurled it over the brink of the monument. It fluttered through the twilight sky and was gone.

I felt (now − n) and (now + n) return.

Selene vanished.

*   *   *

For an hour I stood alone atop Abu Simbel, motionless, baffled, stunned. Suddenly Selene was back. She clutched my arm and whispered, "Quick! Let's go to the hotel!"

"Where have you been?"

"Next Tuesday," she said. "I oscillate in time."

"What?"

"The amulet damped my oscillations. It anchored me to the timeline in the present. I got it in 2459 A.D. Someone I knew there, someone who cared very deeply for me. It was his parting gift, and he gave it knowing we could never meet again. But now—"

She vanished. Gone eighteen minutes.

"I was back in last Tuesday," she said, returning. "I phoned myself and said I should follow you to Istanbul, and then to Tel Aviv, and then to Egypt. You see how I found you?"

We hurried to her hotel overlooking the Nile. We made love, and an instant before the climax I found myself alone in bed. (Now + n) spoke to me and said, "She's been here with me. She should be on her way back to you." Selene returned. "I went to—"

"—this coming Sunday," I said. "I know. Can't you control the oscillations at all?"

"No. I'm swinging free. When the momentum really builds up, I cover centuries. It's torture, Aram. Life has no sequence, no structure. Hold me tight!"

In a frenzy we finished what we could not finish before. We lay clasped close, exhausted. "What will we do?" I cried. "I can't let you oscillate like this!"

"You must. I can't let you sacrifice your livelihood!"

"But—"

She was gone.

I rose and dressed and hurried back to Abu Simbel. In the hours before dawn I searched the sands beside the Nile, crawling, sifting, probing. As the sun's rays crested the mountain I found the amulet. I rushed to the hotel. Selene had reappeared.

"Put it on," I commanded.

"I won't. I can't deprive you of—"

"Put it on."

She disappeared. (Now + n) said, "Never fear. All will work out wondrous well."

Selene came back. "I was in the Friday after next," she said. "I had an idea that will save everything."

"No ideas. Put the amulet on."

She shook her head. "I brought you a present," she said, and handed me a copy of the *Herald-Tribune*, dated the Friday after next. Oscillation seized her. She went and came and handed me November 19's newspaper. Her eyes were bright with excitement. She vanished. She brought me the *Herald-Tribune* of November 8. Of December 4. Of November 11. Of January 18, 1988. Of December 11. Of March 5, 1988. Of December 22. Of June 16, 1997. Of December 14. Of September 8, 1990. "Enough!" I said. "Enough!" She continued to swing through time. The stack of papers grew. "I love you," she gasped, and handed me a transparent cube one inch high. "*The Wall Street Journal*, May 19, 2206," she explained. "I couldn't get the machine that reads it. Sorry." She was gone. She brought me more *Herald-Tribunes*, many dates, 1988–2002. Then a whole microreel. At last she sank down, dazed, exhausted, and said, "Give me the amulet. It must be within twelve inches of my body to neutralize my field." I slipped the disk into her palm. "Kiss me," Selene murmured.

*   *   *

And so. She wears her amulet; we are inseparable; I have no contact with my other selves. In handling my investments I merely consult my file of newspapers, which I have reduced to minicap size and carry in the bezel of a ring I wear. For safety's sake Selene carries a duplicate.

We are very happy. We are very wealthy.

Is only one dilemma. Neither of us uses the special gift with which we were born. Evolution would not have produced such things in us if they were not to be used. What risks do we run by thwarting evolution's design?

I bitterly miss the use of my power, which her amulet negates. Even the company of supreme Selene does not wholly compensate for the loss of the harmoniousness that was

$$\left\{ \begin{array}{l} (\text{now} - n) \\ (\text{now}) \\ (\text{now} + n). \end{array} \right.$$

I could, of course, simply arrange to be away from Selene for an hour here, an hour there, and reopen that contact. I could even have continued playing the market that way, setting aside a transmission hour every 48 hours outside of amulet range. But it is the *continuous* contact that I miss. The always presence of my other selves. If I have that contact, Selene is condemned to oscillate, or else we must part.

I wish also to find some way that her gift will be not terror but joy for her.

Is maybe a solution. Can extrasensory gifts be induced by proximity? Can Selene's oscillation pass to me? I struggle to acquire it. We work together to give me her gift. Just today I felt myself move, perhaps a microsecond into the future, then a microsecond into the past. Selene said I definitely seemed to blur.

Who knows? Will success be ours?

I think yes. I think love will triumph. I think I will learn the secret, and we will coordinate our vanishings, Selene and I, and we will oscillate as one, we will swing together through time, we will soar, we will speed hand in hand across the millennia. She can discard her amulet once I am able to go with her on her journeys.

Pray for us, (now + n), my brother, my other self, and one day soon perhaps I will come to you and shake you by the hand.

3

SOME NOTES ON THE PRE-DYNASTIC EPOCH

We understand some of their languages, but none of them completely. That is one of the great difficulties. What has come down from their epoch to ours is spotted and stained and eroded by time, full of lacunae and static; and so we can only approximately comprehend the nature of their civilization and the reasons for its collapse. Too often, I fear, we project our own values and assumptions back upon them and deceive ourselves into thinking we are making valid historical judgments.

On the other hand there are certain esthetic rewards in the very incompleteness of the record. Their poetry, for example, is heightened and made more mysterious, more strangely appealing, by the tantalizing gaps that result from our faulty linguistic knowledge and from the uncertainties we experience in transliterating their fragmentary written texts, as well as in transcribing their surviving spoken archives. It is as though time itself has turned poet, collaborating belatedly with the ancients to produce something new and fascinating by punching its own inexorable imprint into their work. Consider the resonances and implications of this deformed and defective song, perhaps a chant of a ritual nature, dating from the late pre-dynastic:

Once upon a time you . . . . so fine,
You threw the [?] a [? small unit of currency?]
    in your prime,
Didn't you?
People'd call, say "Beware . . . . to fall,"
You . . . . kidding you.
You . . . . laugh . . . . .

Everybody . . . .
Now you don't . . . . so loud,
Now you don't . . . . so proud
About . . . . for your next meal.
How does it feel, how does it feel
To be . . . . . . home . . . . unknown . . . .
. . . . a rolling stone?

Or examine this, which is an earlier pre-dynastic piece, possibly of Babylonian-American origin:

In my wearied . . . . , me . . . . . .
In my inflamed nostril, me . . . . . .
Punishment, sickness, trouble . . . . . . me
A flail which wickedly afflicts, ... me
A lacerating rod . . . . me
A . . . . hand . . . . . . me
A terrifying message . . . . . . me
A stinging whip . . . . me
. . . .
. . . . in pain I *faint* [?]
. . . .

The Center for Pre-Dynastic Studies is a comfortingly massive building fashioned from blocks of some greasy green synthetic stone and laid out in three spoke-like wings radiating from a common center. It is situated in the midst of the central continental plateau, near what may have been the site of the ancient metropolis of Omahaha. On clear days we take to the air in small solar-powered flying machines and survey the outlines of the city, which are still visible as indistinct white scars on the green breast of the earth. There are more than two thousand staff members. Many of them are women and some are sexually available, even to me. I have been employed here for eleven years. My current title is Metalinguistic Archaeologist, Third Grade. My father before me held that title for much of his life. He died in a professional quarrel while I was a child, and my mother dedicated me to filling his place. I have a small office with several data terminals, a neatly beveled viewing screen, and a modest desk. Upon my desk I keep a collection of artifacts of the so-called Twentieth Century. These serve as talismans spurring me on to greater depth of insight. They include:

One gray communications device ("telephone").

One black inscribing device ("typewriter?") which has been exposed to high temperatures and is somewhat melted.

One metal key, incised with the numerals *1714*, and fastened by a rusted metal ring to a small white plastic plaque that declares, in red letters, IF CARRIED AWAY INADVERTENTLY///DROP IN ANY MAIL BOX///SHERATON BOSTON HOTEL///BOSTON, MASS. 02199.

One coin of uncertain denomination.

It is understood that these items are the property of the Center for Pre-Dynastic Studies and are merely on loan to me. Considering their great age and the harsh conditions to which they must have been exposed after the collapse of Twentieth Century civilization, they are in remarkably fine condition. I am proud to be their custodian.

I am thirty-one years of age, slender, blue-eyed, austere in personal habits, and unmarried. My knowledge of the languages and customs of the so-called Twentieth Century is considerable, although I strive constantly to increase it. My work both saddens and exhilarates me. I see it as a species of poetry, if poetry may be understood to be the imaginative verbal reconstruction of experience; in my case the experiences I reconstruct are not my own, are in fact alien and repugnant to me, but what does that matter? Each night when I go home my feet are moist and chilled, as though I have been wading in swamps all day. Last summer the Dynast visited the Center on Imperial Unity Day, examined our latest findings with care and an apparently sincere show of interest, and said, "We must draw from these researches a profound lesson for our times."

None of the aforegoing is true. I take pleasure in deceiving. I am an extremely unreliable witness.

The heart of the problem, as we have come to understand it, is a pervasive generalized dislocation of awareness. Nightmares break into the fabric of daily life and we no longer notice, or, if we do notice, we fail to make appropriate response. Nothing seems excessive any longer, nothing perturbs our dulled, numbed minds. Predatory giant insects, the products of pointless experiments in mutation, escape from laboratories and devastate the countryside. Rivers are contaminated by lethal microorganisms released accidentally or deliberately by civil servants. Parts of human fetuses obtained from abortions are kept alive in hospital research units; human fetal toes and fingers grow up to four times as fast under controlled conditions as they do *in utero*, starting from single rods of cartilage and becoming fully jointed digits in seven to ten days. These are used in the study of the causes of arthritis. Zoos are vandalized by children, who stone geese and ducks to death and shoot lions in their cages. Sulphuric acid, the result of a combination of rain, mist, and sea-spray with sulphurous industrial effluents, devours the statuary of Venice at a rate of 5 percent a year. The nose is the first part to go when this process, locally termed "marble cancer," strikes. Just off the shores of Manhattan Island, a thick, stinking mass of floating sludge transforms a twenty-square-mile region of the ocean into a dead sea, a sterile soup of dark, poisonous wastes; this pocket of coagulated pollutants has been formed over a forty-year period by the licensed dumping each year of millions of cubic yards of treated sewage, towed by barge to the site, and by the unrestrained discharge of 365 million gallons per day of raw sewage from the Hudson River. All these events are widely deplored but the causative factors are permitted to remain uncorrected, which means a constant widening of their operative zones. (There are no static negative phases; the laws of expansive deterioration decree that bad inevitably becomes worse.) Why is nothing done on any functional level? Because no one believes anything *can* be done. Such a belief in collective impotence is, structurally speaking, identical in effect to actual impotence; one does not need to be helpless, merely to think that one is helpless, in order to reach a condition of surrender to accelerating degenerative conditions. Under such circumstances a withdrawal of attention is the only satisfactory therapy. Along with this emptying of reactive impulse comes a corresponding semantic inflation and devaluation which further speeds the process of general dehumanization. Thus the roving gangs of adolescents who commit random crimes in the streets of New York City say they have "blown away" a victim whom they have in fact murdered, and the President of the United States, announcing an adjustment in the par value of his country's currency made necessary by the surreptitious economic mismanagement of the previous administration, describes it as "the most significant monetary agreement in the history of the world."

Some of the topics urgently requiring detailed analysis:

1. Their poetry
2. Preferred positions of sexual intercourse
3. The street-plans of their major cities
4. Religious beliefs and practices
5. Terms of endearment, heterosexual and homosexual
6. Ecological destruction, accidental and deliberate
7. Sports and rituals
8. Attitudes toward technological progress
9. Forms of government, political processes
10. Their visual art-forms
11. Means of transportation
12. Their collapse and social decay
13. Their terrible last days

One of our amusements here—no, let me be frank, it's more than an amusement, it's a professional necessity—is periodically to enter the vanished pre-dynastic world through the gate of dreams. A drug that leaves a sour, salty taste on the tongue facilitates these journeys. Also we make use of talismans: I clutch my key in my left hand and carry my coin in my right-hand pocket. We never travel alone, but usually go in teams of two or three. A special section of the Center is set aside for those who make these dream-journeys. The rooms are small and brightly lit, with soft rubbery pink walls, rather womb-like in appearance, tuned to a bland heat and an intimate humidity. Alexandra, Jerome, and I enter such a room. We remove our clothing to perform the customary ablutions. Alexandra is plump but her breasts are small and far apart. Jerome's body is hairy and his muscles lie in thick slabs over his bones. I see them both looking at me. We wash and dress; Jerome produces three hexagonal gray tablets and we swallow them. Sour, salty. We lie side by side on the triple couch in the center of the room. I clutch my key, I touch my coin. Backward, backward, backward we drift. Alexandra's soft forearm presses gently against my thin shoulder. Into the dark, into the old times. The pre-dynastic epoch swallows us. This is the kingdom of earth, distorted, broken, twisted, maimed, perjured. The kingdom of hell. A snowbound kingdom. Bright lights on the grease-speckled airstrip. A rusting vehicle jutting from the sand. The eyes and lips of madmen. My feet are sixteen inches above the surface of the ground. Mists curl upward, licking at my soles. I stand before a bleak hotel, and women carrying glossy leather bags pass in and out. Toward us come automobiles, berserk, driverless, with blazing headlights. A blurred column of song rises out of the darkness. Home . . . . unknown . . . . a rolling stone? These ruins are inhabited.

LIFE-SYNTHESIS PIONEER URGES
POLICING OF RESEARCH
Buffalo Doctor Says New Organisms Could Be Peril

USE OF PRIVATE PATROLMEN
ON CITY STREETS INCREASING

MACROBIOTIC COOKING—LEARNING THE
SECRETS OF YANG AND YIN

PATMAN WARNS U.S. MAY CHECK
GAMBLING 'DISEASE' IN THE STATES

SOME AREAS SEEK TO HALT GROWTH

NIXON DEPICTS HIS WIFE
AS STRONG AND SENSITIVE

PSYCHIATRIST IN BELFAST FINDS CHILDREN
ARE DEEPLY DISTURBED BY THE VIOLENCE

GROWING USE OF MIND-AFFECTING
DRUGS STIRS CONCERN

Saigon, Sept. 5—United States Army psychologists said today they are working on a plan to brainwash enemy troops with bars of soap that reveal a new propaganda message practically every time the guerillas lather up. As the soap is used, gradual wear reveals eight messages embedded in layers.

"The Beatles, and their mimicking rock-and-rollers, use the Pavlovian techniques to produce artificial neuroses in our young people," declared Rep. James B. Utt (R-Calif). "Extensive experiments in hypnosis and rhythm have shown how rock and roll music leads to a destruction of the normal inhibitory mechanism of the cerebral cortex and permits easy acceptance of immorality and disregard of all moral norms."

Taylor said the time has come for police "to study and apply so far as possible all the factors that will in any way promote better understanding and a better relationship between citizens and the law enforcement officer, even if it means attempting to enter into the learning and cultural realms of unborn children."

Secretary of Defense Melvin R. Laird formally dedicated a small room in the Pentagon today as a quiet place for meditation and prayer. "In a sense, this ceremony marks the completion of the Pentagon, for until now this building lacked a place where man's inner spirit could find quiet expression," Mr. Laird said.

The meditation room, he said, "is an affirmation that, though we cling to the principle that church and state should be separate, we do not propose to separate man from God."

Moscow, June 19—Oil industry expert says Moses and Joshua were among earth's original polluters, criticizes regulations inhibiting inventiveness and progress.

Much of the interior of the continent lies submerged in a deep sea of radioactive water. The region was deliberately flooded under the policy of "compensating catastrophe" promulgated by the government toward the close of the period of terminal convulsions. Hence, though we come in dreams, we do not dare enter this zone unprotected, and we make use of aquatic robots bearing brain-coupled remote-vision cameras. Without interrupting our slumber we don the equipment, giggling self-consciously as we help one another with the harnesses and snaps. The robots stride into the green, glistening depths, leaving trails of shimmering fiery bubbles. We turn and tilt our heads and our cameras obey, projecting what they see directly upon our retinas. This is a magical realm. Everything sleeps here in a single grave, yet everything throbs and bursts with terrible life. Small boys, glowing, play marbles in the street. Thieves glide on mincing feet past beefy, stolid shopkeepers. A syphilitic whore displays her thighs to potential purchasers. A giant blue screen mounted on the haunch of a colossal glossy-skinned building shows us the face of the President, jowly, earnest, energetic.

His eyes are extraordinarily narrow, almost slits. He speaks but his words are vague and formless, without perceptible syllabic intervals. We are unaware of the pressure of the water. Scraps of paper flutter past us as though driven by the wind. Little girls dance in a ring: their skinny bare legs flash like pistons. Alexandra's robot briefly touches its coppery hand to mine, a gesture of delight, of love. We take turns entering an automobile, sitting at its wheel, depressing its pedals and levers. I am filled with an intense sense of the reality of the pre-dynastic, of its oppressive imminence, of the danger of its return. Who says the past is dead and sealed? Everything comes round at least twice, perhaps even more often, and the later passes are always more grotesque, more deadly, and more comical. Destruction is eternal. Grief is cyclical. Death is undying. We walk the drowned face of the murdered earth and we are tormented by the awareness that past and future lie joined like a lunatic serpent. The sorrows of the pharaohs will be our sorrows. Listen to the voice of Egypt.

The high-born are full of lamentation but the poor are jubilant. Every town sayeth, "Let us drive out the powerful". . . . The splendid judgment-hall has been stripped of its documents. . . . The public offices lie open and their records have been stolen. Serfs have become the masters of serfs. . . . Behold, they that had clothes are now in rags. . . . He who had nothing is now rich and the high official must court the parvenu. . . . Squalor is throughout the land: no clothes are white these days. . . . The Nile is in flood yet no one has the heart to plough. . . . Corn has perished everywhere. . . . Everyone says, "There is no more". . . . The dead are thrown into the river. . . . Laughter has perished. Grief walks the land. A man of character goes in mourning because of what has happened in the land. . . . Foreigners have become people everywhere. There is no man of yesterday.

Alexandra, Jerome, and I waltz in the pre-dynastic streets. We sing the Hymn to the Dynast. We embrace. Jerome couples with Alexandra. We take books, phonograph records, kitchen appliances, and postage stamps, and we leave without paying, for we have no money of this epoch. No one protests. We stare at the clumsy bulk of an airplane soaring over the tops of the buildings. We cup our hands and drink at a public fountain. Naked, I show myself to the veiled green sun. I couple with Jerome. We peer into the pinched, dead faces of the pre-dynastic people we meet outside the grand hotel. We whisper to them in gentle voices, trying to warn them of their danger. Some sand blows across the pavement. Alexandra tenderly kisses an old man's withered cheek and he flees her warmth. Jewelry finer than any our museums own glitters in every window. The great wealth of this epoch is awesome to us. Where did these people go astray? How did they lose the path? What is the source of their pain? Tell us, we beg. Explain yourselves to us. We are historians from a happier time. We seek to know you. What can you reveal to us concerning your poetry, your preferred positions of sexual intercourse, the street-plans of your major cities, your religious beliefs and practices, your terms of endearment, heterosexual and homosexual, your ecological destruction, accidental and deliberate, your sports and rituals, your attitudes toward technological progress, your forms of government, your political processes, your visual art-forms, your means of transportation, your collapse and social decay, your terrible last days? For your last days will be terrible. There is no avoiding that now. The course is fixed; the end is inevitable. The time of the Dynast must come.

I see myself tied into the totality of epochs. I am inextricably linked to the pharaohs, to Assurnasirpal, to Tiglath-Pileser, to the beggars in Calcutta, to Yuri Gagarin and Neil Armstrong, to Caesar, to Adam, to the dwarfed and pallid scrabblers on the bleak shores of the enfamined future. All time converges on this point of now. My soul's core is the universal focus. There is no escape. The swollen reddened moon perpetually climbs the sky. The moment of the Dynast is eternally at hand. All of time and space becomes a cage for now. We are condemned to our own company until death do us part, and perhaps even afterward. Where did we go astray? How did we lose the path? Why can't we escape? Ah. Yes. There's the catch. There is no escape.

They drank wine, and praised the gods of gold, and of silver, of brass, of iron, of wood, and of stone.
In the same hour came forth fingers of a man's hand, and wrote over against the candlestick upon the plaister of the wall of the king's palace: and the king saw the part of the hand that wrote.

Then the king's countenance was changed, and his thoughts troubled him, so that the joints of his loins were loosed, and his knees smote one against another.

And this is the writing that was written, MENE, MENE, TEKEL, UPHARSIN.

This is the interpretation of the thing: MENE; God hath numbered thy kingdom, and finished it.

TEKEL; Thou art weighed in the balances, and art found wanting.

PERES; Thy kingdom is divided, and given to the Medes and Persians.

In that night was Belshazzar the king of the Chaldeans slain.

And Darius the Median took the kingdom, being about threescore and two years old.

We wake. We say nothing to one another as we leave the room of dreams; we avert our eyes from each other's gaze. We return to our separate offices. I spend the remainder of the afternoon analyzing shards of pre-dynastic poetry. The words are muddled and will not cohere. My eyes fill with tears. Why have I become so involved in the fate of these sad and foolish people?

Let me unmask myself. Let me confess everything. There is no Center for Pre-Dynastic Studies. I am no Metalinguistic Archaeologist, Third Grade, living in a remote and idyllic era far in your future and passing my days in pondering the wreckage of the Twentieth Century. The time of the Dynast may be coming, but he does not yet rule. I am your contemporary. I am your brother. These notes are the work of a pre-dynastic man like yourself, a native of the so-called Twentieth Century, who, like you, has lived through dark hours and may live to see darker ones. That much is true. All the rest is fantasy of my own invention. Do you believe that? Do I seem reliable now? Can you trust me, just this once?

All time converges on this point of now.

My . . . . . . hurts me sorely.
The . . . . of my . . . . is decaying.
This is the path that the bison took.
This is the path that the moa took.
This is the . . . . of the dying . . . . [beasts?]
Let us not . . . . that dry path.
Let us not . . . . that bony path.
Let us . . . . another path . . . . . .

O my brother, sharer of my mother's [womb?]
O my sister, whose . . . . I . . . .
Listen . . . . . . close . . . . the wall . . . .
Now the cold winds come.
Now the heavy snows fall.
Now . . . .
. . . . the suffering . . . .
. . . . the solitude . . . .
. . . . blood . . . . sleep . . . . blood . . . .
. . . . blood . . . .
. . . .
. . . . the river, the sea . . . .
. . . . . me . . . .

4

IN THE GROUP

It was a restless time for Murray. He spent the morning sand-trawling on the beach at Acapulco. When it began to seem like lunchtime he popped to Nairobi for mutton curry at the Three Bells. It wasn't lunchtime in Nairobi, but these days any restaurant worth eating at stayed open round the clock. In late afternoon, subjectivewise, he paused for pastis and water in Marseilles, and toward psychological twilight he buzzed back home to California. His inner clock was set to Pacific Time, so reality corresponded to mood: night was falling, San Francisco glittered like a mound of jewels across the bay. He was going to do Group tonight. He got Kay on the screen and said, "Come down to my place tonight, yes?"

"What for?"

"What else? Group."

She lay in a dewy bower of young redwoods, 300 miles up the coast from him. Torrents of unbound milkwhite hair cascaded over her slender bare honeycolored body. A multicarat glitterstone sparkled fraudulently between her flawless little breasts. Looking at her, he felt his hands tightening into desperate fists, his nails ravaging his palms. He loved her beyond all measure. The intensity of his love overwhelmed and embarrassed him.

"You want to do Group together tonight?" she asked. "You and me?" She didn't sound pleased.

"Why not? Closeness is more fun than apartness."

"Nobody's ever apart in Group. What does mere you-and-me physical proximity matter? It's irrelevant. It's obsolete."

46

"I miss you."

"You're with me right now," she pointed out.

"I want to touch you. I want to inhale you. I want to taste you."

"Punch for tactile, then. Punch for olfactory. Punch for any input you think you want."

"I've got all sensory channels open already," Murray said. "I'm flooded with delicious input. It still isn't the same thing. It isn't enough, Kay."

She rose and walked slowly toward the ocean. His eyes tracked her across the screen. He heard the pounding of the surf.

"I want you right beside me when Group starts tonight," he told her. "Look, if you don't feel like coming here, I'll go to your place."

"You're being boringly persistent."

He winced. "I can't help it. I like being close to you."

"You have a lot of old-fashioned attitudes, Murray." Her voice was so cool. "Are you aware of that?"

"I'm aware that my emotional drives are very strong. That's all. Is that such a sin?" Careful, Murray. A serious error in tactics just then. This whole conversation a huge mistake, most likely. He was running big risks with her by pushing too hard, letting too much of his crazy romanticism reveal itself so early. His obsession with her, his impossible new possessiveness, his weird ego-driven exclusivism. His love. *Yes;* his love. She was absolutely right, of course. He was basically old-fashioned. Wallowing in emotional atavism. You-and-me stuff. I, me, me, mine. This unwillingness to share her fully in Group. As though he had some special claim. He was pure nineteenth century underneath it all. He had only just discovered that, and it had come as a surprise to him. His sick archaic fantasies aside, there was no reason for the two of them to be side by side in the same room during Group, not unless they were the ones who were screwing, and the copulation schedule showed Nate and Serena on tonight's ticket. Drop it, Murray. But he couldn't drop it. He said into her stony silence, "All right, but at least let me set up an inner intersex connection for you and me. So I can feel what you're feeling when Nate and Serena get it on."

"Why this frantic need to reach inside my head?" she asked.

"I love you."

"Of course you do. We all love all of Us. But still, when you try to relate to me one-on-one like this, you injure Group."

"No inner connection, then?"

"No."

"Do you love me?"

A sigh. "I love Us, Murray."

That was likely to be the best he'd get from her this evening. All right. All right. He'd settle for that, if he had to. A crumb here, a crumb there. She smiled, blew him an amiable kiss, broke the contact. He stared moodily at the dead screen. All right. Time to get ready for Group. He turned to the lifesize screen on the east wall and keyed in the visuals for preliminary alignment. Right now Group Central was sending its test pattern, stills of all of tonight's couples. Nate and Serena were in the center, haloed by the glowing nimbus that marked them as this evening's performers. Around the periphery Murray saw images of himself, Kay, Van, JoJo, Nikki, Dirk, Conrad, Finn, Lanelle, and Maria. Bruce, Klaus, Mindy, and Lois weren't there. Too busy, maybe. Or too tired. Or perhaps they were in the grip of negative unGrouplike vibes just at the moment. You didn't have to do Group every night, if you didn't feel into it. Murray averaged four nights a week. Only the real bulls, like Dirk and Nate, routinely hit seven out of seven. Also JoJo, Lanelle, Nikki—the Very Hot Ladies, he liked to call them.

He opened up the audio. "This is Murray," he announced. "I'm starting to synchronize."

Group Central gave him a sweet unwavering A for calibration. He tuned his receiver to match the note. "You're at 432," Group Central said. "Bring your pitch up a little. There. There. Steady. 440, fine." The tones locked perfectly. He was synched in for sound. A little fine tuning on the visuals, next. The test pattern vanished and the screen showed only Nate, naked, a big cocky rockjawed man with a thick mat of curly black hair covering him from thighs to throat. He grinned, bowed, preened. Murray made adjustments until it was all but impossible to distinguish the three-dimensional holographic projection of Nate from the actual Nate, hundreds of miles away in his San Diego bedroom.

Murray was fastidious about these adjustments. Any perceptible drop-off in reality approximation dampened the pleasure Group gave him. For some moments he watched Nate striding bouncily back and forth, working off excess energy, fining himself down to performance level; a minor element of distortion crept into the margins of the image, and, cutting in the manual override, Murray fed his own corrections to Central until all was well.

Next came the main brain-wave amplification, delivering data in the emotional sphere: endocrine feeds, neural set, epithelial appercept, erogenous uptake. Diligently Murray keyed in each one. At first he received only a vague undifferentiated blur of formless background cerebration, but then, like intricate figures becoming clear in an elaborate oriental carpet, the specific characteristics of Nate's mental output began to clarify themselves: edginess, eagerness, horniness, alertness, intensity. A sense of Nate's formidable masculine strength came through. At this stage of the evening Murray still had a distinct awareness of himself as an entity independent of Nate, but that would change soon enough.

"Ready," Murray reported. "Holding awaiting Group cut-in."

He had to hold for fifteen intolerable minutes. He was always the quickest to synchronize. Then he had to sit and sweat, hanging on desperately to his balances and line-ups while he waited for the others. All around the circuit, the rest of them were still tinkering with their rigs, adjusting them with varying degrees of competence. He thought of Kay. At this moment making frantic adjustments, tuning herself to Serena as he had done to Nate.

"Group cut-in," Central said finally.

Murray closed the last circuits. Into his consciousness poured, in one wild rush, the mingled consciousnesses of Van, Dirk, Conrad, and Finn, hooked into him via Nate, and, less intensely because less directly, the consciousnesses of Kay, Maria, Lanelle, JoJo, and Nikki, funneled to him by way of their link to Serena. So all twelve of them were in synch. They had attained Group once again. Now the revels could begin.

Now. Nate approaching Serena. The magic moments of foreplay. That buzz of early excitement, that soaring erotic flight, taking everybody upward like a Beethoven adagio, like a solid hit of acid.

Nate. Serena. San Diego. Their bedroom a glittering hall of mirrors. Refracted images everywhere. A thousand quivering breasts. Five hundred jutting cocks. Hands, eyes, tongues, thighs. The circular undulating bed, quivering, heaving. Murray, lying cocooned in his maze of sophisticated amplification equipment, receiving inputs at temples and throat and chest and loins, felt his palate growing dry, felt a pounding in his groin. He licked his lips. His hips began, of their own accord, a slow rhythmic thrusting motion. Nate's hands casually traversed the taut globes of Serena's bosom. Caught the rigid nipples between hairy fingers, tweaked them, thumbed them. Murray felt the firm nodules of engorged flesh with his own empty hands. The merger of identities was starting. He was becoming Nate, Nate was flowing into him, and he was all the others too, Van, JoJo, Dirk, Finn, Nikki, all of them, feedbacks oscillating in interpersonal whirlpools all along the line. Kay. He was part of Kay, she of him, both of them parts of Nate and Serena. Inextricably intertwined. What Nate experienced, Murray experienced. What Serena experienced, Kay experienced. When Nate's mouth descended to cover Serena's, Murray's tongue slid forward. And felt the moist tip of Serena's. Flesh against flesh, skin against skin. Serena was throbbing. Why not? Six men tonguing her at once. She was always quick to arouse, anyway. She was begging for it. Not that Nate was in any hurry: screwing was his thing, he always made a grand production out of it. As well he might, with ten close friends riding as passengers on his trip. Give us a show, Nate. Nate obliged. He was going down on her, now. Inhaling. His stubbly cheeks against her satiny thighs. Oh, the busy tongue! Oh, the sighs and gasps! And then she engulfing him reciprocally. Murray hissed in delight. Her cunning little suctions, her jolly slithers and slides: a skilled fellatrice, that woman was. He trembled. He was fully into it, now, sharing every impulse with Nate. *Becoming* Nate. Yes. Serena's beckoning body gaping for him. His waggling wand poised above her. The old magic of Group never diminishing. Nate doing all his tricks, pulling out the stops. When? Now. *Now.* The thrust. The quick sliding moment of entry. Ah! Ah! *Ah!* Serena simultaneously possessed by Nate, Murray, Van, Dirk, Conrad, Finn. Finn, Conrad, Dirk, Van, Murray, and Nate simultaneously possessing Serena. And, vicariously throbbing in rhythm with

Serena: Kay, Maria, Lanelle, JoJo, Nikki. Kay. Kay. Kay. Through the sorcery of the crossover loop Nate was having Kay while he had Serena, Nate was having Kay, Maria, Lanelle, JoJo, Nikki all at once, they were being had by him, a soup of identities, an *olla podrida* of copulations, and as the twelve of them soared toward a shared and multiplied ecstasy Murray did something dumb. He thought of Kay.

He thought of Kay. Kay alone in her redwood bower, Kay with bucking hips and tossing hair and glistening droplets of sweat between her breasts, Kay hissing and shivering in Nate's simulated embrace. Murray tried to reach across to her through the Group loop, tried to find and isolate the discrete thread of self that was Kay, tried to chisel away the ten extraneous identities and transform this coupling into an encounter between himself and her. It was a plain violation of the spirit of Group; it was also impossible to achieve, since she had refused him permission to establish a special inner link between them that evening, and so at the moment she was accessible to him only as one facet of the enhanced and expanded Serena. At best he could grope toward Kay through Serena and touch the tip of her soul, but the contact was cloudy and uncertain. Instantly on to what he was trying to do, she petulantly pushed him away, at the same time submerging herself more fully in Serena's consciousness. Rejected, reeling, he slid off into confusion, sending jarring crosscurrents through the whole Group. Nate loosed a shower of irritation despite his heroic attempt to remain unperturbed, and pumped his way to climax well ahead of schedule, hauling everyone breathlessly along with him. As the orgasmic frenzy broke loose Murray tried to re-enter the full linkage, but he found himself unhinged, disaffiliated, and mechanically emptied himself without any tremor of pleasure. Then it was over. He lay back, perspiring, feeling soiled, jangled, unsatisfied. After a few moments he uncoupled his equipment and went out for a cold shower.

Kay called half an hour later.

"You crazy bastard," she said. "What were you trying to do?"

He promised not to do it again. She forgave him. He brooded for two days, keeping out of Group. He missed sharing Conrad and JoJo, Klaus and Lois. The third day the Group chart marked him and Kay as that night's performers. He didn't want to let them all share her. It was stronger than ever, this nasty atavistic possessiveness. He didn't have to, of course. Nobody was forced to do Group. He could beg off and continue to sulk, and Dirk or Van or somebody would substitute for him tonight. But Kay wouldn't necessarily pass up her turn. She almost certainly wouldn't. He didn't like the options. If he made it with Kay as per group schedule, he'd be offering her to all the others. If he stepped aside, she'd do it with someone else. Might as well be the one to take her to bed, in that case. Faced with an ugly choice, he decided to stick to the original schedule.

He popped up to her place eight hours early. He found her sprawled on a carpet of redwood needles in a sun-dappled grove, playing with a stack of music cubes. Mozart tinkled in the fragrant air. "Let's go away somewhere tomorrow," he said. "You and me."

"You're still into you-and-me?"

"I'm sorry."

"Where do you want to go?"

He shrugged. "Hawaii. Afghanistan. Poland. Zambia. It doesn't matter. Just to be with you."

"What about Group?"

"They can spare us for a while."

She rolled over, lazily snaffled Mozart into silence, started a cube of Bach. "I'll go," she said. The Goldberg Variations transcribed for glockenspiel. "But only if we take our Group equipment along."

"It means that much to you?"

"Doesn't it to you?"

"I cherish Group," he said. "But it's not all there is to life. I can live without it for a while. I don't need it, Kay. What I need is you."

"That's obscene, Murray."

"No. It isn't obscene."

"It's boring, at any rate."

"I'm sorry you think so," he told her.

"Do you want to drop out of Group?"

I want us both to drop out of Group, he thought, and I want you to live with me. I can't bear to share you any longer, Kay. But he wasn't prepared to move to that level of confrontation. He said, "I want to stay in Group if it's possible, but I'm also interested in extending and developing some one-on-one with you."

"You've already made that excessively clear."

"I love you."

"You've said that before too."

"What do you want, Kay?"

She laughed, rolled over, drew her knees up until they touched her breasts, parted her thighs, opened herself to a stray shaft of sunlight. "I want to enjoy myself," she said.

He started setting up his equipment an hour before sunset. Because he was performing, the calibrations were more delicate than on an ordinary night. Not only did he have to broadcast a full range of control ratios to Central to aid the others in their tuning, he had to achieve a flawless balance of input and output with Kay. He went about his complex tasks morosely, not at all excited by the thought that he and Kay would shortly be making love. It cooled his ardor to know that Nate, Dirk, Van, Finn, Bruce, and Klaus would be having her too. Why did he begrudge it to them so? He didn't know. Such exclusivism, coming out of nowhere, shocked and disgusted him. Yet it wholly controlled him. Maybe I need help, he thought.

Group time, now. Soft sweet ionized fumes drifting through the chamber of Eros. Kay was warm, receptive, passionate. Her eyes sparkled as she reached for him. They had made love five hundred times and she showed no sign of diminished interest. He knew he turned her on. He hoped he turned her on more than anyone else. He caressed her in all his clever ways, and she purred and wriggled and glowed. Her nipples stood tall: no faking that. Yet something was wrong. Not with her, with him. He was aloof, remote. He seemed to be watching the proceedings from a point somewhere outside himself, as though he were just a Group onlooker tonight, badly tuned in, not even as much a part of things as Klaus, Bruce, Finn, Van, Dirk. The awareness that he had an audience affected him for the first time. His technique, which depended more on finesse and grace than on fire and force, became a trap, locking him into a series of passionless arabesques and pirouettes. He was distracted, though he never had been before, by the minute telemetry tapes glued to the side of Kay's neck and the underside of her thigh. He found himself addressing silent messages to the other men. Here, Nate, how do you like that? Grab some haunch, Dirk. Up the old zaboo, Bruce. Uh. Uh. Ah. Oh.

Kay didn't seem to notice anything was amiss. She came three times in the first fifteen minutes. He doubted that he'd ever come at all. He plugged on, in and out, in and out, moving like a mindless piston. A sort of revenge on Group, he realized. You want to share Kay with me, okay, fellows, but this is all you're going to get. This. Oh. Oh. Oh. Now at last he felt the familiar climactic tickle, stepped down to a tenth of its normal intensity. He hardly noticed it when he came.

Kay said afterward, "What about that trip? Are we still going to go away somewhere tomorrow?"

"Let's forget it for the time being," he said.

He popped to Istanbul alone and spent a day in the covered bazaar, buying cheap but intricate trinkets for every woman in Group. At nightfall he popped down to McMurdo Sound, where the merry Antarctic summer was at its height, and spent six hours on the polar ski slopes, coming away with wind-bronzed skin and aching muscles. In the lodge later he met an angular, auburn-haired woman from Portugal and took her to bed. She was very good, in a heartless, mechanically proficient way. Doubtless she thought the same of him. She asked him whether he might be interested in joining her Group, which operated out of Lisbon and Ibiza. "I already have an affiliation," he said. He popped to Addis Ababa after breakfast, checked into the Hilton, slept for a day and a half, and went on to St. Croix for a night of reef-bobbing. When he popped back to California the next day he called Kay at once to learn the news.

"We've been discussing rearranging some of the Group couplings," she said. "Next week, what about you and Lanelle, me and Dirk?"

"Does that mean you're dropping me?"

"No, not at all, silly. But I do think we need some variety."

"Group was designed to provide us with all the variety we'd ever want."

"You know what I mean. Besides, you're developing an unhealthy fixation on me as isolated love-object."

"Why are you rejecting me?"

"I'm not. I'm trying to help you, Murray."

"I love you," he said.

"Love me in a healthier way, then."

That night it was the turn of Maria and Van. The next, Nikki and Finn. After them, Bruce and Mindy. He tuned in for all three, trying to erode his grief in nightly frenzies of lustful fulfillment. By the third night he was very tired and no less grief-smitten. He took the next night off. Then the schedule came up with the first Murray-Lanelle pairing.

He popped to Hawaii and set up his rig in her sprawling beachfront lanai on Molokai. He had bedded her before, of course. Everyone in Group had bedded everyone else during the preliminary months of compatibility testing. But then they all had settled into more-or-less regular pair-bonding, and he hadn't approached her since. In the past year the only Group woman he had slept with was Kay. By choice.

"I've always liked you," Lanelle said. She was tall, heavy-breasted, wide-shouldered, with warm brown eyes, yellow hair, skin the color of fine honey. "You're just a little crazy, but I don't mind that. And I love screwing Scorpios."

"I'm a Capricorn."

"Them too," she said. "I love screwing just about every sign. Except Virgos. I can't stand Virgos. Remember, we were supposed to have a Virgo in Group, at the start. I blackballed him."

They swam and surfed for a couple of hours before doing the calibrating. The water was warm but a brisk breeze blew from the east, coming like a gust of bad news out of California. Lanelle nuzzled him playfully and then not so playfully in the water. She had always been an aggressive woman, a swaggerer, a strutter. Her appetites were enormous. Her eyes glistened with desire. "Come on," she said finally, tugging at him. They ran to the house and he began to adjust the equipment. It was still early. He thought of Kay and his soul drooped. What am I doing here, he wondered? He lined up the Group apparatus with nervous hands, making many errors. Lanelle stood behind him, rubbing her breasts against his bare back. He had to ask her to stop. Eventually everything was ready and she hauled him to the spongy floor with her, covering his body with hers. Lanelle always liked to be the one on top. Her tongue probed his mouth and her hands clutched his hips and she pressed herself against him, but although her body was warm and smooth and alive he felt no onset of excitement, not a shred. She put her mouth to him but it was hopeless. He remained limp, dead, unable to function. With everyone tuned in and waiting. "What is it?" she whispered. "What should I do, love?" He closed his eyes and indulged in a fantasy of Kay coupling with Dirk, pure masochism, and it aroused him as far as a sort of half-erect condition, and he slithered into her like a prurient eel. She rocked her way to ecstasy above him. This is garbage, he thought. I'm falling apart. Kay. Kay. Kay.

Then Kay had her night with Dirk. At first Murray thought he would simply skip it. There was no reason, after all, why he had to subject himself to something like that, if he expected it to give him pain. It had never been painful for him in the past when Kay did it with other men, inside Group or not, but since the onset of his jealousies everything was different. In theory the Group couples were interchangeable, one pair serving as proxies for all the rest each night, but theory and practice coincided less and less in Murray's mind these days. Nobody would be surprised or upset if he happened not to want to participate tonight. All during the day, though, he found himself obsessively fantasizing Kay and Dirk, every motion, every sound, the two of them facing each other, smiling, embracing, sinking down onto her bed, entwining, his hands sliding over her slender body, his mouth on her mouth, his chest crushing her small breasts, Dirk entering her, riding her, plunging, driving, coming, Kay coming, then Kay and Dirk arising, going for a cooling swim, returning to the bedroom, facing each other, smiling, beginning again. By late afternoon it had taken place so many times in his fevered imagination that he saw no risk in experiencing the reality of it; at least he could have Kay, if only at one remove, by doing Group tonight. And it might help him to shake off his obsessiveness. But it was worse than he imagined it could be. The sight of Dirk, all bulging muscles and tapering hips, terrified him; Dirk was ready for making love long before the foreplay started, and Murray somehow came to fear that he, not Kay, was going to be the target of that long rigid spear of his. Then Dirk began to caress Kay. With each insinuating touch of his hand it seemed some vital segment of Murray's relationship with Kay was being obliterated. He was forced to watch Kay through Dirk's eyes, her flushed face, her quivering nostrils, her moist, slack lips, and it killed him. As Dirk drove deep into her Murray coiled into a miserable fetal ball, one hand clutching his loins, the other clapped across his lips, thumb in his mouth. He couldn't stand it at all. To think that every one of them was having Kay at once. Not only Dirk. Nate, Van, Conrad, Finn, Bruce, Klaus, the whole male Group complement, all of them tuning in tonight for this novel Dirk-Kay pairing. Kay giving herself to all of them gladly, willingly, enthusiastically. He had to escape, now, instantly, even though to drop out of Group communion at this point would unbalance everyone's tuning and set up chaotic eddy-currents that might induce nausea or worse in the others. He didn't care. He had to save himself. He screamed and uncoupled his rig.

He waited two days and went to see her. She was at her exercises, floating like a cloud through a dazzling arrangement of metal rings and loops that dangled at constantly varying heights from the ceiling of her solarium. He stood below her, craning his neck. "It isn't any good," he said. "I want us both to withdraw from Group, Kay."

"That was predictable."

"It's killing me. I love you so much I can't bear to share you."

"So loving me means owning me?"

"Let's just drop out for a while. Let's explore the ramifications of one-on-one. A month, two months, six months, Kay. Just until I get this craziness out of my system. Then we can go back in."

"So you admit it's craziness."

"I never denied it." His neck was getting stiff. "Won't you please come down from those rings while we're talking?"

"I can hear you perfectly well from here, Murray."

"Will you drop out of Group and go away with me for a while?"

"No."

"Will you even consider it?"

"No."

"Do you realize that you're addicted to Group?" he asked.

"I don't think that's an accurate evaluation of the situation. But do *you* realize that you're dangerously fixated on me?"

"I realize it."

"What do you propose to do about it?"

"What I'm doing now," he said. "Coming to you, asking you to do a one-on-one with me."

"Stop it."

"One-on-one was good enough for the human race for thousands of years."

"It was a prison," she said. "It was a trap. We're out of the trap at last. You won't get me back in."

He wanted to pull her down from her rings and shake her. "I *love* you, Kay!"

"You take a funny way of showing it. Trying to limit the range of my experience. Trying to hide me away in a vault somewhere. It won't work."

"Definitely no?"

"Definitely no."

She accelerated her pace, flinging herself recklessly from loop to loop. Her glistening nude form tantalized and infuriated him. He shrugged and turned away, shoulders slumping, head drooping. This was precisely how he had expected her to respond. No surprises. Very well. Very well. He crossed from the solarium into the bedroom and lifted her Group rig from its container. Slowly, methodically, he ripped it apart, bending the frame until it split, cracking the fragile leads, uprooting handfuls of connectors, crumpling the control panel. The instrument was already a ruin by the time Kay came in. "What are you *doing?*" she cried. He splintered the lovely gleaming calibration dials under his heel and kicked the wreckage of the rig toward her. It would take months before a replacement rig could be properly attuned and synchronized. "I had no choice," he told her sadly.

They would have to punish him. That was inevitable. But how? He waited at home, and before long they came to him, all of them, Nate, Van, Dirk, Conrad, Finn, Bruce, Klaus, Kay, Serena, Maria, JoJo, Lanelle, Nikki, Mindy, Lois, popping in from many quarters of the world, some of them dressed in evening clothes, some of then naked or nearly so, some of them unkempt and sleepy, all of them angry in a cold, tight way. He tried to stare them down. Dirk said, "You must be terribly sick, Murray. We feel sorry for you."

"We really want to help you," said Lanelle.

"We're here to give you therapy," Finn told him.

Murray laughed. "Therapy. I bet. What kind of therapy?"

"To rid you of your exclusivism," Dirk said. "To burn all the trash out of your mind."

"Shock treatment," Finn said.

"Keep away from me!"

"Hold him," Dirk said.

Quickly they surrounded him. Bruce clamped an arm across his chest like an iron bar. Conrad seized his hands and brought his wrists together behind his back. Finn and Dirk pressed up against his sides. He was helpless.

Kay began to remove her clothing. Naked, she lay down on Murray's bed, flexed her knees, opened her thighs. Klaus got on top of her.

"What the hell is this?" Murray asked.

Efficiently but without passion Kay aroused Klaus, and efficiently but without passion he penetrated her. Murray writhed impotently as their bodies moved together. Klaus made no attempt at bringing Kay off. He reached his climax in four or five minutes, grunting once, and rolled away from her, redfaced, sweating. Van took his place between Kay's legs.

"No," Murray said. "Please, no."

Inexorably Van had his turn, quick, impersonal. Nate was next. Murray tried not to watch, but his eyes would not remain closed. A strange smile glittered on Kay's lips as she gave herself to Nate. Nate arose. Finn approached the bed.

"No!" Murray cried, and lashed out in a backwards kick that sent Conrad screaming across the room. Murray's hands were free. He twisted and wrenched himself away from Bruce. Dirk and Nate intercepted him as he rushed toward Kay. They seized him and flung him to the floor.

"The therapy isn't working," Nate said.

"Let's skip the rest," said Dirk. "It's no use trying to heal him. He's beyond hope. Let him stand up."

Murray got cautiously to his feet. Dirk said, "By unanimous vote, Murray, we expel you from Group for unGrouplike attitudes and especially for your unGrouplike destruction of Kay's rig. All your Group privileges are canceled." At a signal from Dirk, Nate removed Murray's rig from its container and reduced it to unsalvageable rubble. Dirk said, "Speaking as your friend, Murray, I suggest you think seriously about undergoing a total personality reconstruct. You're in trouble, do you know that? You need a lot of help. You're a mess."

"Is there anything else you want to tell me?" Murray asked.

"Nothing else. Goodbye, Murray."

They started to go out. Dirk, Finn, Nate. Bruce, Conrad, Klaus. Van. JoJo. Nikki. Serena, Maria, Lanelle, Mindy. Lois. Kay was the last to leave. She stood by the door, clutching her clothes in a small crumpled bundle. She seemed entirely unafraid of him. There was a peculiar look of—was it tenderness? pity?—on her face. Softly she said, "I'm sorry it had to come to this, Murray. I feel so unhappy for you. I know that what you did wasn't a hostile act. You did it out of love. You were all wrong, but you were doing it out of love." She walked toward him and kissed him lightly, on the cheek, on the tip of the nose, on the lips. He didn't move. She smiled. She touched his arm. "I'm so sorry," she murmured. "Goodbye, Murray." As she went through the door she looked back and said, "Such a damned shame. I could have loved you, you know? I could really have loved you."

He had told himself that he would wait until they all were gone before he let the tears flow. But when the door had closed behind Kay he discovered his eyes remained dry. He had no tears. He was altogether calm. Numb. Burned out.

After a long while he put on fresh clothing and went out. He popped to London, found that it was raining there, and popped to Prague, where there was something stifling about the atmosphere, and went on to Seoul, where he had barbecued beef and kimchi for dinner. Then he popped to New York. In front of a gallery on Lexington Avenue he picked up a complaisant young girl with long black hair. "Let's go to a hotel," he suggested, and she smiled and nodded. He registered for a six-hour stay. Upstairs, she undressed without waiting for him to ask. Her body was smooth and supple, flat belly, pale skin, high full breasts. They lay down together and, in silence, without preliminaries, he took her. She was eager and responsive. Kay, he thought. Kay. Kay. You are Kay. A spasm of culmination shook him with unexpected force.

"Do you mind if I smoke?" she said a few minutes later.

"I love you," he said.

"What?"

"I love you."

"You're sweet."

"Come live with me. Please. Please. I'm serious."

"What?"

"Live with me. Marry me."

"*What?*"

"There's only one thing I ask. No Group stuff. That's all. Otherwise you can do as you please. I'm wealthy. I'll make you happy. I love you."

"You don't even know my name."

"I love you."

"Mister, you must be out of your head."

"Please. Please."

"A lunatic. Unless you're trying to make fun of me."

"I'm perfectly serious, I assure you. Live with me. Be my wife."

"A lunatic," she said. "I'm getting out of here!" She leaped up and looked for her clothes. "Jesus, a madman!"

"No," he said, but she was on her way, not even pausing to get dressed, running helter-skelter from the room, her pink buttocks flashing like beacons as she made her escape. The door slammed. He shook his head. He sat rigid for half an hour, an hour, some long timeless span, thinking of Kay, thinking of Group, wondering what they'd be doing tonight, whose turn it was. At length he rose and put on his clothes and left the hotel. A terrible restlessness assailed him. He popped to Karachi and stayed ten minutes. He popped to Vienna. To Hangchow. He didn't stay. Looking for what? He didn't know. Looking for Kay? Kay didn't exist. Looking. Just looking. Pop. Pop. Pop.

5

CALIBAN

They have all changed their faces to a standard model. It is the latest thing, which should not be confused with the latest Thing. The latest Thing is me. The latest thing, the latest fad, the latest rage, is for them all to change their faces to a standard model. I have no idea how it is done but I think it is genetic, with the RNA, the DNA, the NDA. Only retroactive. They all come out with blond wavy hair and sparkling blue eyes. And long straight faces with sharp cheekbones. And notched chins and thin lips curling in ironic smiles. Even the black ones: thin lips, blue eyes, blond wavy hair. And pink skins. They all look alike now. The sweet Aryanized world. Our entire planet. Except me. Meee.

* * *

I am imperfect. I am blemished. I am unforgiving. I am the latest Thing.

* * *

Louisiana said, Would you like to copulate with me? You are so strange. You are so beautiful. Oh, how I desire you, strange being from a strange time. My orifices are yours.

It was a thoughtful offer. I considered it a while, thinking she might be trying to patronize me. At length I notified her of my acceptance. We went to a public copulatorium. Louisiana is taller than I am and her hair is a torrent of spun gold. Her eyes are blue and her face is long and straight. I would say she is about twenty-three years old. In the copulatorium she dissolved her clothes and stood naked before me. She was wearing gold pubic hair that day and her belly was flat and taut.

Her breasts were round and slightly elongated and the nipples were very small. Go on, she said, now you dissolve your clothes.

I said, I am afraid to because my body is ugly and you will mock me.

Your body is not ugly, she said. Your body is strange but it is not ugly.

My body is ugly, I insisted. My legs are short and they curve outward and my thighs have bulging muscles and I have black hairy hair all over me. Like an ape. And there is this hideous scar on my belly.

A scar?

Where they took out my appendix, I told her.

This aroused her beyond all probability. Her nipples stood up tall and her face became flushed.

Your appendix? Your appendix was removed?

Yes, I said, it was done when I was fourteen years old, and I have a loathsome red scar on my abdomen.

She asked, What year was it when you were fourteen?

I said, It was 1967, I think.

She laughed and clapped her hands and began to dance around the room. Her breasts bounced up and down but her long flowing silken hair soon covered them, leaving only the stubby pinkish nipples poking through like buttons. 1967! she cried. Fourteen! Your appendix was removed! 1967!

Then she turned to me and said, My grandfather was born in 1967, I think. How terribly ancient you are. My helix-father's father on the countermolecular side. I didn't realize you were so very ancient.

Ancient and ugly, I said.

Not ugly, only strange, she said.

Strange and ugly, I said. Strangely ugly.

We think you are beautiful, she said. Will you dissolve your clothes now? It would not be pleasing to me to copulate with you if you keep your clothes on.

There, I said, and boldly revealed myself. The bandy legs. The hairy chest. The scarred belly. The bulging shoulders. The short neck. She has seen my lopsided face, she can see my dismal body as well. If that is what she wants.

She threw herself upon me, gasping and making soft noises.

*   *   *

TABLE 2. AMINO ACID SUBSTITUTIONS IN
POLYPEPTIDE ANTIBIOTICS

ANTIBIOTIC FAMILY	AMINO ACID IN THE MAJOR COMPONENT	REPLACEMENT
Actinomycins	D-Valine	D-Alloisoleucine
	L-Proline	4-Hydroxy-L-proline
		4-Keto-L-proline
		Sarcosine
		Pipecolic acid
		Azetidine-2-carboxylic acid
Bacitracins	L-Valine	L-Isoleucine
Bottromycins	L-Proline	3-Methyl-L-proline
Gramicidin A	L-Leucine	L-Isoleucine
Ilamycins	N-Methyl-L-leucine	N-Methyl-L-formyl-norvaline
Polymyxins	D-Phenylalanine	D-Leucine
	L-Isoleucine	L-Leucine
Quinoxaline antibiotics	N-Methyl-L-valine	N-Methyl-L-isoleucine
Sporidesmolides	D-Valine	A-Alloisoleucine
Tyrocidine	L-Phenylalanine	L-Tryptophan
	D-Phenylalanine	D-Tryptophan
Vernamycin B	D-Alanine	D-Butyrine

*   *   *

What did Louisiana look like before the change came? Did she have dull stringy hair thick lips a hook nose bushy black eyebrows no chin foul breath one breast bigger than the other splay feet crooked teeth little dark hairs around her nipples a bulging navel too many dimples in her buttocks skinny thighs blue veins in her calves protruding ears? And then did they give her the homogenizing treatment and make her the golden creature she is today? How long did it take? What were the costs? Did the government subsidize the process? Were the large corporations involved? How were these matters handled in the socialist countries? Was there anyone who did not care to be changed? Perhaps Louisiana was born this way. Perhaps her beauty is natural. In any society there are always a few whose beauty is natural.

*   *   *

Dr. Habakkuk and Senator Mandragore spent a great deal of time questioning me in the Palazzo of Mirrors. They put a green plastic dome over my head so that everything I said would be recorded with the proper nuance and intensity. Speak to us, they said. We are fascinated by your antique accent. We are enthralled by your primitive odors. Do you realize that you are our sole representative of the nightmare out of which we have awakened? Tell us, said the Senator, tell us about your brutally competitive civilization. Describe in detail the fouling of the environment. Explain the nature of national rivalry. Compare and contrast methods of political discourse in the Soviet Union and in the United States. Let us have your analysis of the sociological implications of the first voyage to the moon. Would you like to see the moon? Can we offer you any psychedelic drugs? Did you find Louisiana sexually satisfying? We are so glad to have you here. We regard you as a unique spiritual treasure. Speak to us of yesterday's yesterdays, while we listen entranced and enraptured.

*   *   *

Louisiana says that she is eighty-seven years old. Am I to believe this? There is about her a springtime freshness. No, she maintains, I am eighty-seven years old. I was born on March-alternate 11, 2022. Does that depress you? Is my great age frightening to you? See how tight my skin is. See how my teeth gleam. Why are you so disturbed? I am, after all, much younger than you.

*   *   *

TABLE XIX

Some Less Likely but Important Possibilities

1. "True" artificial intelligence
2. Practical use of sustained fusion to produce neutrons and/or energy
3. Artificial growth of new limbs and organs (either *in situ* or for later transplantation)
4. Room temperature superconductors
5. Major use of rockets for commercial or private transportation (either terrestrial or extraterrestrial)

6. Effective chemical or biological treatment for most mental illnesses
7. Almost complete control of marginal changes in heredity
8. Suspended animation (for years or centuries)
9. Practical materials with nearly "theoretical limit" strength
10. Conversion of mammals (humans?) to fluid breathers
11. Direct input into human memory banks
12. Direct augmentation of human mental capacity by the mechanical or electrical interconnection of the brain with a computer
13. Major rejuvenation and/or significant extension of vigor and life span—say 100 to 150 years
14. Chemical or biological control of character or intelligence
15. Automated highways
16. Extensive use of moving sidewalks for local transportation
17. Substantial manned lunar or planetary installations
18. Electric power available for less than .3 mill per kilowatt-hour
19. Verification of some extrasensory phenomena
20. Planetary engineering
21. Modification of the solar system
22. Practical laboratory conception and nurturing of animal (human?) foetuses
23. Production of a drug equivalent to Huxley's soma
24. A technological equivalent of telepathy
25. Some direct control of individual thought processes

*   *   *

I understand that in some cases making the great change involved elaborate surgery. Cornea transplants and cosmetic adjustment of the facial structure. A great deal of organ-swapping went on. There is not much permanence among these people. They are forever exchanging segments of themselves for new and improved segments. I am told that among some advanced groups the use of mechanical limb-interfaces has come to be common, in order that new arms and legs may be plugged in with a minimum of trouble. This is truly an astonishing era. Even so, their women seem to copulate in the old ways: knees up thighs apart, lying on right side left leg flexed, back to the man and knees slightly bent, etc., etc., etc. One might think they would have invented something new by this time. But perhaps the possibilities for innovation in the sphere of erotics are not extensive. Can I suggest anything? What if the woman unplugs both arms and both legs and presents her mere torso to the man? Helpless! Vulnerable! Quintessentially feminine! I will discuss it with Louisiana. But it would be just my luck that her arms and legs don't come off.

* * *

On the first para-Wednesday of every month Lieutenant Hotchkiss gives me lessons in fluid-breathing. We go to one of the deepest sub-levels of the Extravagance Building, where there is a special hyperoxygenated pool, for the use of beginners only, circular in shape and not at all deep. The water sparkles like opal. Usually the pool is crowded with children but Lieutenant Hotchkiss arranges for me to have private instruction since I am shy about revealing my body. Each lesson is much like the one before. Lieutenant Hotchkiss descends the gentle ramp that leads one into the pool. He is taller than I am and his hair is golden and his eyes are blue. Sometimes I have difficulties distinguishing him from Dr. Habakkuk and Senator Mandragore. In a casual moment the lieutenant confided that he is ninety-eight years old and therefore not really a contemporary of Louisiana's, although Louisiana has hinted that on several occasions in the past she has allowed the lieutenant to fertilize her ova. I doubt this inasmuch as reproduction is quite uncommon in this era and what probability is there that she would have permitted him to do it more than once? I think she believes that by telling me such things she will stimulate emotions of jealousy in me, since she knows that the primitive ancients were frequently jealous. Regardless of all this Lieutenant Hotchkiss proceeds to enter the water. It reaches his navel, his broad hairless chest, his throat, his chin, his sensitive thin-walled nostrils. He submerges and crawls about on the floor of the pool. I see his golden hair glittering through the opal water. He remains totally submerged for eight or twelve minutes, now and again lifting his hands above the surface and waggling them as if to show me where he is. Then he comes forth. Water streams from his nostrils but he is not in the least out of breath. Come on, now, he says. You can do it. It's as easy as it looks. He beckons me toward the ramp. Any child can do it, the lieutenant assures me. It's a matter of control and determination. I shake my head. No, I say, genetic modification has something to do with it. My lungs aren't equipped to handle water, although I suppose yours are. The lieutenant merely laughs. Come on, come on, into the water. And I go down the ramp. How the water glows and shimmers! It reaches my

navel, my black-matted chest, my throat, my chin, my wide thick
nostrils. I breathe it in and choke and splutter; and I rush up the ramp,
struggling for air. With the water a leaden weight in my lungs, I throw
myself exhausted to the marble floor and cry out, No, no, no, it's
impossible. Lieutenant Hotchkiss stands over me. His body is without
flaw. He says, You've got to try to cultivate the proper attitudes. Your
mental set determines everything. Let's think more positively about this
business of breathing under water. Don't you realize that it's a major
evolutionary step, one of the grand and glorious things separating our
species from the australopithecines? Don't you want to be part of the
great leap forward? Up, now. Try again. Thinking positively all the
time. Carrying in your mind the distinction between yourself and our
bestial ancestors. Go in. In. In. And I go in. And moments later burst
from the water, choking and spluttering. This takes place on the first
para-Wednesday of every month. The same thing, every time.

*   *   *

When you are talking on the telephone and your call is abruptly cut off,
do you worry that the person on the other end will think you have hung
up on him? Do you suspect that the person on the other end has hung
up on you? Such problems are unknown here. These people make very
few telephone calls. We are beyond mere communication in this era,
Louisiana sometimes remarks.

*   *   *

Through my eyes these people behold their shining plastic epoch in
proper historical perspective. They must see it as the present, which is
always the same. But to me it is the future and so I have the true
observer's parallax: I can say, it once was like *that* and now it is like *this.*
They prize my gift. They treasure me. People come from other
continents to run their fingers over my face. They tell me how much
they admire my asymmetry. And they ask me many questions. Most of
them ask about their own era rather than about mine. Such questions
as:

Does suspended animation tempt you?

Was the fusion plant overwhelming in its implications of contained might?

Can you properly describe interconnection of the brain with a computer as an ecstatic experience?

Do you approve of modification of the solar system?

And also there are those who make more searching demands on my critical powers, such as Dr. Habakkuk and Senator Mandragore. They ask such questions as:

Was the brevity of your life span a hindrance to the development of the moral instincts?

Do you find our standardization of appearance at all abhorrent?

What was your typical emotional response to the sight of the dung of some wild animal in the streets?

Can you quantify the intensity of your feelings concerning the transience of human institutions?

I do my best to serve their needs. Often it is a strain to answer them in meaningful ways, but I strive to do so. Wondering occasionally if it would not have been more valuable for them to interrogate a Neanderthal. Or one of Lieutenant Hotchkiss' australopithecines. I am perhaps not primitive enough, though I do have my own charisma, nevertheless.

*   *   *

Members of the new animal phylum, Gnathostomulida, recently discovered in Europe, have now been found in unexpected abundance and diversity along the east coast of the United States.

Two million animal species have been described, but the rate at which new descriptions accumulate indicates that these two million are only about fifty percent of the extant species on earth. The increase in new species of birds (8600 known species) has sunk to less than 0.3 percent a year, but in many other classes (for example, Turbellaria with 2500 known species) the rate of increase indicates that undescribed species probably total more than eighty percent. Although only about half of the existing kinds of animals have been described, eighty percent of the families, ninety-five percent of the orders, and nearly all of the animal classes are presumably already known. Therefore a new phylum should be rare indeed.

☼   ☼   ☼

The first day it was pretty frightening for me. I saw one of them, with his sleek face and all, and I could accept that, but then another one came into the room to give me an injection, and he looked just like the first one. Twins, I thought, my doctors are twins. But then a third and a fourth and a fifth arrived. The same face, the very same fucking face. Imagine my chagrin, me with my blob of a nose, with my uneven teeth, with my eyebrows that meet in the middle, with my fleshy pockmarked cheeks, lying there beneath this convocation of the perfect. Let me tell you I felt out of place. I was never touchy about my looks before—I mean, it's an imperfect world, we all have our flaws—but these bastards *didn't* have flaws, and that was a hard acceptance for me to relate to. I thought I was being clever: I said, You're all multiples of the same gene pattern, right? Modern advances in medicine have made possible an infinite reduplication of genetic information and the five of you belong to one clone, isn't that it? And several of them answered, No, this is not the case, we are in fact wholly unrelated but within the last meta-week we have independently decided to standardize our appearance according to the presently favored model. And then three or four more of them came into my room to get a look at me.

☼   ☼   ☼

In the beginning I kept telling myself: *In the country of the beautiful the ugly man is king.*

☼   ☼   ☼

Louisiana was the first one with whom I had a sexual liaison. We often went to public copulatoria. She was easy to arouse and quite passionate although her friend Calpurnia informed me some months later that Louisiana takes orgasm-inducing drugs before copulating with me. I asked Calpurnia why and she became embarrassed. Dismayed, I bared my body to her and threw myself on top of her. Yes, she cried, rape me, violate me! Calpurnia's vigorous spasms astonished me. The following morning Louisiana asked me if I had noticed Calpurnia swallowing a small purple spansule prior to our intercourse. Calpurnia's face is identical to Louisiana's but her breasts are farther apart. I have also had sexual relations with Helena, Amniota, Drusilla, Florinda, and Vibrissa. Before each episode of copulation I ask them their names so that there will be no mistakes.

*   *   *

At twilight they programmed an hour of red and green rainfall and I queried Senator Mandragore about the means by which I had been brought to this era. Was it by bodily transportation through time? That is, the physical lifting of my very self out of *then* and into *now*? Or was my body dead and kept on deposit in a freezer vault until these people resuscitated and refurbished it? Am I, perhaps, a total genetic reconstruct fashioned from a few fragments of ancient somatic tissue found in a baroque urn? Possibly I am only a simulated and stylized interpretation of twentieth-century man produced by a computer under intelligent and sympathetic guidance. How was it done, Senator? How was it done? The rain ceased. Leaving elegant puddles of blurred hue in the puddle-places.

*   *   *

Walking with Louisiana on my arm down Venus Avenue I imagined that I saw another man with a face like mine. It was the merest flash: a dark visage, thick heavy brows, stubble on the cheeks, the head thrust belligerently forward between the massive shoulders. But he was gone, turning a sudden corner, before I could get a good look. Louisiana suggested I was overindulging in hallucinogens. We went to an underwater theater and she swam below me like a golden fish, revolving lights glinting off the upturned globes of her rump.

*   *   *

This is a demonstration of augmented mental capacity said Vibrissa. I wish to show you what the extent of human potentiality can be. Read me any passage of Shakespeare of your own choice and I will repeat it verbatim and then offer you textual analysis. Shall we try this? Very well I said and delicately put my fingernail to the Shakespeare cube and the words formed and I said out loud, What man dare, I dare: Approach thou like the rugged Russian bear, the arm'd rhinoceros, or the Hyrcan tiger, Take any shape but that, and my firm nerves Shall never tremble. Vibrissa instantly recited the lines to me without error and interpreted them in terms of the poet's penis-envy, offering me footnotes from Seneca and Strindberg. I was quite impressed. But then I was never what you might call an intellectual.

* * *

On the day of the snow-gliding events I distinctly and beyond any possibilities of ambiguity or misapprehension saw two separate individuals who resembled me. Are they importing more of my kind for their amusement? If they are I will be resentful. I cherish my unique status.

* * *

I told Dr. Habakkuk that I wished to apply for transformation to the facial norm of society. Do it, I said, the transplant thing or the genetic manipulation or however you manage it. I want to be golden-haired and have blue eyes and regular features. I want to look like you. Dr. Habakkuk smiled genially and shook his youthful golden head. No, he told me. Forgive us, but we like you as you are.

* * *

Sometimes I dream of my life as it was in the former days. I think of automobiles and pastrami and tax returns and marigolds and pimples and mortgages and the gross national product. Also I indulge in recollections of my childhood my parents my wife my dentist my younger daughter my desk my toothbrush my dog my umbrella my favorite brand of beer my wristwatch my answering service my neighbors my phonograph my ocarina. All of these things are gone. Grinding my flesh against that of Drusilla in the copulatorium I wonder if she could be one of my descendants. I must have descendants somewhere in this civilization, and why not she? She asks me to perform an act of oral perversion with her and I explain that I couldn't possibly engage in such stuff with my own great-grandchild.

*   *   *

I think I remain quite calm at most times considering the extraordinary nature of the stress that this experience has imposed on me. I am still self-conscious about my appearance but I pretend otherwise. Often I go naked just as they do. If they dislike bodily hair or disproportionate limbs, let them look away.

*   *   *

Occasionally I belch or scratch under my arms or do other primitive things to remind them that I am the authentic man from antiquity. For now there can be no doubt that I have my imitators. There are at least five. Calpurnia denies this but I am no fool.

*   *   *

Dr. Habakkuk revealed that he was going to take a holiday in the Carpathians and would not return until the 14th of June-surrogate. In the meantime Dr. Clasp would minister to my needs. Dr. Clasp entered my suite and I remarked on his startling resemblance to Dr. Habakkuk. He asked, What would you like? and I told him I wanted him to operate on me so that I looked like everybody else. I am tired of appearing bestial and primordial, I said. To my surprise Dr. Clasp smiled warmly and told me that he'd arrange for the transformation at once, since it violated his principles to allow any organism needlessly to suffer. I was taken to the operating room and given a sour-tasting anesthetic. Seemingly without the passing of time I awakened and was wheeled into a dome of mirrors to behold myself. Even as I had requested they had redone me into one of them, blond-haired, blue-eyed, with a slim, agile body and a splendidly symmetrical face. Dr. Clasp came in after a while and we stood side by side: we might have been twins. How do you like it? he asked. Tears brimmed in my eyes and I said that this was the most wonderful moment of my life. Dr. Clasp pummeled my shoulder jovially and said, You know, I am not Dr.

Clasp at all, I am really Dr. Habakkuk and I never went to the Carpathians. This entire episode has been a facet of our analysis of your pattern of responses.

* * *

Louisiana was astonished by my changed appearance. Are you truly he? she kept asking Are you truly he? I'll prove it I said and mounted her with my old prehistoric zeal, snorting and gnawing her breasts. But she shook me free with a deft flip of her pelvis and rushed from the chamber. You'll never see me again she shouted but I merely shrugged and called after her, So what I can see lots of others just like you. I never saw her again.

* * *

TABLE I
Composition of isocaloric diet

Substance	Composition (%)
Barley meal	70.0
Fine Millars Offal	20.0
Extracted soya bean meal	7.5
Salt	0.5
Ground limestone	0.5
Sterilized bone meal	1.0
"Eves" No. 32 (totally digestible)	0.25

* * *

Plausible attitudes upon discovering that one has been ripped from one's proper cultural matrix:

a) Fear
b) Indignation
c) Incredulity
d) Uncertainty
e) Aggressive hostility

f) Withdrawal
g) Compulsive masturbation
h) Cool acceptance
i) Suspicion
j) None of these

*   *   *

So now they have all changed themselves again to the new standard model. It happened gradually over a period of months but the transition is at last complete. Their heavy brows, their pockmarked cheeks, their hairy chests. It is the latest thing. I make my way through the crowded streets and wherever I turn I see faces that mirror my own lopsidedness. Only I am not lopsided myself any more, of course. I am symmetrical and flawless, and I am the only one. I cannot find Dr. Habakkuk and Dr. Clasp is in the Pyrenees; Senator Mandragore was defeated in the primary. So I must remain beautiful. Walking among them. They are all alike. Thick lips uneven teeth noses like blobs. How I despise them! I the only golden one. And all of them mocking me by their metamorphosis. All of them. Mocking me. Meee.

6

MANY MANSIONS

It's been a rough day. Everything gone wrong. A tremendous tieup on the freeway going to work, two accounts canceled before lunch, now some inconceivable botch by the weather programmers. It's snowing outside. Actually snowing. He'll have to go out and clear the driveway in the morning. He can't remember when it last snowed. And of course a fight with Alice again. She never lets him alone. She's at her most deadly when she sees him come home exhausted from the office. Ted why don't you this, Ted get me that. Now, waiting for dinner, working on his third drink in forty minutes, he feels one of his headaches coming on. Those miserable killer headaches that can destroy a whole evening. What a life! He toys with murderous fantasies. Take her out by the reservoir for a friendly little stroll, give her a quick hard shove with his shoulder. She can't swim. Down, down, down. Glub. Goodbye, Alice. Free at last.

In the kitchen she furiously taps the keys of the console, programming dinner just the way he likes it. Cold vichyssoise, baked potato with sour cream and chives, sirloin steak blood-rare inside and charcoal-charred outside. Don't think it isn't work to get the meal just right, even with the autochef. All for him. The bastard. Tell me, why do I sweat so hard to please him? Has he made me happy? What's he ever done for me except waste the best years of my life? And he thinks I don't know about his other women. Those lunchtime quickies. Oh, I wouldn't mind at all if he dropped dead tomorrow. I'd be a great widow—so dignified at the funeral, so strong, hardly crying at all. And everybody thinks we're such a close couple. Married eleven years and they're still

in love. I heard someone say that only last week. If they only knew the
truth about us. If they only knew.

Martin peers out the window of his third-floor apartment in Sunset
Village. Snow. I'll be damned. He can't remember the last time he saw
snow. Thirty, forty years back, maybe, when Ted was a baby. He
absolutely can't remember. White stuff on the ground—when? The
mind gets wobbly when you're past eighty. He still can't believe he's an
old man. It rocks him to realize that his grandson Ted, Martha's boy, is
almost forty. I bounced that kid on my knee and he threw up all over
my suit. Four years old then. Nixon was President. Nobody talks much
about Tricky Dick these days. Ancient history. McKinley, Coolidge,
Nixon. Time flies. Martin thinks of Ted's wife Alice. What a nice tight
little ass she has. What a cute pair of jugs. I'd like to get my hands on
them. I really would. You know something, Martin? You're not such an
old ruin yet. Not if you can get it up for your grandson's wife.

His dreams of drowning her fade as quickly as they came. He is not a
violent man by nature. He knows he could never do it. He can't even
bring himself to step on a spider; how then could he kill his wife? If
she'd die some other way, of course, without the need of his taking
direct action, that would solve everything. She's driving to the
hairdresser on one of those manual-access roads she likes to use and her
car swerves on an icy spot, and she goes into a tree at 80 kilometers an
hour. Good. She's shopping on Union Boulevard and the bank is blown
up by an activist; she's nailed by flying debris. Good. The dentist gives
her a new anesthetic and it turns out she's fatally allergic to it. Puffs up
like a blowfish and dies in five minutes. Good. The police come, long
faces, snuffly noses. Terribly sorry, Mr. Porter. There's been an awful
accident. Don't tell me it's my wife, he cries. They nod lugubriously.
He bears up bravely under the loss, though.

"You can come in for dinner now," she says. He's sitting slouched on
the sofa with another drink in his hand. He drinks more than any man
she knows, not that she knows all that many. Maybe he'll get cirrhosis
and die. Do people still die of cirrhosis, she wonders, or do they give

them liver transplants now? The funny thing is that he still turns her on, after eleven years. His eyes, his face, his hands. She despises him but he still turns her on.

The snow reminds him of his young manhood, of his days long ago in the East. He was quite the ladies' man then. And it wasn't so easy to get some action back in those days, either. The girls were always worried about what people would say if anyone found out. *What people would say!* As if doing it with a boy you liked was something shameful. Or they'd worry about getting knocked up. They made you wear a rubber. How awful that was: like wearing a sock. The pill was just starting to come in, the original pill, the old one-a-day kind. Imagine a world without the pill! ("Did they have dinosaurs when you were a boy, grandpa?") Still, Martin had made out all right. Big muscular frame, strong earnest features, warm inquisitive eyes. You'd never know it to look at me now. I wonder if Alice realizes what kind of stud I used to be. If I had the money I'd rent one of those time machines they've got now and send her back to visit myself around 1950 or so. A little gift to my younger self. He'd really rip into her. It gives Martin a quick riffle of excitement to think of his younger self ripping into Alice. But of course he can't afford any such thing.

As he forks down his steak he imagines being single again. Would I get married again? Not on your life. Not until I'm good and ready, anyway, maybe when I'm fifty-five or sixty. Me for bachelorhood for the time being, just screwing around like a kid. To hell with responsibilities. I'll wait two, three weeks after the funeral, a decent interval, and then I'll go off for some fun. Hawaii, Tahiti, Fiji, someplace out there. With Nolie. Or Maria. Or Ellie. Yes, with Ellie. He thinks of Ellie's pink thighs, her soft heavy breasts, her long radiant auburn hair. Two weeks in Fiji with Ellie. Two weeks in Ellie with Fiji. Yes. Yes. Yes. "Is the steak rare enough for you, Ted?" Alice asks. "It's fine," he says.

She goes upstairs to check the children's bedroom. They're both asleep, finally. Or else faking it so well that it makes no difference. She stands by their beds a moment, thinking, I love you, Bobby, I love you, Tink.

Tink and Bobby, Bobby and Tink. I love you even though you drive me crazy sometimes. She tiptoes out. Now for a quiet evening of television. And then to bed. The same old routine. Christ. I don't know why I go on like this. There are times when I'm ready to explode. I stay with him for the children's sake, I guess. Is that enough of a reason?

He envisions himself running hand in hand along the beach with Ellie. Both of them naked, their skins bronzed and gleaming in the tropical sunlight. Palm trees everywhere. Grains of pink sand under foot. Soft transparent wavelets lapping the shore. A quiet cove. "No one can see us here," Ellie murmurs. He sinks down on her firm sleek body and enters her.

A blazing band of pain tightens like a strip of hot metal across Martin's chest. He staggers away from the window, dropping into a low crouch as he stumbles toward a chair. The heart. Oh, the heart! That's what you get for drooling over Alice. Dirty old man. "Help," he calls feebly. "Come on, you filthy machine, help me!" The medic, activated by the key phrase, rolls silently toward him. Its sensors are already at work scanning him, searching for the cause of the discomfort. A telescoping steel-jacketed arm slides out of the medic's chest and, hovering above Martin, extrudes an ultrasonic injection snout. "Yes," Martin murmurs, "that's right, damn you, hurry up and give me the drug!" Calm. I must try to remain calm. The snout makes a gentle whirring noise as it forces the relaxant into Martin's vein. He slumps in relief. The pain slowly ebbs. Oh, that's much better. Saved again. Oh. Oh. Oh. Dirty old man. Ought to be ashamed of yourself.

Ted knows he won't get to Fiji with Ellie or anybody else. Any realistic assessment of the situation brings him inevitably to the same conclusion. Alice isn't going to die in an accident, any more than he's likely to murder her. She'll live forever. Unwanted wives always do. He could ask for a divorce, of course. He'd probably lose everything he owned, but he'd win his freedom. Or he could simply do away with himself. That was always a temptation for him. The easy way out, no lawyers, no hassles. So it's that time of the evening again. It's the same every night. Pretending to watch television, he secretly indulges in suicidal fantasies.

Bare-bodied dancers in gaudy luminous paint gyrate lasciviously on the screen, nearly large as life. Alice scowls. The things they show on TV nowadays! It used to be that you got this stuff only on the X-rated channels, but now it's everywhere. And look at him, just lapping it up! Actually she knows she wouldn't be so stuffy about the sex shows except that Ted's fascination with them is a measure of his lack of interest in her. Let them show screwing and all the rest on TV, if that's what people want. I just wish Ted had as much enthusiasm for me as he does for the television stuff. So far as sexual permissiveness in general goes, she's no prude. She used to wear nothing but trunks at the beach, until Tink was born and she started to feel a little less proud of her figure. But she still dresses as revealingly as anyone in their crowd. And gets stared at by everyone but her own husband. *He* watches the TV cuties. His other women must use him up. Maybe I ought to step out a bit myself, Alice thinks. She's had her little affairs along the way. Not many, nothing very serious, but she's had some. Three lovers in eleven years, that's not a great many, but it's a sign that she's no puritan. She wonders if she ought to get involved with somebody now. It might move her life off dead center while she still has the chance, before boredom destroys her entirely. "I'm going up to wash my hair," she announces. "Will you be staying down here till bedtime?"

There are so many ways he could do it. Slit his wrists. Drive his car off the bridge. Swallow Alice's whole box of sleeping tabs. Of course those are all old-fashioned ways of killing yourself. Something more modern would be appropriate. Go into one of the black taverns and start making loud racial insults? No, nothing modern about that. It's very 1975. But something genuinely contemporary does occur to him. Those time machines they've got now: suppose he rented one and went back, say, sixty years, to a time when one of his parents hadn't yet been born. And killed his grandfather. Find old Martin as a young man and slip a knife into him. If I do that, Ted figures, I should instantly and painlessly cease to exist. I would never have existed, because my mother wouldn't ever have existed. Poof. Out like a light. Then he realizes he's fantasizing a murder again. Stupid: if he could ever murder anyone, he'd murder Alice and be done with it. So the whole fantasy is foolish. Back to the starting point is where he is.

She is sitting under the hair-dryer when he comes upstairs. He has a peculiarly smug expression on his face and as soon as she turns the dryer off she asks him what he's thinking about. "I may have just invented a perfect murder method," he tells her. "Oh?" she says. He says, "You rent a time machine. Then you go back a couple of generations and murder one of the ancestors of your intended victim. That way you're murdering the victim too, because he won't ever have been born if you kill off one of his immediate progenitors. Then you return to your own time. Nobody can trace you because you don't have any fingerprints on file in an era before your own birth. What do you think of it?" Alice shrugs. "It's an old one," she says. "It's been done on television a dozen times. Anyway, I don't like it. Why should an innocent person have to die just because he's the grandparent of somebody you want to kill?"

They're probably in bed together right now, Martin thinks gloomily. Stark naked side by side. The lights are out. The house is quiet. Maybe they're smoking a little grass. Do they still call it grass, he wonders, or is there some new nickname now? Anyway the two of them turn on. Yes. And then he reaches for her. His hands slide over her cool, smooth skin. He cups her breasts. Plays with the hard little nipples. Sucks on them. The other hand wandering down to her parted thighs. And then she. And then he. And then they. And then they. Oh, Alice, he murmurs. Oh, Ted, *Ted*, she cries. And then they. Go to it. Up and down, in and out. Oh. Oh. Oh. She claws his back. She pumps her hips. Ted! Ted! Ted! The big moment is arriving now. For her, for him. Jackpot! Afterward they lie close for a few minutes, basking in the afterglow. And then they roll apart. Goodnight, Ted. Goodnight, Alice. Oh, Jesus. They do it every night, I bet. They're so young and full of juice. And I'm all dried up. Christ, I hate being old. When I think of the man I once was. When I think of the women I once had. Jesus. Jesus. God, let me have the strength to do it just once more before I die. And leave me alone for two hours with Alice.

She has trouble falling asleep. A strange scene keeps playing itself out obsessively in her mind. She sees herself stepping out of an upright coffin-sized box of dark gray metal, festooned with dials and levers. The time machine. It delivers her into a dark, dirty alleyway, and when she walks forward to the street she sees scores of little antique automobiles buzzing around. Only they aren't antiques: they're the current models. This is the year 1947. New York City. Will she be conspicuous in her futuristic clothes? She has her breasts covered, at any rate. That's essential back here. She hurries to the proper address, resisting the temptation to browse in shop windows along the way. How quaint and ancient everything looks. And how dirty the streets are. She comes to a tall building of red brick. This is the place. No scanners study her as she enters. They don't have annunciators yet or any other automatic home-protection equipment. She goes upstairs in an elevator so creaky and unstable that she fears for her life. Fifth floor. Apartment 5-J. She rings the doorbell. *He* answers. He's terribly young, only 24, but she can pick out signs of the Martin of the future in his face, the strong cheekbones, the searching blue eyes. "Are you Martin Jamieson?" she asks. "That's right," he says. She smiles. "May I come in?" "Of course," he says. He bows her into the apartment. As he momentarily turns his back on her to open the coat closet she takes the heavy steel pipe from her purse and lifts it high and brings it down on the back of his head. *Thwock.* She takes the heavy steel pipe from her purse and lifts it high and brings it down on the back of his head. *Thwock.* She takes the heavy steel pipe from her purse and lifts it high and brings it down on the back of his head. *Thwock.*

Ted and Alice visit him at Sunset Village two or three times a month. He can't complain about that; it's as much as he can expect. He's an old old man and no doubt a boring one, but they come dutifully, sometimes with the kids, sometimes without. He's never gotten used to the idea that he's a great-grandfather. Alice always gives him a kiss when she arrives and another when she leaves. He plays a private little game with her, copping a feel at each kiss. His hand quickly stroking her butt. Or sometimes when he's really rambunctious it travels lightly over her breasts. Does she notice? Probably. She never lets on, though. Pretends it's an accidental touch. Most likely she thinks it's charming that a man of his age would still have at least a vestige of sexual desire left. Unless she thinks it's disgusting, that is.

The time-machine gimmick, Ted tells himself, can be used in ways that don't quite amount to murder. For instance. "What's that box?" Alice asks. He smiles cunningly. "It's called a panchronicon," he says. "It gives you a kind of televised reconstruction of ancient times. The salesman loaned me a demonstration sample." She says, "How does it work?" "Just step inside," he tells her. "It's all ready for you." She starts to enter the machine, but then, suddenly suspicious, she hesitates on the threshold. He pushes her in and slams the door shut behind her. *Wham!* The controls are set. Off goes Alice on a one-way journey to the Pleistocene. The machine is primed to return as soon as it drops her off. That isn't murder, is it? She's still alive, wherever she may be, unless the saber-tooth tigers have caught up with her. So long, Alice.

In the morning she drives Bobby and Tink to school. Then she stops at the bank and the post office. From ten to eleven she has her regular session at the identity-reinforcement parlor. Ordinarily she would go right home after that, but this morning she strolls across the shopping-center plaza to the office that the time-machine people have just opened. TEMPONAUTICS, LTD., the sign over the door says. The place is empty except for two machines, no doubt demonstration models, and a bland-faced, smiling salesman. "Hello," Alice says nervously. "I just wanted to pick up some information about the rental costs of one of your machines."

Martin likes to imagine Alice coming to visit him by herself some rainy Saturday afternoon. "Ted isn't able to make it today," she explains. "Something came up at the office. But I knew you were expecting us, and I didn't want you to be disappointed. Poor Martin, you must lead such a lonely life." She comes close to him. She is trembling. So is he. Her face is flushed and her eyes are bright with the unmistakable glossiness of desire. He feels a sense of sexual excitement too, for the first time in ten or twenty years, that tension in the loins, that throbbing of the pulse. Electricity. Chemistry. His eyes lock on hers. Her nostrils flare, her mouth goes taut. "Martin," she whispers huskily. "Do you feel what I feel?" "You know I do," he tells her. She says, "If only I could have known you when you were in your prime!" He chuckles. "I'm not altogether senile yet," he cries exultantly. Then she is in his arms and his lips are seeking her fragrant breasts.

"Yes, it came as a terrible shock to me," Ted tells Ellie. "Having her disappear like that. She simply vanished from the face of the earth, as far as anyone can determine. They've tried every possible way of tracing her and there hasn't been a clue." Ellie's flawless forehead furrows in a fitful frown. "Was she unhappy?" she asks. "Do you think she may have done away with herself?" Ted shakes his head. "I don't know. You live with a person for eleven years and you think you know her pretty well, and then one day something absolutely incomprehensible occurs and you realize how impossible it is ever to know another human being at all. Don't you agree?" Ellie nods gravely. "Yes, oh, yes, certainly!" she says. He smiles down at her and takes her hands in his. Softly he says, "Let's not talk about Alice any more, shall we? She's gone and that's all I'll ever know." He hears a pulsing symphonic crescendo of shimmering angelic choirs as he embraces her and murmurs, "I love you, Ellie. I love you."

She takes the heavy steel pipe from her purse and lifts it high and brings it down on the back of his head. *Thwock*. Young Martin drops instantly, twitches once, lies still. Dark blood begins to seep through the dense blond curls of his hair. How strange to see Martin with golden hair, she thinks, as she kneels beside his body. She puts her hand to the bloody place, probes timidly, feels the deep indentation. Is he dead? She isn't sure how to tell. He isn't moving. He doesn't seem to be breathing. She wonders if she ought to hit him again, just to make certain. Then she remembers something she's seen on television, and takes her mirror from her purse. Holds it in front of his face. No cloud forms. That's pretty conclusive: you're dead, Martin. R.I.P. Martin Jamieson, 1923–1947. Which means that Martha Jamieson Porter (1948–   ) will never now be conceived, and that automatically obliterates the existence of her son Theodore Porter (1968–   ). Not bad going, Alice, getting rid of unloved husband and miserable shrewish mother-in-law all in one shot. Sorry, Martin. Bye-bye, Ted. (R.I.P. Theodore Porter, 1968–1947. Eh?) She rises, goes into the bathroom with the steel pipe, and carefully rinses it off. Then she puts it back into her purse. Now to go back to the machine and return to 2006, she thinks. To start my new life. But as she leaves the apartment, a tall, lean man steps out of the hallway shadows and clamps his hand powerfully around her wrist. "Time Patrol," he says crisply, flashing an identification badge. "You're under arrest for temponautic murder, Mrs. Porter."

Today has been a better day than yesterday, low on crises and depressions, but he still feels a headache coming on as he lets himself into the house. He is braced for whatever bitchiness Alice may have in store for him this evening. But, oddly, she seems relaxed and amiable. "Can I get you a drink, Ted?" she asks. "How did your day go?" He smiles and says, "Well, I think we may have salvaged the Hammond account after all. Otherwise nothing special happened. And you? What did you do today, love?" She shrugs. "Oh, the usual stuff," she says. "The bank, the post office, my identity-reinforcement session."

If you had the money, Martin asks himself, how far back would you send her? 1947, that would be the year, I guess. My last year as a single man. No sense complicating things. Off you go, Alice baby, to 1947. Let's make it March. By June I was engaged and by September Martha was on the way, though I didn't find that out until later. Yes: March, 1947. So. Young Martin answers the doorbell and sees an attractive girl in the hall, a woman, really, older than he is, maybe 30 or 32. Slender, dark-haired, nicely constructed. Odd clothing: a clinging gray tunic, very short, made of some strange fabric that flows over her body like a stream. How it achieves that liquid effect around the pleats is beyond him. "Are you Martin Jamieson?" she asks. And quickly answers herself.

"Yes, of course, you must be. I recognize you. How handsome you were!" He is baffled. He knows nothing, naturally, about this gift from his aged future self. "Who are you?" he asks. "May I come in first?" she says. He is embarrassed by his lack of courtesy and waves her inside. Her eyes glitter with mischief. "You aren't going to believe this," she tells him, "but I'm your grandson's wife."

"Would you like to try out one of our demonstration models?" the salesman asks pleasantly. "There's absolutely no cost or obligation." Ted looks at Alice. Alice looks at Ted. Her frown mirrors his inner uncertainty. She also must be wishing that they had never come to the Temponautics showroom. The salesman, pattering smoothly onward, says, "In these demonstrations we usually send our potential customers fifteen or twenty minutes into the past. I'm sure you'll find it fascinating. While remaining in the machine, you'll be able to look through a viewer and observe your own selves actually entering this very showroom a short while ago. Well? Will you give it a try? You go first, Mrs. Porter. I assure you it's going to be the most unique experience you've ever had." Alice, uneasy, tries to back off, but the salesman prods her in a way that is at once gentle and unyielding, and she steps reluctantly into the time machine. He closes the door. A great business of adjusting fine controls ensues. Then the salesman throws a master switch. A green glow envelops the machine and it disappears, although something transparent and vague—a retinal after-image? the ghost of the machine?—remains dimly visible. The salesman says, "She's now gone a short distance into her own past. I've programmed the machine to take her back eighteen minutes and keep her there for a total elapsed interval of six minutes, so she can see the entire opening moments of your visit here. But when I return her to Now Level, there's no need to match the amount of elapsed time in the past, so that from our point of view she'll have been absent only some thirty seconds. Isn't that remarkable, Mr. Porter? It's one of the many extraordinary paradoxes we encounter in the strange new realm of time travel." He throws another switch. The time machine once more assumes solid form. "*Voila!*" cries the salesman. "Here is Mrs. Porter, returned safe and sound from her voyage into the past." He flings open the door of the time machine. The passenger compartment is empty. The salesman's face crumbles. "Mrs. Porter?" he shrieks in consternation. "Mrs. Porter? I don't understand! How could there have been a malfunction? This is impossible! Mrs. Porter? *Mrs. Porter?*"

She hurries down the dirty street toward the tall brick building. This is the place. Upstairs. Fifth floor, apartment 5-J. As she starts to ring the doorbell, a tall, lean man steps out of the shadows and clamps his hand powerfully around her wrist. "Time Patrol," he says crisply, flashing an identification badge. "You're under arrest for contemplated tempo-nautic murder, Mrs. Porter."

"But I haven't any grandson," he sputters. "I'm not even mar—" She laughs. "Don't worry about it!" she tells him. "You're going to have a daughter named Martha and she'll have a son named Ted and I'm going to marry Ted and we'll have two children named Bobby and Tink. And you're going to live to be an old, old man. And that's all you need to know. Now let's have a little fun." She touches a catch at the side of her tunic and the garment falls away in a single fluid cascade. Beneath it she is naked. Her nipples stare up at him like blind pink eyes. She beckons to him. "Come on!" she says hoarsely. "Get undressed, Martin! You're wasting time!"

Alice giggles nervously. "Well, as a matter of fact," she says to the salesman, "I think I'm willing to let my husband be the guinea pig. How about it, Ted?" She turns toward him. So does the salesman. "Certainly, Mr. Porter. I know you're eager to give our machine a test run, yes?" No, Ted thinks, but he feels the pressure of events propelling him willy-nilly. He gets into the machine. As the door closes on him he fears that claustrophobic panic will overwhelm him; he is reassured by the sight of a handle on the door's inner face. He pushes on it and the door opens, and he steps out of the machine just in time to see his earlier self coming into the Temponautics showroom with Alice. The salesman is going forward to greet them. Ted is now eighteen minutes into his own past. Alice and the other Ted stare at him, aghast. The salesman whirls and exclaims, "Wait a second, you aren't supposed to get out of——" How stupid they all look! How bewildered! Ted laughs in their faces. Then he rushes past them, nearly knocking his other self down, and erupts into the shopping-center plaza. He sprints in a wild frenzy of exhilaration toward the parking area. Free, he thinks. I'm free at last. And I didn't have to kill anybody.

Suppose I rent a machine, Alice thinks, and go back to 1947 and kill Martin. Suppose I really do it. What if there's some way of tracing the crime to me? After all, a crime committed by a person from 2006 who goes back to 1947 will have consequences in our present day. It might change all sorts of things. So they'd want to catch the criminal and punish him, or better yet prevent the crime from being committed in the first place. And the time-machine company is bound to know what year I asked them to send me to. So maybe it isn't such an easy way of committing a perfect crime. I don't know. God, I can't understand any of this. But perhaps I can get away with it. Anyway, I'm going to give it a try. I'll show Ted he can't go on treating me like dirt.

They lie peacefully side by side, sweaty, drowsy, exhausted in the good exhaustion that comes after a first-rate screw. Martin tenderly strokes her belly and thighs. How smooth her skin is, how pale, how transparent! The little blue veins so clearly visible. "Hey," he says suddenly. "I just thought of something. I wasn't wearing a rubber or anything. What if I made you pregnant? And if you're really who you say you are. Then you'll go back to the year 2006 and you'll have a kid and he'll be his own grandfather, won't he?" She laughs. "Don't worry much about it," she says.

A wave of timidity comes over her as she enters the Temponautics office. This is crazy, she tells herself. I'm getting out of here. But before she can turn around, the salesman she spoke to the day before materializes from a side room and gives her a big hello. Mr. Friesling. He's practically rubbing his hands together in anticipation of landing a contract. "So nice to see you again, Mrs. Porter." She nods and glances worriedly at the demonstration models. "How much would it cost," she asks, "to spend a few hours in the spring of 1947?"

Sunday is the big family day. Four generations sitting down to dinner together: Martin, Martha, Ted and Alice, Bobby and Tink. Ted rather enjoys these reunions, but he knows Alice loathes them, mainly because of Martha. Alice hates her mother-in-law. Martha has never cared much for Alice, either. He watches them glaring at each other across the table. Meanwhile old Martin stares lecherously at the gulf between Alice's breasts. You have to hand it to the old man, Ted thinks. He's never lost the old urge. Even though there's not a hell of a lot he can do about gratifying it, not at his age. Martha says sweetly, "You'd look ever so much better, Alice dear, if you'd let your hair grow out to its natural color." A sugary smile from Martha. A sour scowl from Alice. She glowers at the older woman. "This *is* its natural color," she snaps.

Mr. Friesling hands her the standard contract form. Eight pages of densely packed type. "Don't be frightened by it, Mrs. Porter. It looks formidable but actually it's just a lot of empty legal rhetoric. You can show it to your lawyer, if you like. I can tell you, though, that most of our customers find no need for that." She leafs through it. So far as she can tell, the contract is mainly a disclaimer of responsibility. Tempo-nautics, Ltd., agrees to bear the brunt of any malfunction caused by its own demonstrable negligence, but wants no truck with acts of God or with accidents brought about by clients who won't obey the safety regulations. On the fourth page Alice finds a clause warning the prospective renter that the company cannot be held liable for any consequences of actions by the renter which wantonly or wilfully interfere with the already-determined course of history. She translates that for herself: *If you kill your husband's grandfather, don't blame us if you get in trouble.* She skims the remaining pages. "It looks harmless enough," she says. "Where do I sign?"

As Martin comes out of the bathroom he finds Martha blocking his way. "Excuse me," he says mildly, but she remains in his path. She is a big fleshy woman. At 58 she affects the fashions of the very young, with grotesque results; he hates that aspect of her. He can see why Alice dislikes her so much. "Just a moment," Martha says. "I want to talk to you, Father." "About what?" he asks. "About those looks you give

Alice. Don't you think that's a little too much? How tasteless can you get?" "Tasteless? Are you anybody to talk about taste, with your face painted green like a 15-year-old?" She looks angry: he's scored a direct hit. She replies, "I just think that at the age of 82 you ought to have a greater regard for decency than to go staring down your own grandson's wife's front." Martin sighs. "Let me have the staring, Martha. It's all I've got left."

He is at the office, deep in complicated negotiations, when his autosecretary bleeps him and announces that a call has come in from a Mr. Friesling, of the Union Boulevard Plaza office of Temponautics, Ltd. Ted is puzzled by that: what do the time-machine people want with him? Trying to line him up as a customer? "Tell him I'm not interested in time-trips," Ted says. But the autosecretary bleeps again a few moments later. Mr. Friesling, it declares, is calling in reference to Mr. Porter's credit standing. More baffled than before, Ted orders the call switched over to him. Mr. Friesling appears on the desk screen. He is small-featured and bright-eyed, rather like a chipmunk. "I apologize for troubling you, Mr. Porter," he begins. "This is strictly a routine credit check, but it's altogether necessary. As you surely know, your wife has requested rental of our equipment for a 59-year time-jaunt, and inasmuch as the service fee for such a trip exceeds the level at which we extend automatic credit, our policy requires us to ask you if you'll confirm the payment schedule that she has requested us to—" Ted coughs violently. "Hold on," he says. "My wife's going on a time-jaunt? What the hell, this is the first time I've heard of that!"

She is surprised by the extensiveness of the preparations. No wonder they charge so much. Getting her ready for the jaunt takes hours. They inoculate her to protect her against certain extinct diseases. They provide her with clothing in the style of the mid-twentieth century, ill-fitting and uncomfortable. They give her contemporary currency, but warn her that she would do well not to spend any except in an emergency, since she will be billed for it at its present-day numismatic value, which is high. They make her study a pamphlet describing the customs and historical background of the era and quiz her in detail. She learns that she is not under any circumstances to expose her breasts or genitals in public while she is in 1947. She must not attempt to obtain any mind-stimulating drugs other than alcohol. She should not say anything that might be construed as praise of the Soviet Union or of Marxist philosophy. She must bear in mind that she is entering the past solely as an observer, and should engage in minimal social interaction with the citizens of the era she is visiting. And so forth. At last they decide it's safe to let her go. "Please come this way, Mrs. Porter," Friesling says.

After staring at the telephone a long while, Martin punches out Alice's number. Before the second ring he loses his nerve and disconnects. Immediately he calls her again. His heart pounds so furiously that the medic, registering alarm on its delicate sensing apparatus, starts toward him. He waves the robot away and clings to the phone. Two rings. Three. Ah. "Hello?" Alice says. Her voice is warm and rich and feminine. He has his screen switched off. "Hello? Who's there?" Martin breathes heavily into the mouthpiece. Ah. Ah. Ah. Ah. "Hello? Hello? Hello? Listen, you pervert, if you phone me once more—" *Ah. Ah. Ah.* A smile of bliss appears on Martin's withered features. Alice hangs up. Trembling, Martin sags in his chair. Oh, that was good! He signals fiercely to the medic. "Let's have the injection now, you metal monster!" He laughs. Dirty old man.

Ted realizes that it isn't necessary to kill a person's grandfather in order to get rid of that person. Just interfere with some crucial event in that person's past, is all. Go back and break up the marriage of Alice's grandparents, for example. (How? Seduce the grandmother when she's 18? "I'm terribly sorry to inform you that your intended bride is no virgin, and here's the documentary evidence." They were very grim about virginity back then, weren't they?) Nobody would have to die. But Alice wouldn't ever be born.

Martin still can't believe any of this, even after she's slept with him. It's some crazy practical joke, most likely. Although he wishes all practical jokes were as sexy as this one. "Are you really from the year 2006?" he asks her. She laughs prettily. "How can I prove it to you?" Then she leaps from the bed. He tracks her with his eyes as she crosses the room, breasts jiggling gaily. What a sweet little body. How thoughtful of my older self to ship her back here to me. If that's what really happened. She fumbles in her purse and extracts a handful of coins. "Look here," she says. "Money from the future. Here's a dime from 1993. And this is a two-dollar piece from 2001. And here's an old one, a 1979 Kennedy half dollar." He studies the unfamiliar coins. They have a greasy look, not silvery at all. Counterfeits? They won't necessarily be striking coins out of silver forever. And the engraving job is very professional. A two-dollar piece, eh? Well, you never can tell. And this. The half dollar. A handsome young man in profile. "Kennedy?" he says. "Who's Kennedy?"

So this is it at last. Two technicians in gray smocks watch her, sober-faced, as she clambers into the machine. It's very much like a coffin, just as she imagined it would be. She can't sit down in it: it's too narrow. Gives her the creeps, shut up in here. Of course, they've told her the trip won't take any apparent subjective time, only a couple of seconds. *Woosh!* and she'll be there. All right. They close the door. She hears the lock clicking shut. Mr. Friesling's voice comes to her over a loudspeaker. "We wish you a happy voyage, Mrs. Porter. Keep calm and you won't get into any difficulties." Suddenly the red light over the door is glowing. That means the jaunt has begun: she's traveling backward in time. No sense of acceleration, no sense of motion. One, two, three. The light goes off. That's it. I'm in 1947, she tells herself. Before she opens the door, she closes her eyes and runs through her history lessons. World War II has just ended. Europe is in ruins. There are 48 states. Nobody has been to the moon yet or even thinks much about going there. Harry Truman is President. Stalin runs Russia and Churchill—is Churchill still Prime Minister of England? She isn't sure. Well, no matter. I didn't come here to talk about prime ministers. She touches the latch and the door of the time machine swings outward.

He steps from the machine into the year 2006. Nothing has changed in the showroom. Friesling, the two poker-faced technicians, the sleek

desks, the thick carpeting, all the same as before. He moves bouncily.
His mind is still back there with Alice's grandmother. The taste of her
lips, the soft urgent cries of her fulfillment. Who ever said all women
were frigid in the old days? They ought to go back and find out.
Friesling smiles at him. "I hope you had a very enjoyable journey,
Mr.—ah—" Ted nods. "Enjoyable and useful," he says. He goes out.
Never to see Alice again—how beautiful! The car isn't where he
remembers leaving it in the parking area. You have to expect certain
small peripheral changes, I guess. He hails a cab, gives the driver his
address. His key does not fit the front door. Troubled, he thumbs the
annunciator. A woman's voice, not Alice's, asks him what he wants. "Is
this the Ted Porter residence?" he asks. "No, it isn't," the woman says,
suspicious and irritated. The name on the doorplate, he notices now, is
McKenzie. So the changes are not all so small. Where do I go now? If I
don't live here, then where? "Wait!" he yells to the taxi, just pulling
away. It takes him to a downtown cafe, where he phones Ellie. Her
face, peering out of the tiny screen, wears an odd frowning expression.
"Listen, something very strange has happened," he begins, "and I need
to see you as soon as—" "I don't think I know you," she says. "I'm
Ted," he tells her. "Ted who?" she asks.

How peculiar this is, Alice thinks. Like walking into a museum diorama
and having it come to life. The noisy little automobiles. The ugly
clothing. The squat, dilapidated twentieth-century buildings. The
chaos. The oily, smoky smell of the polluted air. Wisps of dirty snow in
the streets. Cans of garbage just sitting around as if nobody's ever heard
of the plague. Well, I won't stay here long. In her purse she carries her
kitchen carver, a tiny nickel-jacketed laser-powered implement. Steel
pipes are all right for dream-fantasies, but this is the real thing, and she
wants the killing to be quick and efficient. Criss, cross, with the laser
beam, and Martin goes. At the street corner she pauses to check the
address. There's no central info number to ring for all sorts of useful
data, not in these primitive times; she must use a printed telephone
directory, a thick tattered book with small smeary type. Here he is:
Martin Jamieson, 504 West 45th. That's not far. In ten minutes she's
there. A dark brick structure, five or six stories high, with spidery metal

fire escapes running down its face. Even for its day it appears unusually run down. She goes inside. A list of tenants is posted just within the front door. Jamieson, 3-A. There's no elevator and of course no liftshaft. Up the stairs. A musty hallway lit by a single dim incandescent bulb. This is Apartment 3-A. Jamieson. She rings the bell.

Ten minutes later Friesling calls back, sounding abashed and looking dismayed: "I'm sorry to have to tell you that there's been some sort of error, Mr. Porter. The technicians were apparently unaware that a credit check was in process and they sent Mrs. Porter off on her trip while we were still talking." Ted is shaken. He clutches the edge of the desk. Controlling himself with an effort, he says, "How far back was it that she wanted to go?" Friesling says, "It was 59 years. To 1947." Ted nods grimly. A horrible idea has occurred to him. 1947 was the year that his mother's parents met and got married. What is Alice up to?

The doorbell rings. Martin, freshly showered, is sprawled out naked on his bed, leafing through the new issue of *Esquire* and thinking vaguely of going out for dinner. He isn't expecting any company. Slipping into his bathrobe, he goes toward the door. "Who's there?" he calls. A youthful, pleasant female voice replies, "I'm looking for Martin Jamieson." Well, okay. He opens the door. She's perhaps 27, 28 years old, *very* sexy, on the slender side but well built. Dark hair, worn in a strangely boyish short cut. He's never seen her before. "Hi," he says tentatively. She grins warmly at him. "You don't know me," she tells him, "but I'm a friend of an old friend of yours. Mary Chambers? Mary and I grew up together in—ah—Ohio. I'm visiting New York for the first time, and Mary once told me that if I ever come to New York I should be sure to look up Martin Jamieson, and so—may I come in?" "You bet," he says. He doesn't remember any Mary Chambers from Ohio. But what the hell, sometimes you forget a few. What the hell.

He's much more attractive than she expected him to be. She has always known Martin only as an old man, made unattractive as much by his coarse lechery as by what age has done to him. Hollow-chested, stoop-shouldered, pleated jowly face, sparse strands of white hair, beady eyes of faded blue—a wreck of a man. But this Martin in the doorway is sturdy, handsome, untouched by time, brimming with life and vigor and virility. She thinks of the carver in her purse and feels a genuine pang of regret at having to cut this robust boy off in his prime. But there isn't such a great hurry, is there? First we can enjoy each other, Martin. And then the laser.

"When is she due back?" Ted demands. Friesling explains that all concepts of time are relative and flexible; so far as elapsed time at Now Level goes, she's already returned. "What?" Ted yells. "Where is she?" Friesling does not know. She stepped out of the machine, bade the Temponautics staff a pleasant goodbye, and left the showroom. Ted puts his hand to his throat. What if she's already killed Martin? Will I just wink out of existence? Or is there some sort of lag, so that I'll fade gradually into unreality over the next few days? "Listen," he says raggedly, "I'm leaving my office right now and I'll be down at your place in less than an hour. I want you to have your machinery set up so that you can transport me to the exact point in space and time where you just sent my wife." "But that won't be possible," Friesling protests. "It takes hours to prepare a client properly for—" Ted cuts him off. "Get everything set up, and to hell with preparing me properly," he snaps. "Unless you feel like getting slammed with the biggest negligence suit since this time-machine thing got started, you better have everything ready when I get there."

He opens the door. The girl in the hallway is young and good-looking, with close-cropped dark hair and full lips. Thank you, Mary Chambers, whoever you may be. "Pardon the bathrobe," he says, "but I wasn't expecting company." She steps into his apartment. Suddenly he notices how strained and tense her face is. Country girl from Ohio, suddenly having second thoughts about visiting a strange man in a strange city? He tries to put her at her ease. "Can I get you a drink?" he asks. "Not much of a selection, I'm afraid, but I have scotch, gin, some blackberry cordial—" She reaches into her purse and takes something out. He frowns. Not a gun, exactly, but it does seem like a weapon of some sort, a little glittering metal device that fits neatly in her hand. "Hey," he says, "what's—" "I'm so terribly sorry, Martin," she whispers, and a bolt of terrible fire slams into his chest.

She sips the drink. It relaxes her. The glass isn't very clean, but she isn't worried about picking up a disease, not after all the injections Friesling gave her. Martin looks as if he can stand some relaxing too. "Aren't you drinking?" she asks. "I suppose I will," he says. He pours himself some gin. She comes up behind him and slips her hand into the front of his bathrobe. His body is cool, smooth, hard. "Oh, Martin," she murmurs. "Oh! Martin!"

Ted takes a room in one of the commercial hotels downtown. The first thing he does is try to put a call through to Alice's mother in Chillicothe. He still isn't really convinced that his little time-jaunt flirtation has retroactively eliminated Alice from existence. But the call convinces him, all right. The middle-aged woman who answers is definitely not Alice's mother. Right phone number, right address—he badgers her for the information—but wrong woman. "You don't have a daughter named Alice Porter?" he asks three or four times. "You don't know anyone in the neighborhood who does? It's important." All right. Cancel the old lady, ergo cancel Alice. But now he has a different problem. How much of the universe has he altered by removing Alice and her mother? Does he live in some other city, now, and hold some other job? What has happened to Bobby and Tink? Frantically he begins phoning people. Friends, fellow workers, the man at the bank. The same response from all of them: blank stares, shakings of the head. We don't know you, fellow. He looks at himself in the mirror. Okay, he asks himself. Who am I?

Martin moves swiftly and purposefully, the way they taught him to do in the army when it's necessary to disarm a dangerous opponent. He lunges forward and catches the girl's arm, pushing it upward before she can fire the shiny whatzis she's aiming at him. She turns out to be stronger than he anticipated, and they struggle fiercely for the weapon. Suddenly it fires. Something like a lightning-bolt explodes between them and knocks him to the floor, stunned. When he picks himself up he sees her lying near the door with a charred hole in her throat.

The telephone's jangling clatter brings Martin up out of a dream in which he is ravishing Alice's luscious young body. Dry-throated, gummy-eyed, he reaches a palsied hand toward the receiver. "Yes?" he says. Ted's face blossoms on the screen. "Grandfather!" he blurts. "Are you all right?" "Of course I'm all right," Martin says testily. "Can't you tell? What's the matter with you, boy?" Ted shakes his head. "I don't know," he mutters. "Maybe it was only a bad dream. I imagined that Alice rented one of those time machines and went back to 1947. And tried to kill you so that I wouldn't ever have existed." Martin snorts. "What idiotic nonsense! How can she have killed me in 1947 when I'm here alive in 2006?"

Naked, Alice sinks into Martin's arms. His strong hands sweep eagerly over her breasts and shoulders and his mouth descends to hers. She shivers with desire. "Yes," she murmurs tenderly, pressing herself against him. "Oh, yes, yes, yes!" They'll do it and it'll be fantastic. And afterward she'll kill him with the kitchen carver while he's lying there savoring the event. But a troublesome thought occurs. If Martin dies in 1947, Ted doesn't get to be born in 1968. Okay. But what about Tink and Bobby? They won't get born either, not if I don't marry Ted. I'll be married to someone else when I get back to 2006, and I suppose I'll have different children. Bobby? Tink? What am I doing to you? Sudden fear congeals her, and she pulls back from the vigorous young man nuzzling her throat. "Wait," she says. "Listen, I'm sorry. It's all a big mistake. I'm sorry, but I've got to get out of here right away!"

So this is the year 1947. Well, well, well. Everything looks so cluttered and grimy and ancient. He hurries through the chilly streets toward his grandfather's place. If his luck is good and if Friesling's technicians have calculated things accurately, he'll be able to head Alice off. That might even be her now, that slender woman walking briskly half a block ahead of him. He steps up his pace. Yes, it's Alice, on her way to Martin's.

Well done, Friesling! Ted approaches her warily, suspecting that she's armed. If she's capable of coming back to 1947 to kill Martin, she'd kill him just as readily. Especially back here where neither one of them has any legal existence. When he's close to her he says in a low, hard, intense voice, "Don't turn around, Alice. Just keep walking as if everything's perfectly normal." She stiffens. "Ted?" she cries, astonished. "Is that you, Ted?" "Damned right it is." He laughs harshly. "Come on. Walk to the corner and turn to your left around the block. You're going back to your machine and you're going to get the hell out of the twentieth century without harming anybody. I know what you were trying to do, Alice. But I caught you in time, didn't I?"

Martin is just getting down to real business when the door of his apartment bursts open and a man rushes in. He's middle-aged, stocky, with weird clothes—the ultimate in zoot suits, a maze of vividly contrasting colors and conflicting patterns, shoulders padded to resemble shelves—and a wild look in his eyes. Alice leaps up from the bed. "Ted!" she screams. "My God, what are you doing here?" "You murderous bitch," the intruder yells. Martin, naked and feeling vulnerable, his nervous system stunned by the interruption, looks on in amazement as the stranger grabs her and begins throttling her. "Bitch! Bitch! Bitch!" he roars, shaking her in a mad frenzy. The girl's face is turning black. Her eyes are bugging. After a long moment Martin breaks finally from his freeze. He stumbles forward, seizes the man's fingers, peels them away from the girl's throat. Too late. She falls limply and lies motionless. "Alice!" the intruder moans. "Alice, Alice, what have I done?" He drops to his knees beside her body, sobbing. Martin blinks. "You killed her," he says, not believing that any of this can really be happening. "You actually killed her!"

Alice's face appears on the telephone screen. Christ, how beautiful she is, Martin thinks, and his decrepit body quivers with lust. "There you are," he says. "I've been trying to reach you for hours. I had such a strange dream—that something awful had happened to Ted—and then your phone didn't answer, and I began to think maybe the dream was a premonition of some kind, an omen, you know—" Alice looks puzzled. "I'm afraid you have the wrong number, sir," she says sweetly, and hangs up.

She draws the laser and the naked man cowers back against the wall in bewilderment. "What the hell is this?" he asks, trembling. "Put that thing down, lady. You've got the wrong guy." "No," she says. "You're the one I'm after. I hate to do this to you, Martin, but I've got no choice. You have to die." "Why?" he demands. "*Why?*" "You wouldn't understand it even if I told you," she says. She moves her finger toward the discharge stud. Abruptly there is a frightening sound of cracking wood and collapsing plaster behind her, as though an earthquake has struck. She whirls and is appalled to see her husband breaking down the door of Martin's apartment. "I'm just in time!" Ted exclaims. "Don't move, Alice!" He reaches for her. In panic she fires without thinking. The dazzling beam catches Ted in the pit of the stomach and he goes down, gurgling in agony, clutching at his belly as he dies.

The door falls with a crash and this character in peculiar clothing materializes in a cloud of debris, looking crazier than Napoleon. It's incredible, Martin thinks. First an unknown broad rings his bell and invites herself in and takes her clothes off, and then, just as he's about to screw her, this happens. It's pure Marx Brothers, only dirty. But Martin's not going to take any crap. He pulls himself away from the panting, gasping girl on the bed, crosses the room in three quick strides, and seizes the newcomer. "Who the hell are you?" Martin demands, slamming him hard against the wall. The girl is dancing around behind him. "Don't hurt him!" she wails. "Oh, please, don't hurt him!"

Ted certainly hadn't expected to find them in bed together. He understood why she might have wanted to go back in time to murder Martin, but simply to have an affair with him, no, it didn't make sense. Of course, it was altogether likely that she had come here to kill and had paused for a little dalliance first. You never could tell about women, even your own wife. Alleycats, all of them. Well, a lucky thing for him that she had given him these few extra minutes to get here. "Okay," he says. "Get your clothes on, Alice. You're coming with me." "Just a second, mister," Martin growls. "You've got your goddamned nerve, busting in like this." Ted tries to explain, but the words won't come. It's all too complicated. He gestures mutely at Alice, at himself, at Martin. The next moment Martin jumps him and they go tumbling together to the floor.

"Who are you?" Martin yells, banging the intruder repeatedly against the wall. "You some kind of detective? You trying to work a badger game on me?" Slam. Slam. Slam. He feels the girl's small fists pounding on his own back. "Stop it!" she screams. "Let him alone, will you? He's my husband!" "*Husband!*" Martin cries. Astounded, he lets go of the stranger and swings around to face the girl. A moment later he realizes his mistake. Out of the corner of his eye he sees that the intruder has raised his fists high above his head like clubs. Martin tries to get out of the way, but no time, no time, and the fists descend with awful force against his skull.

Alice doesn't know what to do. They're rolling around on the floor, fighting like wildcats, now Martin on top, now Ted. Martin is younger and bigger and stronger, but Ted seems possessed by the strength of the insane; he's gone berserk. Both men are bloody-faced and furniture is crashing over everywhere. Her first impulse is to get between them and stop this crazy fight somehow. But then she remembers that she has come here as a killer, not as a peacemaker. She gets the laser from her purse and aims it at Martin, but then the combatants do a flipflop and it is Ted who is in the line of fire. She hesitates. It doesn't matter which one she shoots, she realizes after a moment. They both have to die, one way or another. She takes aim. Maybe she can get them both with one bolt. But as her finger starts to tighten on the discharge stud Martin suddenly gets Ted in a bearhug and, half lifting him, throws him five feet across the room. The back of Ted's neck hits the wall and there is a loud *crack*. Ted slumps and is still. Martin gets shakily to his feet. "I think I killed him," he says. "Christ, who the hell was he?" "He was your grandson," Alice says, and begins to shriek hysterically.

Ted stares in horror at the crumpled body at his feet. His hands still tingle from the impact. The left side of Martin's head looks as though a pile-driver has crushed it. "Good God in heaven," Ted says thickly, "what have I done? I came here to protect him and I've killed him! I've killed my own grandfather!" Alice, wide-eyed, futilely trying to cover her nakedness by folding one arm across her breasts and spreading her other hand over her loins, says, "If he's dead, why are you still here? Shouldn't you have disappeared?" Ted shrugs. "Maybe I'm safe as long as I remain here in the past. But the moment I try to go back to 2006, I'll vanish as though I've never been. I don't know. I don't understand any of this. What do you think?"

Alice steps uncertainly from the machine into the Temponautics showroom. There's Friesling. There are the technicians. Friesling says, smiling, "I hope you had a very enjoyable journey, Mrs.—ah—uh—" He falters. "I'm sorry," he says, reddening, "but your name seems to have escaped me." Alice says, "It's—ah—Alice—uh—do you know, the second name escapes me too?"

The whole clan has gathered to celebrate Martin's 83rd birthday. He cuts the cake and then one by one they go to him to kiss him. When it's Alice's turn, he deftly spins her around so that he screens her from the others, and gives her rump a good hearty pinch. "Oh, if I were only fifty years younger!" he sighs.

It's a warm springlike day. Everything has been lovely at the office—three new accounts all at once—and the trip home on the freeway was a breeze. Alice is waiting for him, dressed in her finest and most sexy outfit, all ready to go out. It's a special day. Their eleventh anniversary. How beautiful she looks! He kisses her, she kisses him, he takes the tickets from his pocket with a grand flourish. "Surprise," he says. "Two weeks in Hawaii, starting next Tuesday! Happy anniversary!" "Oh, Ted!" she cries. "How marvelous! I love you, Ted darling!" He pulls her close to him again. "I love you, Alice dear."

7

GOOD NEWS FROM THE VATICAN

This is the morning everyone has waited for, when at last the robot cardinal is to be elected Pope. There can no longer be any doubt of the outcome. The conclave has been deadlocked for many days between the obstinate advocates of Cardinal Asciuga of Milan and Cardinal Carciofo of Genoa, and word has gone out that a compromise is in the making. All factions now are agreed on the selection of the robot. This morning I read in *Osservatore Romano* that the Vatican computer itself has taken a hand in the deliberations. The computer has been strongly urging the candidacy of the robot. I suppose we should not be surprised by this loyalty among machines. Nor should we let it distress us. We *absolutely must not* let it distress us.

"Every era gets the Pope it deserves," Bishop FitzPatrick observed somewhat gloomily today at breakfast. "The proper Pope for our times is a robot, certainly. At some future date it may be desirable for the Pope to be a whale, an automobile, a cat, a mountain." Bishop FitzPatrick stands well over two meters in height and his normal facial expression is a morbid, mournful one. Thus it is impossible for us to determine whether any particular pronouncement of his reflects existential despair or placid acceptance. Many years ago he was a star player for the Holy Cross championship basketball team. He has come to Rome to do research for a biography of St. Marcellus the Righteous.

We have been watching the unfolding drama of the papal election from an outdoor cafe several blocks from the Square of St. Peter's. For all of us, this has been an unexpected dividend of our holiday in Rome;

the previous Pope was reputed to be in good health and there was no reason to suspect that a successor would have to be chosen for him this summer.

Each morning we drive across by taxi from our hotel near the Via Veneto and take up our regular positions around "our" table. From where we sit, we all have a clear view of the Vatican chimney through which the smoke of the burning ballots rises: black smoke if no Pope has been elected, white if the conclave has been successful. Luigi, the owner and head waiter, automatically brings us our preferred beverages: fernet branca for Bishop FitzPatrick, campari and soda for Rabbi Mueller, Turkish coffee for Miss Harshaw, lemon squash for Kenneth and Beverly, and pernod on the rocks for me. We take turns paying the check, although Kenneth has not paid it even once since our vigil began. Yesterday, when Miss Harshaw paid, she emptied her purse and found herself 350 lire short; she had nothing else except hundred-dollar travelers' checks. The rest of us looked pointedly at Kenneth but he went on calmly sipping his lemon squash. After a brief period of tension Rabbi Mueller produced a 500-lire coin and rather irascibly slapped the heavy silver piece against the table. The rabbi is known for his short temper and vehement style. He is 28 years old, customarily dresses in a fashionable plaid cassock and silvered sunglasses, and frequently boasts that he has never performed a bar mitzvah ceremony for his congregation, which is in Wicomico County, Maryland. He believes that the rite is vulgar and obsolete, and invariably farms out all his bar mitzvahs to a franchised organization of itinerant clergymen who handle such affairs on a commission basis. Rabbi Mueller is an authority on angels.

Our group is divided over the merits of electing a robot as the new Pope. Bishop FitzPatrick, Rabbi Mueller, and I are in favor of the idea. Miss Harshaw, Kenneth, and Beverly are opposed. It is interesting to note that both of our gentlemen of the cloth, one quite elderly and one fairly young, support this remarkable departure from tradition. Yet the three "swingers" among us do not.

I am not sure why I align myself with the progressives. I am a man of mature years and fairly sedate ways. Nor have I ever concerned myself with the doings of the Church of Rome. I am unfamiliar with Catholic dogma and unaware of recent currents of thought within the Church.

Still, I have been hoping for the election of the robot since the start of the conclave.

Why, I wonder? Is it because the image of a metal creature upon the Throne of St. Peter's stimulates my imagination and tickles my sense of the incongruous? That is, is my support of the robot purely an esthetic matter? Or is it, rather, a function of my moral cowardice? Do I secretly think that this gesture will buy the robots off? Am I privately saying, Give them the papacy and maybe they won't want other things for a while? No. I can't believe anything so unworthy of myself. Possibly I am for the robot because I am a person of unusual sensitivity to the needs of others.

"If he's elected," says Rabbi Mueller, "he plans an immediate time-sharing agreement with the Dalai Lama and a reciprocal plug-in with the head programmer of the Greek Orthodox Church, just for starters. I'm told he'll make ecumenical overtures to the Rabbinate as well, which is certainly something for all of us to look forward to."

"I don't doubt that there'll be many corrections in the customs and practices of the hierarchy," Bishop FitzPatrick declares. "For example we can look forward to superior information-gathering techniques as the Vatican computer is given a greater role in the operations of the Curia. Let me illustrate by—"

"What an utterly ghastly notion," Kenneth says. He is a gaudy young man with white hair and pink eyes. Beverly is either his wife or his sister. She rarely speaks. Kenneth makes the sign of the Cross with offensive brusqueness and murmurs, "In the name of the Father, the Son, and the Holy Automaton." Miss Harshaw giggles but chokes the giggle off when she sees my disapproving face.

Dejectedly, but not responding at all to the interruption, Bishop FitzPatrick continues, "Let me illustrate by giving you some figures I obtained yesterday afternoon. I read in the newspaper *Oggi* that during the last five years, according to a spokesman for the *Missiones Catholicae*, the Church has increased its membership in Yugoslavia from 19,381,403 to 23,501,062. But the government census taken last year gives the total population of Yugoslavia at 23,575,194. That leaves only 74,132 for the other religious and irreligious bodies. Aware of the large Moslem population of Yugoslavia, I suspected an inaccuracy in the published statistics and consulted the computer in St. Peter's, which informed me"—the bishop, pausing, produces a lengthy print-out and unfolds it across much of the table—"that the last count of the Faithful in Yugoslavia, made a year and a half ago, places our numbers at 14,206,198. Therefore an overstatement of 9,294,864 has been made. Which is absurd. And perpetuated. Which is damnable."

"What does he look like?" Miss Harshaw asks. "Does anyone have any idea?"

"He's like all the rest," says Kenneth. "A shiny metal box with wheels below and eyes on top."

"You haven't seen him," Bishop FitzPatrick interjects. "I don't think it's proper for you to assume that—"

"They're all alike," Kenneth says. "Once you've seen one, you've seen all of them. Shiny boxes. Wheels. Eyes. And voices coming out of their bellies like mechanized belches. Inside, they're all cogs and gears." Kenneth shudders delicately. "It's too much for me to accept. Let's have another round of drinks, shall we?"

Rabbi Mueller says, "It so happens that I've seen him with my own eyes."

"You *have?*" Beverly exclaims.

Kenneth scowls at her. Luigi, approaching, brings a tray of new drinks for everyone. I hand him a 5000-lire note. Rabbi Mueller removes his sunglasses and breathes on their brilliantly reflective surfaces. He has small, watery gray eyes and a bad squint. He says, "The cardinal was the keynote speaker at the Congress of World Jewry that was held last fall in Beirut. His theme was 'Cybernetic Ecumenicism for Contemporary Man.' I was there. I can tell you that His Eminency is tall and distinguished, with a fine voice and a gentle smile. There's something inherently melancholy about his manner that reminds me greatly of our friend the bishop, here. His movements are graceful and his wit is keen."

"But he's mounted on wheels, isn't he?" Kenneth persists.

"On treads," replies the rabbi, giving Kenneth a fiery, devastating look and resuming his sunglasses. "Treads, like a tractor has. But I don't think that treads are spiritually inferior to feet, or, for that matter, to wheels. If I were a Catholic I'd be proud to have a man like that as my Pope."

"Not a man," Miss Harshaw puts in. A giddy edge enters her voice whenever she addresses Rabbi Mueller. "A robot," she says. "He's not a man, remember?"

"A *robot* like that as my Pope, then," Rabbi Mueller says, shrugging at the correction. He raises his glass. "To the new Pope!"

"To the new Pope!" cries Bishop FitzPatrick.

Luigi comes rushing from his cafe. Kenneth waves him away. "Wait a second," Kenneth says. "The election isn't over yet. How can you be so sure?"

"The *Osservatore Romano*," I say, "indicates in this morning's edition that everything will be decided today. Cardinal Carciofo has agreed to withdraw in his favor, in return for a larger real-time allotment when the new computer hours are decreed at next year's consistory."

"In other words, the fix is in," Kenneth says.

Bishop FitzPatrick sadly shakes his head. "You state things much too harshly, my son. For three weeks now we have been without a Holy Father. It is God's Will that we shall have a Pope; the conclave, unable to choose between the candidacies of Cardinal Carciofo and Cardinal Asciuga, thwarts that Will; if necessary, therefore, we must make certain accommodations with the realities of the times so that His Will shall not be further frustrated. Prolonged politicking within the conclave now becomes sinful. Cardinal Carciofo's sacrifice of his personal ambitions is not as self-seeking an act as you would claim."

Kenneth continues to attack poor Carciofo's motives for withdrawing. Beverly occasionally applauds his cruel sallies. Miss Harshaw several times declares her unwillingness to remain a communicant of a Church whose leader is a machine. I find this dispute distasteful and swing my chair away from the table to have a better view of the Vatican. At this moment the cardinals are meeting in the Sistine Chapel. How I wish I were there! What splendid mysteries are being enacted in that gloomy, magnificent room! Each prince of the Church now sits on a small throne surmounted by a violet-hued canopy. Fat wax tapers glimmer on

the desk before each throne. Masters-of-ceremonies move solemnly
through the vast chamber, carrying the silver basins in which the blank
ballots repose. These basins are placed on the table before the altar.
One by one the cardinals advance to the table, take ballots, return to
their desks. Now, lifting their quill pens, they begin to write. "I,
Cardinal ———, elect to the Supreme Pontificate the Most Reverend
Lord my Lord Cardinal ———." What name do they fill in? Is it
Carciofo? Is it Asciuga? Is it the name of some obscure and shriveled
prelate from Madrid or Heidelberg, some last-minute choice of the
anti-robot faction in its desperation? Or are they writing *his* name? The
sound of scratching pens is loud in the chapel. The cardinals are
completing their ballots, sealing them at the ends, folding them, folding
them again and again, carrying them to the altar, dropping them into
the great gold chalice. So have they done every morning and every
afternoon for days, as the deadlock has prevailed.

"I read in the *Herald-Tribune* a couple of days ago," says Miss
Harshaw, "that a delegation of 250 young Catholic robots from Iowa is
waiting at the Des Moines airport for news of the election. If their man
gets in, they've got a chartered flight ready to leave, and they intend to
request that they be granted the Holy Father's first public audience."

"There can be no doubt," Bishop FitzPatrick agrees, "that his
election will bring a great many people of synthetic origin into the fold
of the Church."

"While driving out plenty of flesh-and-blood people!" Miss Harshaw
says shrilly.

"I doubt that," says the bishop. "Certainly there will be some feelings
of shock, of dismay, of injury, of loss, for some of us at first. But these
will pass. The inherent goodness of the new Pope, to which Rabbi
Mueller alluded, will prevail. Also I believe that technologically–
minded young folk everywhere will be encouraged to join the Church.
Irresistible religious impulses will be awakened throughout the world."

"Can you imagine 250 robots clanking into St. Peter's?" Miss
Harshaw demands.

I contemplate the distant Vatican. The morning sunlight is brilliant
and dazzling, but the assembled cardinals, walled away from the world,

cannot enjoy its gay sparkle. They all have voted, now. The three cardinals who were chosen by lot as this morning's scrutators of the vote have risen. One of them lifts the chalice and shakes it, mixing the ballots. Then he places it on the table before the altar; a second scrutator removes the ballots and counts them. He ascertains that the number of ballots is identical to the number of cardinals present. The ballots now have been transferred to a ciborium, which is a goblet ordinarily used to hold the consecrated bread of the Mass. The first scrutator withdraws a ballot, unfolds it, reads its inscription; passes it to the second scrutator, who reads it also; then it is given to the third scrutator, who reads the name aloud. Asciuga? Carciofo? Some other? *His?*

Rabbi Mueller is discussing angels. "Then we have the Angels of the Throne, known in Hebrew as *arelim* or *ophanim*. There are 70 of them, noted primarily for their steadfastness. Among them are the angels Orifiel, Ophaniel, Zabkiel, Jophiel, Ambriel, Tychagar, Barael, Quelamia, Paschar, Boel, and Raum. Some of these are no longer found in Heaven and are numbered among the fallen angels in Hell."

"So much for their steadfastness," says Kenneth.

"Then, too," the rabbi goes on, "there are the Angels of the Presence, who apparently were circumcised at the moment of their creation. These are Michael, Metatron, Suriel, Sandalphon, Uriel, Saraqael, Astanphaeus, Phanuel, Jehoel, Zagzagael, Yefefiah, and Akatriel. But I think my favorite of the whole group is the Angel of Lust, who is mentioned in Talmud *Bereshith Rabba* 85 as follows, that when Judah was about to pass by—"

They have finished counting the votes by this time, surely. An immense throng has assembled in the Square of St. Peter's. The sunlight gleams off hundreds if not thousands of steel-jacketed crania. This must be a wonderful day for the robot population of Rome. But most of those in the piazza are creatures of flesh and blood: old women in black, gaunt young pickpockets, boys with puppies, plump vendors of sausages, and an assortment of poets, philosophers, generals, legislators, tourists, and fishermen. How has the tally gone? We will have our answer shortly. If no candidate has had a majority, they will mix the

ballots with wet straw before casting them into the chapel stove, and
black smoke will billow from the chimney. But if a Pope has been
elected, the straw will be dry, the smoke will be white.

The system has agreeable resonances. I like it. It gives me the
satisfactions one normally derives from a flawless work of art: the
Tristan chord, let us say, or the teeth of the frog in Bosch's *Temptation
of St. Anthony.* I await the outcome with fierce concentration. I am
certain of the result; I can already feel the irresistible religious impulses
awakening in me. Although I feel, also, an odd nostalgia for the days of
flesh-and-blood popes. Tomorrow's newspapers will have no interviews
with the Holy Father's aged mother in Sicily, nor with his proud
younger brother in San Francisco. And will this grand ceremony of
election ever be held again? Will we need another Pope, when this one
whom we will soon have can be repaired so easily?

Ah. The white smoke! The moment of revelation comes!

A figure emerges on the central balcony of the facade of St. Peter's,
spreads a web of cloth-of-gold, and disappears. The blaze of light
against that fabric stuns the eye. It reminds me perhaps of moonlight
coldly kissing the sea at Castellamare, or, perhaps even more, of the
noonday glare rebounding from the breast of the Caribbean off the
coast of St. John. A second figure, clad in ermine and vermillion, has
appeared on the balcony. "The cardinal-archdeacon," Bishop FitzPatrick whispers. People have started to faint. Luigi stands beside me,
listening to the proceedings on a tiny radio. Kenneth says, "It's all been
fixed." Rabbi Mueller hisses at him to be still. Miss Harshaw begins to
sob. Beverly softly recites the Pledge of Allegiance, crossing herself
throughout. This is a wonderful moment for me. I think it is the most
truly contemporary moment I have ever experienced.

The amplified voice of the cardinal-archdeacon cries, "I announce to
you great joy. We have a Pope."

Cheering commences, and grows in intensity as the cardinal-archdeacon tells the world that the newly chosen Pontiff is indeed *that*
cardinal, that noble and distinguished person, that melancholy and
austere individual, whose elevation to the Holy See we have all awaited
so intensely for so long. "He has imposed upon himself," says the
cardinal-archdeacon, "the name of—"

Lost in the cheering. I turn to Luigi. "Who? What name?"

"Sisto Settimo," Luigi tells me.

Yes, and there he is, Pope Sixtus the Seventh, as we now must call him. A tiny figure clad in the silver and gold papal robes, arms outstretched to the multitude, and, yes! the sunlight glints on his cheeks, his lofty forehead, there is the brightness of polished steel. Luigi is already on his knees. I kneel beside him. Miss Harshaw, Beverly, Kenneth, even the rabbi, all kneel, for beyond doubt this is a miraculous event. The Pope comes forward on his balcony. Now he will deliver the traditional apostolic benediction to the city and to the world. "Our help is in the Name of the Lord," he declares gravely. He activates the levitator-jets beneath his arms; even at this distance I can see the two small puffs of smoke. White smoke, again. He begins to rise into the air. "Who hath made heaven and earth," he says. "May Almighty God, Father, Son, and Holy Ghost, bless you." His voice rolls majestically toward us. His shadow extends across the whole piazza. Higher and higher he goes, until he is lost to sight. Kenneth taps Luigi. "Another round of drinks," he says, and presses a bill of high denomination into the innkeeper's fleshy palm. Bishop FitzPatrick weeps. Rabbi Mueller embraces Miss Harshaw. The new Pontiff, I think, has begun his reign in an auspicious way.

8

PUSH NO MORE

I push . . . and the shoe moves. Will you look at that? It really moves!
All I have to do is give a silent inner nudge, no hands, just reaching
from the core of my mind, and my old worn-out brown shoe, the left
one, goes sliding slowly across the floor of my bedroom. Past the chair,
past the pile of beaten-up textbooks (Geometry, Second Year Spanish,
Civic Studies, Biology, etc.), past my sweaty heap of discarded clothes.
Indeed the shoe obeys me. Making a little swishing sound as it snags
against the roughnesses of the elderly linoleum floor-tiling. Look at it
now, bumping gently into the far wall, tipping edge-up, stopping. Its
voyage is over. I bet I could make it climb right up the wall. But don't
bother doing it, man. Not just now. This is hard work. Just relax, Harry.
Your arms are shaking. You're perspiring all over. Take it easy for a
while. You don't have to prove everything all at once.

What have I proven, anyway?

It seems that I can make things move with my mind. How about that,
man? Did you ever imagine that you had freaky powers? Not until this
very night. This very lousy night. Standing there with Cindy Klein and
finding that terrible knot of throbbing tension in my groin, like needing
to take a leak only fifty times more intense, a zone of anguish spinning
off some kind of fearful energy like a crazy dynamo implanted in my
crotch. And suddenly, without any conscious awareness, finding a way
of tapping that energy, drawing it up through my body to my head,
amplifying it, and . . . *using* it. As I just did with my shoe. As I did a
couple of hours earlier with Cindy. So you aren't just a dumb gawky
adolescent schmuck, Harry Blaufeld. You are somebody very special.

You have power. You are potent.

How good it is to lie here in the privacy of my own musty bedroom
and be able to make my shoe slide along the floor, simply by looking at
it in that special way. The feeling of strength that I get from that!
Tremendous. I am potent. I have power. That's what potent means, to
have power, out of the Latin *potentia*, derived from *posse*. To be able. I
am able. I can do this most extraordinary thing. And not just in fitful
unpredictable bursts. It's under my conscious control. All I have to do is
dip into that reservoir of tension and skim off a few watts of *push*. Far
out! What a weird night this is.

Let's go back three hours. To a time when I know nothing of this
potentia in me. Three hours ago I know only from horniness. I'm
standing outside Cindy's front door with her at half past ten. We have
done the going-to-the-movies thing, we have done the cappucino-after-
ward thing, now I want to do the make-out thing. I'm trying to get
myself invited inside, knowing that her parents have gone away for the
weekend and there's nobody home except her older brother, who is
seeing his girl in Scarsdale tonight and won't be back for hours, and
once I'm past Cindy's front door I hope, well, to get invited inside.
(What a coy metaphor! You know what I mean.) So three cheers for
Casanova Blaufeld, who is suffering a bad attack of inflammation of the
cherry. Look at me, stammering, fumbling for words, shifting my weight
from foot to foot, chewing on my lips, going red in the face. All my
pimples light up like beacons when I blush. Come on, Blaufeld, pull
yourself together. Change your image of yourself. Try this on for size:
you're 23 years old, tall, strong, suave, a man of the world, veteran of so
many beds you've lost count. Bushy beard that girls love to run their
hands through. Big drooping handlebar mustachios. And you aren't
asking her for any favors. You aren't whining and wheedling and saying
please, Cindy, let's do it, because you know you don't need to say
please. It's no boon you seek: you give as good as you get, right, so it's a
mutually beneficial transaction, right? Right? Wrong. You're as suave
as a pig. You want to exploit her for the sake of your own grubby needs.
You know you'll be inept. But let's pretend, at least. Straighten the
shoulders, suck in the gut, inflate the chest. Harry Blaufeld, the devilish
seducer. Get your hands on her sweater for starters. No one's around;

it's a dark night. Go for the boobs, get her hot. Isn't that what Jimmy the Greek told you to do? So you try it. Grinning stupidly, practically apologizing with your eyes. Reaching out. The grabby fingers connecting with the fuzzy purple fabric.

Her face, flushed and big-eyed. Her mouth, thin-lipped and wide. Her voice, harsh and wire-edged. She says, "Don't be disgusting, Harry. Don't be *silly*." Silly. Backing away from me like I've turned into a monster with eight eyes and green fangs. Don't be disgusting. She tries to slip into the house fast, before I can paw her again. I stand there watching her fumble for her key, and this terrible rage starts to rise in me. Why disgusting? Why silly? All I wanted was to show her my love, right? That I really care for her, that I *relate* to her. A display of affection through physical contact. Right? So I reached out. A little caress. Prelude to tender intimacy. "Don't be disgusting," she said. "Don't be *silly*." The trivial little immature bitch. And now I feel the anger mounting. Down between my legs there's this hideous pain, this throbbing sensation of anguish, this purely sexual tension, and it's pouring out into my belly, spreading upward along my gut like a stream of flame. A dam has broken somewhere inside me. I feel fire blazing under the top of my skull. And there it is! The power! The strength! I don't question it. I don't ask myself what it is or where it came from. I just push her, hard, from ten feet away, a quick furious shove. It's like an invisible hand against her breasts—I can see the front of her sweater flatten out—and she topples backwards, clutching at the air, and goes over on her ass. I've knocked her sprawling without touching her. "Harry," she mumbles. "Harry?"

My anger's gone. Now I feel terror. What have I done? How? *How?* Down on her ass, *boom*. From ten feet away!

I run all the way home, never looking back.

Footsteps in the hallway, *clickety-clack*. My sister is home from her date with Jimmy the Greek. That isn't his name. Aristides Pappas is who he really is. Ari, she calls him. Jimmy the Greek, I call him, but not to his face. He's nine feet tall with black greasy hair and a tremendous beak of a nose that comes straight out of his forehead. He's 27 years old and he's laid a thousand girls. Sara is going to marry him next year. Meanwhile they see each other three nights a week and they screw a lot. She's never said a word to me about that, about the screwing, but I know. Sure they screw. Why not? They're going to get married, aren't they? And they're adults. She's 19 years old, so it's legal for her to screw. I won't be 19 for four years and four months. It's legal for me to screw now, I think. If only. If only I had somebody. If only.

Clickety-clickety-clack. There she goes, into her room. *Blunk.* That's her door closing. She doesn't give a damn if she wakes the whole family up. Why should she care? She's all turned on now. Soaring on her memories of what she was just doing with Jimmy the Greek. That warm feeling. The afterglow, the book calls it.

I wonder how they do it when they do it.

They go to his apartment. Do they take off all their clothes first? Do they talk before they begin? A drink or two? Smoke a joint? Sara claims she doesn't smoke it. I bet she's putting me on. They get naked. Christ, he's so tall, he must have a dong a foot long. Doesn't it scare her? They lie down on the bed together. Or on a couch. The floor, maybe? A thick fluffy carpet? He touches her body. Doing the foreplay stuff. I've read about it. He strokes the breasts, making the nipples go erect. I've seen her nipples. They aren't any bigger than mine. How tall do they get when they're erect? An inch? Three inches? Standing up like a couple of pink pencils? And his hand must go down below, too. There's this thing you're supposed to touch, this tiny bump of flesh hidden inside there. I've studied the diagrams and I still don't know where it is. Jimmy the Greek knows where it is, you can bet your ass. So he touches her there. Then what? She must get hot, right? How can he tell when it's time to go inside her? The time arrives. They're finally doing it. You know, I can't visualize it. He's on top of her and they're moving up and down, sure, but I still can't imagine how the bodies fit together, how they really move, how they do it.

She's getting undressed now, right across the hallway. Off with the shirt, the slacks, the bra, the panties, whatever the hell she wears. I can hear her moving around. I wonder if her door is really closed tight. It's a long time since I've had a good look at her. Who knows, maybe her nipples are still standing up. Even if her door's open only a few inches, I can see into her room from mine, if I hunch down here in the dark and peek.

But her door's closed. What if I reach out and give it a little nudge? From here. I pull the power up into my head, yes . . . reach . . . *push* . . . ah . . . yes! Yes! It moves! One inch, two, three. That's good enough. I can see a slice of her room. The light's on. Hey, there she goes! Too fast, out of sight. I think she was naked. Now she's coming back. Naked, yes. Her back is to me. You've got a cute ass, Sis, you know that? Turn around, turn around, turn around . . . ah. Her nipples look the same as always. Not standing up at all. I guess they must go back down after it's all over. *Thy two breasts are like two young roes that are twins, which feed among the lilies.* (I don't really read the Bible a lot, just the dirty parts.) Cindy's got bigger ones than you, Sis, I bet she has. Unless she pads them. I couldn't tell tonight. I was too excited to notice whether I was squeezing flesh or rubber.

Sara's putting her housecoat on. One last flash of thigh and belly, then no more. Damn. Into the bathroom now. The sound of water running. She's getting washed. Now the tap is off. And now . . . *tinkle, tinkle, tinkle.* I can picture her sitting there, grinning to herself, taking a happy piss, thinking cozy thoughts about what she and Jimmy the Greek did tonight. Oh, Christ, I hurt! I'm jealous of my own sister! That she can do it three times a week while I . . . am nowhere . . . with nobody . . . no one . . . nothing. . . .

Let's give Sis a little surprise.

Hmm. Can I manipulate something that's out of my direct line of sight? Let's try it. The toilet seat is in the right-hand corner of the bathroom, under the window. And the flush knob is—let me think—on the side closer to the wall, up high—yes. Okay, reach out, man. Grab it before she does. *Push* . . . down . . . *push.* Yeah! Listen to that, man! You flushed it for her without leaving your own room!

She's going to have a hard time figuring that one out.

Sunday: a rainy day, a day of worrying. I can't get the strange events of last night out of my mind. This power of mine—where did it come from, what can I use it for? And I can't stop fretting over the awareness that I'll have to face Cindy again first thing tomorrow morning, in our Biology class. What will she say to me? Does she realize I actually wasn't anywhere near her when I knocked her down? If she knows I have a power, is she frightened of me? Will she report me to the Society for the Prevention of Supernatural Phenomena, or whoever looks after such things? I'm tempted to pretend I'm sick, and stay home from school tomorrow. But what's the sense of that? I can't avoid her forever.

The more tense I get, the more intensely I feel the power surging within me. It's very strong today. (The rain may have something to do with that. Every nerve is twitching. The air is damp and maybe that makes me more conductive.) When nobody is looking, I experiment. In the bathroom, standing far from the sink, I unscrew the top of the toothpaste tube. I turn the water taps on and off. I open and close the window. How fine my control is! Doing these things is a strain: I tremble, I sweat, I feel the muscles of my jaws knotting up, my back teeth ache. But I can't resist the kick of exercising my skills. I get riskily mischievous. At breakfast, my mother puts four slices of bread in the toaster; sitting with my back to it, I delicately work the toaster's plug out of the socket, so that when she goes over to investigate five minutes later, she's bewildered to find the bread still raw. "How did the plug slip out?" she asks, but of course no one tells her. Afterward, as we all sit around reading the Sunday papers, I turn the television set on by remote control, and the sudden blaring of a cartoon show makes everyone jump. And a few hours later I unscrew a light bulb in the hallway, gently, gently, easing it from its fixture, holding it suspended close to the ceiling for a moment, then letting it crash to the floor. "What was that?" my mother says in alarm. My father inspects the hall. "Bulb fell out of the fixture and smashed itself to bits." My mother shakes her head. "How could a bulb fall out? It isn't possible." And my father says, "It must have been loose." He doesn't sound convinced. It must be occurring to him that a bulb loose enough to fall to the floor couldn't have been lit. And this bulb had been lit.

How soon before my sister connects these incidents with the episode of the toilet that flushed by itself?

Monday is here. I enter the classroom through the rear door and skulk to my seat. Cindy hasn't arrived yet. But now here she comes. God, how beautiful she is! The gleaming, shimmering red hair, down to her shoulders. The pale flawless skin. The bright, mysterious eyes. The purple sweater, same one as Saturday night. My hands have touched that sweater. I've touched that sweater with my power, too.

I bend low over my notebook. I can't bear to look at her. I'm a coward.

But I force myself to look up. She's standing in the aisle, up by the front of the room, staring at me. Her expression is strange—edgy, uneasy, the lips clamped tight. As if she's thinking of coming back here to talk to me but is hesitating. The moment she sees me watching her, she glances away and takes her seat. All through the hour I sit hunched forward, studying her shoulders, the back of her neck, the tips of her ears. Five desks separate her from me. I let out a heavy romantic sigh. Temptation is tickling me. It would be so easy to reach across that distance and touch her. Gently stroking her soft cheek with an invisible fingertip. Lightly fondling the side of her throat. Using my special power to say a tender hello to her. See, Cindy? See what I can do to show my love? Having imagined it, I find myself unable to resist doing it. I summon the force from the churning reservoir in my depths; I pump it upward and simultaneously make the automatic calculations of intensity of push. Then I realize what I'm doing. Are you crazy, man? She'll scream. She'll jump out of her chair like she was stung. She'll roll on the floor and have hysterics. Hold back, hold back, you lunatic! At the last moment I manage to deflect the impulse. Gasping, grunting, I twist the force away from Cindy and hurl it blindly in some other direction. My random thrust sweeps across the room like a whiplash and intersects the big framed chart of the plant and animal kingdoms that hangs on the classroom's left-hand wall. It rips loose as though kicked by a tornado and soars twenty feet on a diagonal arc that sends it crashing into the blackboard. The frame shatters. Broken glass sprays everywhere. The class is thrown into panic. Everybody yelling, running around, picking up pieces of glass, exclaiming in awe, asking questions. I sit like a statue. Then I start to shiver. And Cindy, very slowly, turns and looks at me. A chilly look of horror freezes her face.

She knows, then. She thinks I'm some sort of freak. She thinks I'm some sort of monster.

Poltergeist. That's what I am. That's me.

I've been to the library. I've done some homework in the occultism section. So: Harry Blaufeld, boy poltergeist. From the German, *poltern*, "to make a noise," and *geist*, "spirit." Thus, *poltergeist* = "noisy spirit." Poltergeists make plates go smash against the wall, pictures fall suddenly to the floor, doors bang when no one is near them, rocks fly through the air.

I'm not sure whether it's proper to say that I *am* a poltergeist, or that I'm merely the host for one. It depends on which theory you prefer. True-blue occultists like to think that poltergeists are wandering demons or spirits that occasionally take up residence in human beings, through whom they focus their energies and play their naughty tricks. On the other hand, those who hold a more scientific attitude toward paranormal extrasensory phenomena say that it's absurdly medieval to believe in wandering demons; to them, a poltergeist is simply someone who's capable of harnessing a paranormal ability within himself that allows him to move things without touching them. Myself, I incline toward the latter view. It's much more flattering to think that I have an extraordinary psychic gift than that I've been possessed by a marauding demon. Also less scary.

Poltergeists are nothing new. A Chinese book about a thousand years old called *Gossip from the Jade Hall* tells of one that disturbed the peace of a monastery by flinging crockery around. The monks hired an exorcist to get things under control, but the noisy spirit gave him the works: "His cap was pulled off and thrown against the wall; his robe was loosed, and even his trousers pulled off, which caused him to retire precipitately." Right on, poltergeist! "Others tried where he had failed, but they were rewarded for their pains by a rain of insolent missives from the air, upon which were written words of malice and bitter odium."

The archives bulge with such tales from many lands and many eras. Consider the Clarke case, Oakland, California, 1874. On hand: Mr.

Clarke, a successful businessman of austere and reserved ways, and his wife and adolescent daughter and eight-year-old son, plus two of Mr. Clarke's sisters and two male house-guests. On the night of April 23, as everyone prepares for bed, the front doorbell rings. No one there. Rings again a few minutes later. No one there. Sound of furniture being moved in the parlor. One of the house-guests, a banker named Bayley, inspects, in the dark, and is hit by a chair. No one there. A box of silverware comes floating down the stairs and lands with a bang. (*Poltergeist* = "noisy spirit.") A heavy box of coal flies about next. A chair hits Bayley on the elbow and lands against a bed. In the dining room a massive oak chair rises two feet in the air, spins, lets itself down, chases the unfortunate Bayley around the room in front of three witnesses. And so on. Much spooked, everybody goes to bed, but all night they hear crashes and rumbling sounds; in the morning they find all the downstairs furniture in a scramble. Also the front door, which was locked and bolted, has been ripped off its hinges. More such events the next night. Likewise on the next, culminating in a female shriek out of nowhere, so terrible that it drives the Clarkes and guests to take refuge in another house. No explanation for any of this ever offered.

A man named Charles Fort, who died in 1932, spent much of his life studying poltergeist phenomena and similar mysteries. Fort wrote four fat books which so far I've only skimmed. They're full of newspaper accounts of strange things like the sudden appearance of several young crocodiles on English farms in the middle of the nineteenth century, and rainstorms in which the earth was pelted with snakes, frogs, blood, or stones. He collected clippings describing instances of coal-heaps and houses and even human beings suddenly and spontaneously bursting into flame. Luminous objects sailing through the sky. Invisible hands that mutilate animals and people. "Phantom bullets" shattering the windows of houses. Inexplicable disappearances of human beings, and equally inexplicable reappearances far away. Et cetera, et cetera, et cetera. I gather that Fort believed that most of these phenomena were the work of beings from interplanetary space who meddle in events on our world for their own amusement. But he couldn't explain away everything like that. Poltergeists in particular didn't fit into his bogeymen-from-space fantasy, and so, he wrote, "Therefore I regard poltergeists as evil or false or discordant or absurd. . . ." Still, he said, "I don't care to deny poltergeists, because I suspect that later, when we're more enlightened, or when we widen the range of our credulities, or take on more of that increase of ignorance that is called knowledge, poltergeists may become assimilable. Then they'll be as reasonable as trees."

I like Fort. He was eccentric and probably very gullible, but he wasn't foolish or crazy. I don't think he's right about beings from interplanetary space, but I admire his attitude toward the inexplicable.

Most of the poltergeist cases on record are frauds. They've been exposed by experts. There was the 1944 episode in Wild Plum, North Dakota, in which lumps of burning coal began to jump out of a bucket in the one-room schoolhouse of Mrs. Pauline Rebel. Papers caught fire on the pupils' desks and charred spots appeared on the curtains. The class dictionary moved around of its own accord. There was talk in town of demonic forces. A few days later, after an assistant state attorney general had begun interrogating people, four of Mrs. Rebel's pupils confessed that they had been tossing the coal around to terrorize their teacher. They'd done most of the dirty work while her back was turned or when she had had her glasses off. A prank. A hoax. Some people would tell you that all poltergeist stories are equally phony. I'm here to testify that they aren't.

One pattern is consistent in all genuine poltergeist incidents: an adolescent is invariably involved, or a child on the edge of adolescence. This is the "naughty child" theory of poltergeists, first put forth by Frank Podmore in 1890 in the *Proceedings of the Society for Psychical Research.* (See, I've done my homework very thoroughly.) The child is usually unhappy, customarily over sexual matters, and suffers either from a sense of not being wanted or from frustration, or both. There are no statistics on the matter but the lore indicates that teenagers involved in poltergeist activity are customarily virgins.

The 1874 Clarke case, then, becomes the work of the adolescent daughter, who—I would guess—had a yen for Mr. Bayley. The multitude of cases cited by Fort, most of them dating from the nineteenth century, show a bunch of poltergeist kids flinging stuff around in a sexually repressed era. That seething energy had to go somewhere. I discovered my own poltering power while in an acute state of palpitating lust for Cindy Klein, who wasn't having any part of me. Especially *that* part. But instead of exploding from the sheer force of my bottled-up yearnings I suddenly found a way of channeling all that drive outward. And pushed. . . .

Fort again: "Wherein children are atavistic, they may be in rapport with forces that mostly human beings have outgrown." Atavism: a strange recurrence to the primitive past. Perhaps in Neanderthal times we were all poltergeists, but most of us lost it over the millennia. But see Fort, also: "There are of course other explanations of the 'occult power' of children. One is that children, instead of being atavistic, may occasionally be far in advance of adults, foreshadowing coming human powers, because their minds are not stifled by conventions. After that, they go to school and lose their superiority. Few boy-prodigies have survived an education."

I feel reassured, knowing I'm just a statistic in a long-established pattern of paranormal behavior. Nobody likes to think he's a freak, even when he is a freak. Here I am, virginal, awkward, owlish, quirky, precocious, edgy, uncertain, timid, clever, solemn, socially inept, stumbling through all the standard problems of the immediately post-pubescent years. I have pimples and wet dreams and the sort of fine fuzz that isn't worth shaving, only I shave it anyway. Cindy Klein thinks I'm silly and disgusting. And I've got this hot core of fury and frustration in my gut, which is my great curse and my great supremacy. I'm a poltergeist, man. Go on, give me a hard time, make fun of me, call me silly and disgusting. The next time I may not just knock you on your ass. I might heave you all the way to Pluto.

An unavoidable humiliating encounter with Cindy today. At lunchtime I go into Schindler's for my usual bacon-lettuce-tomato; I take a seat in one of the back booths and open a book and someone says, "Harry," and there she is at the booth just opposite, with three of her friends. What do I do? Get up and run out? Poltergeist her into the next county? Already I feel the power twitching in me. Mrs. Schindler brings me my sandwich. I'm stuck. I can't bear to be here. I hand her the money and mutter, "Just remembered, got to make a phone call."

Sandwich in hand, I start to leave, giving Cindy a foolish hot-cheeked grin as I go by. She's looking at me fiercely. Those deep green eyes of hers terrify me.

"Wait," she says. "Can I ask you something?"

She slides out of her booth and blocks the aisle of the luncheonette. She's nearly as tall as I am, and I'm tall. My knees are shaking. God in heaven, Cindy, don't trap me like this, I'm not responsible for what I might do.

She says in a low voice, "Yesterday in Bio, when that chart hit the blackboard. You did that, didn't you?"

"I don't understand."

"You made it jump across the room."

"That's impossible," I mumble. "What do you think I am, a magician?"

"I don't know. And Saturday night, that dumb scene outside my house—"

"I'd rather not talk about it."

"I would. How did you do that to me, Harry? Where did you learn the trick?"

"Trick? Look, Cindy, I've absolutely got to go."

"You pushed me over. You just looked at me and I felt a push."

"You tripped," I say. "You just fell down."

She laughs. Right now she seems about nineteen years old and I feel about nine years old. "Don't put me on," she says, her voice a deep sophisticated drawl. Her girlfriends are peering at us, trying to overhear. "Listen, this interests me. I'm involved. I want to know how you do that stuff."

"There isn't any stuff," I tell her, and suddenly I know I have to escape. I give her the tiniest push, not touching her, of course, just a wee mental nudge, and she feels it and gives ground, and I rush miserably past her, cramming my sandwich into my mouth. I flee the store. At the door I look back and see her smiling, waving to me, telling me to come back.

I have a rich fantasy life. Sometimes I'm a movie star, 22 years old with a palace in the Hollywood hills, and I give parties that Peter Fonda and

Dustin Hoffman and Julie Christie and Faye Dunaway come to, and we all turn on and get naked and swim in my pool and afterward I make it with five or six starlets all at once. Sometimes I'm a famous novelist, author of the book that really gets it together and speaks for My Generation, and I stand around in Brentano's in a glittering science-fiction costume signing thousands of autographs, and afterward I go to my penthouse high over First Avenue and make it with a dazzling young lady editor. Sometimes I'm a great scientist, four years out of Harvard Medical School and already acclaimed for my pioneering research in genetic reprogramming of unborn children, and when the phone rings to notify me of my Nobel Prize I'm just about to reach my third climax of the evening with a celebrated Metropolitan Opera soprano who wants me to design a son for her who'll eclipse Caruso. And sometimes—

But why go on? That's all fantasy. Fantasy is dumb because it encourages you to live a self-deluding life, instead of coming to grips with reality. Consider reality, Harry. Consider the genuine article that is Harry Blaufeld. The genuine article is something pimply and ungainly and naive, something that shrieks with every molecule of his skinny body that he's not quite fifteen and has never made it with a girl and doesn't know how to go about it and is terribly afraid that he never will. Mix equal parts of desire and self-pity. Add a dash of incompetence and a dollop of insecurity. Season lightly with extrasensory powers. You're a long way from the Hollywood hills, boy.

Is there some way I can harness my gift for the good of mankind? What if all these ghastly power plants, belching black smoke into the atmosphere, could be shut down forever, and humanity's electrical needs were met by a trained corps of youthful poltergeists, volunteers living a monastic life and using their sizzling sexual tensions as the fuel that keeps the turbines spinning? Or perhaps NASA wants a poltergeist-driven spaceship. There I am, lean and bronzed and jaunty, a handsome figure in my white astronaut suit, taking my seat in the command capsule of the *Mars One*. T minus thirty seconds and counting. An anxious world awaits the big moment. Five. Four. Three. Two. One. Lift-off. And I grin my world-famous grin and coolly summon my power and open the mental throttle and *push,* and the mighty vessel rises, hovering serenely a moment above the launching pad, rises and climbs, slicing like a giant glittering needle through the ice-blue Florida sky, soaring up and away on man's first voyage to the red planet. . . .

Another experiment is called for. I'll try to send a beer can to the moon. If I can do that, I should be able to send a spaceship. A simple Newtonian process, a matter of attaining escape velocity; and I don't think thrust is likely to be a determining quantitative function. A push is a push is a push, and so far I haven't noticed limitations of mass, so if I can get it up with a beer can, I ought to succeed in throwing anything of any mass into space. I think. Anyway, I raid the family garbage and go outside clutching a crumpled Schlitz container. A mild misty night; the moon isn't visible. No matter. I place the can on the ground and contemplate it. Five. Four. Three. Two. One. Lift-off. I grin my world-famous grin. I coolly summon my power and open the mental throttle. *Push.* Yes, the beer can rises. Hovering serenely a moment above the pavement. Rises and climbs, end over end, slicing like a crumpled beer can through the muggy air. Up. Up. Into the darkness. Long after it disappears, I continue to push. Am I still in contact? Does it still climb? I have no way of telling. I lack the proper tracking stations. Perhaps it does travel on and on through the lonely void, on a perfect lunar trajectory. Or maybe it has already tumbled down, a block away, skulling some hapless cop. I shot a beer can into the air, it fell to earth I know not where. Shrugging, I go back into the house. So much for my career as a spaceman. Blaufeld, you've pulled off another dumb fantasy. Blaufeld, how can you stand being such a silly putz?

Clickety-clack. Four in the morning, Sara's just coming in from her date. Here I am lying awake like a worried parent. Notice that the parents themselves don't worry: they're fast asleep, I bet, giving no damns about the hours their daughter keeps. Whereas I brood. She got laid again tonight, no doubt of it. Possibly twice. Grimly I try to reconstruct the event in my imagination. The positions, the sounds of flesh against flesh, the panting and moaning. How often has she done it now? A hundred times? Three hundred? She's been doing it at least since she was sixteen. I'm sure of that. For girls it's so much easier; they

don't need to chase and coax, all they have to do is say yes. Sara says yes
a lot. Before Jimmy the Greek there was Greasy Kid Stuff, and before
him there was the Spade Wonder, and before him. . . .

Out there tonight in this city there are three million people at the
very minimum who just got laid. I detest adults and their easy screwing.
They devalue it by doing it so much. They just have to roll over and
grab some meat, and away they go, in and out, in and out, oooh oooh
oooh ahhh. Christ, how boring it must get! If they could only look at it
from the point of view of a frustrated adolescent again. The hungry
virgin, on the outside peering in. Excluded from the world of screwing.
Feeling that delicious sweet tension of wanting and not knowing how
to get. The fiery knot of longing, sitting like a ravenous tapeworm in my
belly, devouring my soul. I magnify sex. I exalt it. I multiply its
wonders. It'll never live up to my anticipations. But I love the tension
of anticipating and speculating and not getting. In fact, I think
sometimes I'd like to spend my whole life on the edge of the blade,
looking forward always to being deflowered but never quite taking the
steps that would bring it about. A dynamic stasis, sustaining and
enhancing my special power. Harry Blaufeld, virgin and poltergeist.
Why not? Anybody at all can screw. Idiots, morons, bores, uglies.
Everybody does it. There's magic in renunciation. If I keep myself
aloof, pure, unique. . . .

Push. . . .

I do my little poltergeisty numbers. I stack and restack my textbooks
without leaving my bed. I move my shirt from the floor to the back of
the chair. I turn the chair around to face the wall. Push . . . push . . .
push. . . .

Water running in the john. Sara's washing up. What's it like, Sara?
How does it feel when he puts it in you? We don't talk much, you and
I. You think I'm a child; you patronize me, you give me cute winks,
your voice goes up half an octave. Do you wink at Jimmy the Greek like
that? Like hell. And you talk husky contralto to him. Sit down and talk
to me some time, Sis. I'm teetering on the brink of manhood. Guide me
out of my virginity. Tell me what girls like guys to say to them. Sure.
You won't tell me shit, Sara. You want me to stay your baby brother
forever, because that enhances your own sense of being grown up. And

you screw and screw and screw, you and Jimmy the Greek, and you don't even understand the mystical significance of the act of intercourse. To you it's just good sweaty fun, like going bowling. Right? Right? Oh, you miserable bitch! Screw you, Sara!

A shriek from the bathroom. Christ, what have I done now? I better go see.

Sara, naked, kneels on the cold tiles. Her head is in the bathtub and she's clinging with both hands to the bathtub's rim, and she's shaking violently.

"You okay?" I ask. "What happened?"

"Like a kick in the back," she says hoarsely. "I was at the sink, washing my face, and I turned around and something hit me like a kick in the back and knocked me halfway across the room."

"You okay, though? You aren't hurt?"

"Help me up."

She's upset but not injured. She's so upset that she forgets that she's naked, and without putting on her robe she cuddles up against me, trembling. She seems small and fragile and scared. I stroke her bare back where I imagine she felt the blow. Also I sneak a look at her nipples, just to see if they're still standing up after her date with Jimmy the Greek. They aren't. I soothe her with my fingers. I feel very manly and protective, even if it's only my cruddy dumb sister I'm protecting.

"What could have happened?" she asks. "You weren't pulling any tricks, were you?"

"I was in bed," I say, totally sincere.

"A lot of funny things been going on around this house lately," she says.

Cindy, catching me in the hallway between Geometry and Spanish: "How come you never call me any more?"

"Been busy."

"Busy how?"

"Busy."

"I guess you must be," she says. "Looks to me like you haven't slept in a week. What's her name?"

"Her? No her. I've just been busy." I try to escape. Must I push her again? "A research project."

"You could take some time out for relaxing. You could keep in touch with old friends."

"Friends? What kind of friend are you? You said I was silly. You said I was disgusting. Remember, Cindy?"

"The emotions of the moment. I was off balance. I mean, psychologically. Look, let's talk about all this some time, Harry. Some time soon."

"Maybe."

"If you're not doing anything Saturday night—"

I look at her in astonishment. She's actually asking *me* for a date! Why is she pursuing me? What does she want from me? Is she itching for another chance to humiliate me? Silly and disgusting, disgusting and silly. I look at my watch and quirk up my lips. Time to move along.

"I'm not sure," I tell her. "I may have some work to do."

"Work?"

"Research," I say. "I'll let you know."

A night of happy experiments. I unscrew a light bulb, float it from one side of my room to the other, return it to the fixture, and efficiently *screw it back in*. Precision control. I go up to the roof and launch another beer can to the moon, only this time I loft it a thousand feet, bring it back, kick it up even higher, bring it back, send it off a third time with a tremendous accumulated kinetic energy, and I have no doubt it'll cleave through space. I pick up trash in the street from a hundred yards away and throw it in the trash basket. Lastly—most scary of all—I polt *myself*. I levitate a little, lifting myself five feet into the air. That's as high as I dare go. (What if I lose the power and fall?) If I had the courage, I could fly. I can do anything. Give me the right fulcrum and I'll move the world. O, *potentia!* What a fantastic trip this is!

After two awful days of inner debate I phone Cindy and make a date for Saturday. I'm not sure whether it's a good idea. Her sudden new aggressiveness turns me off, slightly, but nevertheless it's a novelty to have a girl chasing me, and who am I to snub her? I wonder what she's up to, though. Coming on so interested in me after dumping me mercilessly on our last date. I'm still angry with her about that, but I can't hold a grudge, not with *her*. Maybe she wants to make amends. We did have a pretty decent relationship in the non-physical sense, until that one stupid evening. Jesus, what if she really *does* want to make amends, all the way? She scares me. I guess I'm a little bit of a coward. Or a lot of a coward. I don't understand any of this, man. I think I'm getting into something very heavy.

I juggle three tennis balls and keep them all in the air at once, with my hands in my pockets. I see a woman trying to park her car in a space that's too small, and as I pass by I give her a sneaky little assist by pushing against the car behind her space; it moves backward a foot and a half and she has room to park. Friday afternoon, in my gym class, I get into a basketball game and on five separate occasions when Mike Kisiak goes driving in for one of his sure-thing lay-ups I flick the ball away from the hoop. He can't figure out why he's off form and it really kills him. There seem to be no limits to what I can do. I'm awed at it myself. I gain skill from day to day. I might just be an authentic superman.

Cindy and Harry, Harry and Cindy, warm and cozy, sitting on her living-room couch. Christ, I think I'm being seduced! How can this be happening? To me? Christ. Christ. Christ. Cindy and Harry. Harry and Cindy. Where are we heading tonight?

In the movie house Cindy snuggles close. Midway through the flick I take the hint. A big bold move: slipping my arm around her shoulders. She wriggles so that my hand slides down through her armpit and comes to rest grasping her right breast. My cheeks blaze. I do as if to pull back, as if I've touched a hot stove, but she clamps her arm over my forearm. Trapped. I explore her yielding flesh. No padding there, just authentic Cindy. She's so eager and easy that it terrifies me. Afterwards we go for sodas. In the shop she turns on the body language something frightening—gleaming eyes, suggestive smiles, little steamy twistings of her shoulders. I feel like telling her not to be so obvious about it. It's like living one of my own wet dreams.

Back to her place, now. It starts to rain. We stand outside, in the very spot where I stood when I polted her the last time. I can write the script effortlessly. "Why don't you come inside for a while, Harry?" "I'd love to." "Here, dry your feet on the doormat. Would you like some hot chocolate?" "Whatever you're having, Cindy." "No, whatever you'd like to have." "Hot chocolate would be fine, then." Her parents aren't home. Her older brother is fornicating in Scarsdale. The rain hammers at the windows. The house is big, expensive-looking, thick carpets, fancy draperies. Cindy in the kitchen, puttering at the stove. Harry in the living-room, fidgeting at the bookshelves. Then Cindy and Harry, Harry and Cindy, warm and cozy, together on the couch. Hot chocolate: two sips apiece. Her lips near mine. Silently begging me. Come on, dope, bend forward. Be a *mensh*. We kiss. We've kissed before, but this time it's with tongues. Christ. Christ. I don't believe this. Suave old Casanova Blaufeld swinging into action like a well-oiled seducing machine. Her perfume in my nostrils, my tongue in her mouth, my hand on her sweater, and then, unexpectedly, my hand is *under* her sweater, and then, astonishingly, my other hand is on her knee, and up under her skirt, and her thigh is satiny and cool, and I sit there having this weird two-dimensional feeling that I'm not an autonomous human being but just somebody on the screen in a movie rated X, aware that thousands of people out there in the audience are watching me with held breath, and I don't dare let them down. I continue, not letting myself pause to examine what's happening, not thinking at all, turning off my mind completely, just going forward step by step. I know that if I ever halt and back off to ask myself if this is real, it'll all blow up in my face. She's helping me. She knows much more about this than I do. Murmuring softly. Encouraging me. My fingers scrabbling at our undergarments. "Don't rush it," she whispers. "We've got all the time in the world." My body pressing urgently against hers. Somehow now I'm not puzzled by the mechanics of the thing. So this is how it happens. What a miracle of evolution that we're designed to fit together this way! "Be gentle," she says, the way girls always say in the novels, and I want to be gentle, but how can I be gentle when I'm riding a runaway chariot? I push, not with my mind but with my body, and suddenly I feel this wondrous velvety softness enfolding me, and I begin to move fast, unable to hold back, and she moves too and we clasp each other and I'm swept helter-skelter along into a whirlpool. Down and down and down. "Harry!" she gasps and I explode uncontrollably and I know it's over. Hardly begun, and it's over. Is that it? That's it. That's all there is to it, the moving, the clasping, the gasping, the explosion. It felt good, but not *that* good, not as good as in my feverish virginal hallucinations I hoped it would be, and a backwash of letdown rips through me at the realization that it isn't transcendental after all, it isn't a mystic thing, it's just a body thing that starts and continues and ends. Abruptly I want to pull away and be alone to think. But I know I mustn't, I have to be tender and grateful now, I hold her in my arms, I whisper soft things to her, I tell her how good it was, she tells me how good it was. We're both lying, but so what? It *was* good. In retrospect it's starting to seem fantastic, overwhelming, all the things I wanted it to be. The *idea* of what we've done blows my mind. If only it hadn't been over so fast. No matter. Next time will be better. We've crossed a frontier; we're in unfamiliar territory now.

Much later she says, "I'd like to know how you make things move without touching them."

I shrug. "Why do you want to know?"

"It fascinates me. *You* fascinate me. I thought for a long time you were just another fellow, you know, kind of clumsy, kind of immature. But then this gift of yours. It's ESP, isn't it, Harry? I've read a lot about it. I know. The moment you knocked me down, I knew what it must have been. Wasn't it?"

Why be coy with her?

"Yes," I say, proud in my new manhood. "As a matter of fact, it's a classic poltergeist manifestation. When I gave you that shove, it was the first I knew I had the power. But I've been developing it. You wouldn't believe some of the things I've been able to do lately." My voice is deep; my manner is assured. I have graduated into my own fantasy self tonight.

"Show me," she says. "Poltergeist something, Harry!"

"Anything. You name it."

"That chair."

"Of course." I survey the chair. I reach for the power. It does not come. The chair stays where it is. What about the saucer, then? No. The spoon? No. "Cindy, I don't understand it, but—it doesn't seem to be working right now—"

"You must be tired."

"Yes. That's it. Tired. A good night's sleep and I'll have it again. I'll phone you in the morning and give you a real demonstration." Hastily buttoning my shirt. Looking for my shoes. Her parents will walk in any minute. Her brother. "Listen, a wonderful evening, unforgettable, tremendous—"

"Stay a little longer."

"I really can't."

Out into the rain.

Home. Stunned. I push . . . and the shoe sits there. I look up at the light fixture. Nothing. The bulb will not turn. The power is gone. What will become of me now? Commander Blaufeld, space hero! No. No. Nothing. I will drop back into the ordinary rut of mankind. I will be . . . *a husband.* I will be . . . *an employee.* And push no more. And push no more. Can I even lift my shirt and flip it to the floor? No. No. Gone. Every shred, gone. I pull the covers over my head. I put my hands to my deflowered maleness. That alone responds. There alone am I still potent. Like all the rest. Just one of the common herd, now. Let's face it: I'll push no more. I'm ordinary again. Fighting off tears, I coil tight against myself in the darkness, and, sweating, moaning a little, working hard, I descend numbly into the quicksand, into the first moments of the long colorless years ahead.

9

THE MUTANT SEASON

It snowed yesterday, three inches. Today a cruel wind comes ripping off the ocean, kicking up the snowdrifts. This is the dead of winter, the low point of the year. This is the season when the mutants arrive. They showed up ten days ago, the same six families as always, renting all the beach houses on the north side of Dune Crest Road. They like to come here in winter when the vacationers are gone and the beaches are empty. I guess they don't enjoy having a lot of normals around. In winter here there's just the little hard core of year-round residents like us. And we don't mind the mutants so long as they don't bother us.

I can see them now, frolicking along the shore, kids and grownups. The cold doesn't seem to affect them at all. It would affect me plenty, being outside in this weather, but they don't even trouble themselves with wearing overcoats. Just light windbreakers and pullovers. They have thicker skins than we do, I guess—leathery-looking, shiny, apple-green—and maybe a different metabolism. They could almost be people from some other planet, but no, they're all natives of the U.S.A., just like you and me. Mutants, that's all. Freaks is what we used to call them. But of course you mustn't call them that now.

Doing their mutant tricks. They can fly, you know. Oh, it isn't really flying, it's more a kind of jumping and soaring, but they can go twenty, thirty feet in the air and float up there about three or four minutes. Levitation, they call it. A bunch of them are levitating right out over the ocean, hanging high above the breakers. It would serve them right to drop and get a soaking. But they don't ever lose control. And look, two of them are having a snowball fight without using their hands, just

133

picking up the snow with their minds and wadding it into balls and tossing it around. Telekinesis, that's called.

I learn these terms from my older daughter Ellen. She's 17. She spends a lot of time hanging around with one of the mutant kids. I wish she'd stay away from him.

Levitation. Telekinesis. Mutants renting beach houses. It's a crazy world these days.

Look at them jumping around. They look happy, don't they?

It's three weeks since they came. Cindy, my younger girl—she's 9—asked me today about mutants. What they are. Why they exist.

I said, There are all different kinds of human beings. Some have brown skins and woolly hair, some have yellow skins and slanted eyes, some have—

Those are the races, she said. I know about races. The races look different outside but inside they're pretty much all the same. But the mutants are really different. They have special powers and some of them have strange bodies. They're more different from us than other races are, and that's what I don't understand.

They're a special kind of people, I told her. They were born different from everybody else.

Why?

You know what genes are, Cindy?

Sort of, she said. We're just starting to study about them.

Genes are what determine how our children will look. Your eyes are brown because I have the gene for brown eyes, see? But sometimes there are sudden changes in a family's genes. Something strange gets in. Yellow eyes, maybe. That would be a mutation. The mutants are people who had something strange happen to their genes some time back, fifty, a hundred, three hundred years ago, and the change in the genes became permanent and was handed down from parents to children. Like the gene for the floating they do. Or the gene for their shiny skin. There are all sorts of different mutant genes.

Where did the mutants come from?

They've always been here, I said.

But why didn't anybody ever talk about them? Why isn't there anything about the mutants in my schoolbooks?

It takes time for things to get into schoolbooks, Cindy. Your books were written ten or fifteen years ago. People didn't know much about mutants then and not much was said about them, especially to children your age. The mutants were still in hiding. They lived in out-of-the-way places and disguised themselves and concealed their powers.

Why don't they hide any more?

Because they don't need to, I said. Things have changed. The normal people accept them. We've been getting rid of a lot of prejudices in the last hundred years. Once upon a time anybody who was even a little strange made other people uncomfortable. Any sort of difference—skin color, religion, language—caused trouble, Cindy. Well, we learned to accept people who aren't like ourselves. We even accept people who aren't quite human, now. Like the mutants.

If you accept them, she said, why do you get angry when Ellen goes walking on the beach with what's-his-name?

Ellen's friend went back to college right after the Christmas holidays. Tim, his name is. He's a junior at Cornell. I think she's spending too much time writing long letters to him, but what can I do?

My wife thinks we ought to be more sociable toward them. They've been here a month and a half and we've just exchanged the usual token greetings—friendly nods, smiles, nothing more. We don't even know their names. I could get along without knowing them, I said. But all right. Let's go over and invite them to have drinks with us tonight.

We went across to the place Tim's family is renting. A man who might have been anywhere from 35 to 55 answered the door. It was the first time I ever saw any of them up close. His features were flat and his eyes were set oddly far apart, and his skin was so glossy it looked like it had been waxed. He didn't ask us in. I was able to see odd things going on behind him in the house—people floating near the ceiling, stuff like that. Standing there at the door, feeling very uneasy and awkward, we hemmed and hawed and finally said what we had come to say. He wasn't interested. You can tell when people aren't interested in being mixed with. Very coolly he said they were busy now, expecting guests, and couldn't drop by. But they'd be in touch.

I bet that's the last we hear of them. A standoffish bunch, keeping to themselves, setting up their own ghetto.

Well, never mind. I don't need to socialize with them. They'll be leaving in another couple of weeks anyway.

How fast the cycle of the months goes round. First snowstorm of the season today, a light one, but it's not really winter yet. I guess our weird friends will be coming back to the seashore soon.

Three of the families moved in on Friday and the other three came today. Cindy's already been over visiting. She says this year Tim's family has a pet, a mutant dog, no less, a kind of poodle only with scaly skin and bright red eyes, like marbles. Gives me the shivers. I didn't know there were mutant dogs.

I was hoping Tim had gone into the army or something. No such luck. He'll be here for two weeks at Christmastime. Ellen's already counting the days.

I saw the mutant dog out on the beach. If you ask me, that's no dog, that's some kind of giant lizard. But it barks. It does bark. And wags its tail. I saw Cindy hugging it. She plays with the younger mutant kids just as though they're normals. She accepts them and they accept her. I suppose it's healthy. I suppose their attitudes are right and mine are wrong. But I can't help my conditioning, can I? I don't *want* to be prejudiced. But some things are ingrained when we're very young.

Ellen stayed out way past midnight tonight with Tim.

Tim at our house for dinner this evening. He's a nice kid, have to admit. But *so* strange-looking. And Ellen made him show off levitation for us. He frowns a little and floats right up off the ground. A freak, a circus freak. And my daughter's in love with him.

His winter vacation will be over tomorrow. Not a moment too soon, either.

Another winter nearing its end. The mutants clear out this week. On Saturday they had a bunch of guests—mutants of some other type, no less! A different tribe. The visitors were tall and thin, like walking skeletons, very pale, very solemn. They don't speak out loud: Cindy says they talk with their minds. Telepaths. They seem harmless enough but I find this whole thing very scary. I imagine dozens of bizarre strains existing within mankind, alongside mankind, all kinds of grotesque mutant types breeding true and multiplying. Now that they've finally surfaced, now that we're discovering how many of them there really are, I start to wonder what new surprises lie ahead for us so-called normals. Will we find ourselves in a minority in another couple of generations? Will those of us who lack superpowers become third-class citizens?

I'm worried.

Summer. Fall. Winter. And here they come again. Maybe we can be friendlier with them this year.

Last year, seven houses. This year they've rented nine. It's good to have so many people around, I guess. Before they started coming it was pretty lonesome here in the winters.

Looks like snow. Soon they'll be here. Letter from Ellen, saying to get her old room ready. Time passes. It always does. Things change. They always do. Winter comes round in its season, and with it come our strange friends. Their ninth straight year here. Can't wait to see Ellen.

Ellen and Tim arrived yesterday. You see them down on the beach? Yes, they're a good-looking young couple. That's my grandson with them. The one in the blue snowsuit. Look at him floating—I bet he's nine feet off the ground! Precocious, that's him. Not old enough to walk yet. But he can levitate pretty well, let me tell you.

10

WHEN WE WENT TO SEE THE END OF THE WORLD

Nick and Jane were glad that they had gone to see the end of the world, because it gave them something special to talk about at Mike and Ruby's party. One always likes to come to a party armed with a little conversation. Mike and Ruby give marvelous parties. Their home is superb, one of the finest in the neighborhood. It is truly a home for all seasons, all moods. Their very special corner-of-the-world. With more space indoors and out . . . more wide-open freedom. The living room with its exposed ceiling beams is a natural focal point for entertaining. Custom-finished, with a conversation pit and fireplace. There's also a family room with beamed ceiling and wood paneling . . . plus a study. And a magnificent master suite with 12-foot dressing room and private bath. Solidly impressive exterior design. Sheltered courtyard. Beautifully wooded ⅓-acre grounds. Their parties are highlights of any month. Nick and Jane waited until they thought enough people had arrived. Then Jane nudged Nick and Nick said gaily, "You know what we did last week? Hey, we went to see the end of the world!"

"The end of the world?" Henry asked.

"You went to see it?" said Henry's wife Cynthia.

"How did you manage that?" Paula wanted to know.

"It's been available since March," Stan told her. "I think a division of American Express runs it."

Nick was put out to discover that Stan already knew. Quickly, before

Stan could say anything more, Nick said, "Yes, it's just started. Our travel agent found out for us. What they do is they put you in this machine, it looks like a tiny teeny submarine, you know, with dials and levers up front behind a plastic wall to keep you from touching anything, and they send you into the future. You can charge it with any of the regular credit cards."

"It must be very expensive," Marcia said.

"They're bringing the costs down rapidly," Jane said. "Last year only millionaires could afford it. Really, haven't you heard about it before?"

"What did you see?" Henry asked.

"For a while, just grayness outside the porthole," said Nick. "And a kind of flickering effect." Everybody was looking at him. He enjoyed the attention. Jane wore a rapt, loving expression. "Then the haze cleared and a voice said over a loudspeaker that we had now reached the very end of time, when life had become impossible on Earth. Of course we were sealed into the submarine thing. Only looking out. On this beach, this empty beach. The water a funny gray color with a pink sheen. And then the sun came up. It was red like it sometimes is at sunrise, only it stayed red as it got to the middle of the sky, and it looked lumpy and sagging at the edges. Like a few of us, hah hah. Lumpy and sagging at the edges. A cold wind blowing across the beach."

"If you were sealed in the submarine, how did you know there was a cold wind?" Cynthia asked.

Jane glared at her. Nick said, "We could see the sand blowing around. And it *looked* cold. The gray ocean. Like in winter."

"Tell them about the crab," said Jane.

"Yes, and the crab. The last life-form on Earth. It wasn't really a crab, of course, it was something about two feet wide and a foot high, with thick shiny green armor and maybe a dozen legs and some curving horns coming up, and it moved slowly from right to left in front of us. It took all day to cross the beach. And toward nightfall it died. Its horns went limp and it stopped moving. The tide came in and carried it away. The sun went down. There wasn't any moon. The stars didn't seem to be in the right places. The loudspeaker told us we had just seen the death of Earth's last living thing."

"How *eerie!*" cried Paula.

"Were you gone very long?" Ruby asked.

"Three hours," Jane said. "You can spend weeks or days at the end of the world, if you want to pay extra, but they always bring you back to a point three hours after you went. To hold down the babysitter expenses."

Mike offered Nick some pot. "That's really something," he said. "To have gone to the end of the world. Hey, Ruby, maybe we'll talk to the travel agent about it."

Nick took a deep drag and passed the joint to Jane. He felt pleased with himself about the way he had told the story. They had all been very impressed. That swollen red sun, that scuttling crab. The trip had cost more than a month in Japan, but it had been a good investment. He and Jane were the first in the neighborhood who had gone. That was important. Paula was staring at him in awe. Nick knew that she regarded him in a completely different light now. Possibly she would meet him at a motel on Tuesday at lunchtime. Last month she had turned him down but now he had an extra attractiveness for her. Nick winked at her. Cynthia was holding hands with Stan. Henry and Mike both were crouched at Jane's feet. Mike and Ruby's 12-year-old son came into the room and stood at the edge of the conversation pit. He said, "There just was a bulletin on the news. Mutated amoebas escaped from a government research station and got into Lake Michigan. They're carrying a tissue-dissolving virus and everybody in seven states is supposed to boil his water until further notice." Mike scowled at the boy and said, "It's after your bedtime, Timmy." The boy went out. The doorbell rang. Ruby answered it and returned with Eddie and Fran.

Paula said, "Nick and Jane went to see the end of the world. They've just been telling us all about it."

"Gee," said Eddie, "we did that too, on Wednesday night."

Nick was crestfallen. Jane bit her lip and asked Cynthia quietly why Fran always wore such flashy dresses. Ruby said, "You saw the whole works, eh? The crab and everything?"

"The crab?" Eddie said. "What crab? We didn't see the crab."

"It must have died the time before," Paula said. "When Nick and Jane were there."

Mike said, "A fresh shipment of Cuernavaca Lightning is in. Here, have a toke."

"How long ago did you do it?" Eddie said to Nick.

"Sunday afternoon. I guess we were about the first."

"Great trip, isn't it?" Eddie said. "A little somber, though. When the last hill crumbles into the sea."

"That's not what we saw," said Jane. "And you didn't see the crab? Maybe we were on different trips."

Mike said, "What was it like for you, Eddie?"

Eddie put his arms around Cynthia from behind. He said, "They put us into this little capsule, with a porthole, you know, and a lot of instruments and—"

"We heard that part," said Paula. "What did you *see?*"

"The end of the world," Eddie said. "When water covers everything. The sun and the moon were in the sky at the same time—"

"We didn't see the moon at all," Jane remarked. "It just wasn't there."

"It was on one side and the sun was on the other," Eddie went on. "The moon was closer than it should have been. And a funny color, almost like bronze. And the ocean creeping up. We went halfway around the world and all we saw was ocean. Except in one place, there was this chunk of land sticking up, this hill, and the guide told us it was the top of Mount Everest." He waved to Fran. "That was groovy, huh, floating in our tin boat next to the top of Mount Everest. Maybe ten feet of it sticking up. And the water rising all the time. Up, up, up. Up and over the top. Glub. No land left. I have to admit it was a little disappointing, except of course the *idea* of the thing. That human ingenuity can design a machine that can send people billions of years forward in time and bring them back, wow! But there was just this ocean."

"How strange," said Jane. "We saw an ocean too, but there was a beach, a kind of nasty beach, and the crab-thing walking along it, and the sun—it was all red, was the sun red when you saw it?"

"A kind of pale green," Fran said.

"Are you people talking about the end of the world?" Tom asked. He and Harriet were standing by the door taking off their coats. Mike's son must have let them in. Tom gave his coat to Ruby and said, "Man, what a spectacle!"

"So you did it too?" Jane asked, a little hollowly.

"Two weeks ago," said Tom. "The travel agent called and said, Guess what we're offering now, the end of the goddamned world! With all the extras it didn't really cost so much. So we went right down there to the office, Saturday, I think—was it a Friday?—the day of the big riot, anyway, when they burned St. Louis—"

"That was a Saturday," Cynthia said. "I remember I was coming back from the shopping center when the radio said they were using nuclears—"

"Saturday, yes," Tom said. "And we told them we were ready to go, and off they sent us."

"Did you see a beach with crabs," Stan demanded, "or was it a world full of water?"

"Neither one. It was like a big ice age. Glaciers covered everything. No oceans showing, no mountains. We flew clear around the world and it was all a huge snowball. They had floodlights on the vehicle because the sun had gone out."

"I was sure I could see the sun still hanging up there," Harriet put in. "Like a ball of cinders in the sky. But the guide said no, nobody could see it."

"How come everybody gets to visit a different kind of end of the world?" Henry asked. "You'd think there'd be only one kind of end of the world. I mean, it ends, and this is how it ends, and there can't be more than one way."

"Could it be a fake?" Stan asked. Everybody turned around and looked at him. Nick's face got very red. Fran looked so mean that Eddie let go of Cynthia and started to rub Fran's shoulders. Stan shrugged. "I'm not suggesting it is," he said defensively. "I was just wondering."

"Seemed pretty real to me," said Tom. "The sun burned out. A big ball of ice. The atmosphere, you know, frozen. The end of the goddamned world."

The telephone rang. Ruby went to answer it. Nick asked Paula about lunch on Tuesday. She said yes. "Let's meet at the motel," he said, and she grinned. Eddie was making out with Cynthia again. Henry looked very stoned and was having trouble staying awake. Phil and Isabel arrived. They heard Tom and Fran talking about their trips to the end of the world and Isabel said she and Phil had gone only the day before yesterday. "Goddamn," Tom said, "everybody's doing it! What was your trip like?"

Ruby came back into the room. "That was my sister calling from Fresno to say she's safe. Fresno wasn't hit by the earthquake at all."

"Earthquake?" Paula said.

"In California," Mike told her. "This afternoon. You didn't know? Wiped out most of Los Angeles and ran right up the coast practically to Monterey. They think it was on account of the underground bomb test in the Mohave Desert."

"California's always having such awful disasters," Marcia said.

"Good thing those amoebas got loose back east," said Nick. "Imagine how complicated it would be if they had them in L.A. now too."

"They will," Tom said. "Two to one they reproduce by airborne spores."

"Like the typhoid germs last November," Jane said.

"That was typhus," Nick corrected.

"Anyway," Phil said, "I was telling Tom and Fran about what we saw at the end of the world. It was the sun going nova. They showed it very cleverly, too. I mean, you can't actually sit around and *experience* it, on account of the heat and the hard radiation and all. But they give it to you in a peripheral way, very elegant in the McLuhanesque sense of the word. First they take you to a point about two hours before the blowup, right? It's I don't know how many jillion years from now, but a long way, anyhow, because the trees are all different, they've got blue scales and ropy branches, and the animals are like things with one leg that jump on pogo sticks—"

"Oh, I don't *believe* that," Cynthia drawled.

Phil ignored her gracefully. "And we didn't see any sign of human beings, not a house, not a telephone pole, nothing, so I suppose we must have been extinct a long time before. Anyway, they let us look at that for a while. Not getting out of our time machine, naturally, because they said the atmosphere was wrong. Gradually the sun started to puff up. We were nervous—weren't we, Iz?—I mean, suppose they miscalculated things? This whole trip is a very new concept and things might go wrong. The sun was getting bigger and bigger, and then this thing like an arm seemed to pop out of its left side, a big fiery arm reaching out across space, getting closer and closer. We saw it through smoked glass, like you do an eclipse. They gave us about two minutes of the explosion, and we could feel it getting hot already. Then we jumped a couple of years forward in time. The sun was back to its regular shape, only it was smaller, sort of like a little white sun instead of a big yellow one. And on Earth everything was ashes."

"Ashes," Isabel said, with emphasis.

"It looked like Detroit after the union nuked Ford," Phil said. "Only much, much worse. Whole mountains were melted. The oceans were dried up. Everything was ashes." He shuddered and took a joint from Mike. "Isabel was crying."

"The things with one leg," Isabel said. "I mean, they must have all been wiped *out*." She began to sob. Stan comforted her. "I wonder why it's a different way for everyone who goes," he said. "Freezing. Or the oceans. Or the sun blowing up. Or the thing Nick and Jane saw."

"I'm convinced that each of us had a genuine experience in the far future," said Nick. He felt he had to regain control of the group somehow. It had been so good when he was telling his story, before those others had come. "That is to say, the world suffers a variety of natural calamities, it doesn't just have *one* end of the world, and they keep mixing things up and sending people to different catastrophes. But never for a moment did I doubt that I was seeing an authentic event."

"We have to do it," Ruby said to Mike. "It's only three hours. What about calling them first thing Monday and making an appointment for Thursday night?"

"Monday's the President's funeral," Tom pointed out. "The travel agency will be closed."

"Have they caught the assassin yet?" Fran asked.

"They didn't mention it on the four o'clock news," said Stan. "I guess he'll get away like the last one."

"Beats me why anybody wants to be President," Phil said.

Mike put on some music. Nick danced with Paula. Eddie danced with Cynthia. Henry was asleep. Dave, Paula's husband, was on crutches because of his mugging, and he asked Isabel to sit and talk with him. Tom danced with Harriet even though he was married to her. She hadn't been out of the hospital more than a few months since the transplant and he treated her extremely tenderly. Mike danced with Fran. Phil danced with Jane. Stan danced with Marcia. Ruby cut in on Eddie and Cynthia. Afterward Tom danced with Jane and Phil danced with Paula. Mike and Ruby's little girl woke up and came out to say hello. Mike sent her back to bed. Far away there was the sound of an explosion. Nick danced with Paula again, but he didn't want her to get bored with him before Tuesday, so he excused himself and went to talk with Dave. Dave handled most of Nick's investments. Ruby said to Mike, "The day after the funeral, will you call the travel agent?" Mike said he would, but Tom said somebody would probably shoot the new President too and there'd be another funeral. These funerals were demolishing the gross national product, Stan observed, on account of how everything had to close all the time. Nick saw Cynthia wake Henry up and ask him sharply if he would take her on the end-of-the-world trip. Henry looked embarrassed. His factory had been blown up at Christmas in a peace demonstration and everybody knew he was in bad shape financially. "You can *charge* it," Cynthia said, her fierce voice carrying above the chitchat. "And it's so *beautiful*, Henry. The ice. Or the sun exploding. I want to go."

"Lou and Janet were going to be here tonight too," Ruby said to Paula. "But their younger boy came back from Texas with that new kind of cholera and they had to cancel."

Phil said, "I understand that one couple saw the moon come apart. It got too close to the Earth and split into chunks and the chunks fell like meteors. Smashing everything up, you know. One big piece nearly hit their time machine."

"I wouldn't have liked that at all," Marcia said.

"Our trip was very lovely," said Jane. "No violent things at all. Just the big red sun and the tide and that crab creeping along the beach. We were both deeply moved."

"It's amazing what science can accomplish nowadays," Fran said.

Mike and Ruby agreed they would try to arrange a trip to the end of the world as soon as the funeral was over. Cynthia drank too much and got sick. Phil, Tom, and Dave discussed the stock market. Harriet told Nick about her operation. Isabel flirted with Mike, tugging her neckline lower. At midnight someone turned on the news. They had some shots of the earthquake and a warning about boiling your water if you lived in the affected states. The President's widow was shown visiting the last President's widow to get some pointers for the funeral. Then there was an interview with an executive of the time-trip company. "Business is phenomenal," he said. "Time-tripping will be the nation's number one growth industry next year." The reporter asked him if his company would soon be offering something beside the end-of-the-world trip. "Later on, we hope to," the executive said. "We plan to apply for Congressional approval soon. But meanwhile the demand for our present offering is running very high. You can't imagine. Of course, you have to expect apocalyptic stuff to attain immense popularity in times like these." The reporter said, "What do you mean, times like these?" but as the time-trip man started to reply, he was interrupted by the commercial. Mike shut off the set. Nick discovered that he was extremely depressed. He decided that it was because so many of his friends had made the journey, and he had thought he and Jane were the only ones who had. He found himself standing next to Marcia and tried to describe the way the crab had moved, but Marcia only shrugged. No one was talking about time-trips now. The party had moved beyond that point. Nick and Jane left quite early and went right to sleep, without making love. The next morning the Sunday paper wasn't delivered because of the Bridge Authority strike, and the radio said that the mutant amoebas were proving harder to eradicate than originally anticipated. They were spreading into Lake Superior and everyone in the region would have to boil all drinking water. Nick and Jane discussed where they would go for their next vacation. "What about going to see the end of the world all over again?" Jane suggested, and Nick laughed quite a good deal.

11

WHAT WE LEARNED
FROM THIS MORNING'S
NEWSPAPER

[1]

I got home from the office as usual at 6:47 this evening and discovered that our peaceful street has been in some sort of crazy uproar all day. The newsboy it seems came by today and delivered the New York *Times* for Wednesday December 1 to every house on Redbud Crescent. Since today is Monday November 22 it follows therefore that Wednesday December 1 is the middle of next week. I said to my wife are you sure that this really happened? Because I looked at the newspaper myself before I went off to work this morning and it seemed quite all right to me.

At breakfast time the newspaper could be printed in Albanian and it would seem quite all right to you my wife replied. Here look at this. And she took the newspaper from the hall closet and handed it all folded up to me. It looked just like any other edition of the New York *Times* but now I saw what I had failed to notice at breakfast time, that it said Wednesday December 1.

Is today the 22nd of November I asked? Monday?

It certainly is my wife told me. Yesterday was Sunday and tomorrow is going to be Tuesday and we haven't even come to Thanksgiving yet. Bill what are we going to do about this?

I glanced through the newspaper. The front page headlines were
nothing remarkable I must admit, just the same old New York *Times*
stuff that you get any day when there hasn't been some event of cosmic
importance. NIXON, WITH WIFE, TO VISIT 3 CHINESE CITIES
IN 7 DAYS. Yes. 10 HURT AS GUNMEN SHOOT WAY INTO
AND OUT OF BANK. All right. GROUP OF 10, IN ROME,
BEGINS NEGOTIATING REALIGNMENT OF CURRENCIES.
Okay. The same old New York *Times* stuff and no surprises. But the
paper was dated Wednesday December 1 and that was a surprise of
sorts I guess.

This is only a joke I told my wife.

Who would do such a thing for a joke? To print up a whole
newspaper? It's impossible Bill.

It's also impossible to get next week's newspaper delivered this week
you know or hadn't you considered what I said?

She shrugged and I picked up the second section. I opened to page 50
which contained the obituary section and I admit I felt quite queasy for
a moment since after all this might not be any joke and what would it
be like to find my own name there? To my relief the people whose
obituaries I saw were Harry Rogoff Terry Turner Dr. M. A. Feinstein
and John Millis. I will not say that the deaths of these people gave me
any pleasure but better them than me of course. I even looked at the
death notices in small type but there was no listing for me. Next I
turned to the sports section and saw KNICKS' STREAK ENDED,
110-109. We had been talking about going to get tickets for that game
at the office and my first thought now was that it isn't worth bothering
to see it. Then I remembered you can bet on basketball games and I
knew who was going to win and that made me feel very strange. So also
I felt odd to look at the bottom of page 64 where they had the results
of the racing at Yonkers Raceway and then quickly flip flip flip I was on
page 69 and the financial section lay before my eyes. DOW INDEX
RISES BY 1.61 TO 831.34 the headline said. National Cash Register
was the most active stock closing at 27⅜ off ¼. Then Eastman Kodak
88⅞ down 1⅛. By this time I was starting to sweat very hard and I gave
my wife the paper and took off my jacket and tie.

I said how many people have this newspaper?

Everybody on Redbud Crescent she said that's eleven houses altogether.

And nowhere beyond our street?

No the others got the ordinary paper today we've been checking on that.

Who's we I asked?

Marie and Cindy and I she said. Cindy was the one who noticed about the paper first and called me and then we all got together and talked about it. Bill what are we going to do? We have the stock market prices and everything Bill.

If it isn't a joke I told her.

It looks like the real paper doesn't it Bill?

I think I want a drink I said. My hands were shaking all of a sudden and the sweat was still coming. I had to laugh because it was just the other Saturday night some of us were talking about the utter predictable regularity of life out here in the suburbs the dull smooth sameness of it all. And now this. The newspaper from the middle of next week. It's like God was listening to us and laughed up His sleeve and said to Gabriel or whoever it's time to send those stuffed shirts on Redbud Crescent a little excitement.

[2]

After dinner Jerry Wesley called and said we're having a meeting at our place tonight Bill can you and your lady come?

I asked him what the meeting was about and he said it's about the newspaper.

Oh yes I said. The newspaper. What about the newspaper?

Come to the meeting he said I really don't want to talk about this on the phone.

Of course we'll have to arrange a sitter Jerry.

No you won't we've already arranged it he told me. The three Fischer girls are going to look after all the kids on the block. So just come over around quarter to nine.

Jerry is an insurance broker very successful at that he has the best house on the Crescent, two-story Tudor style with almost an acre of land and a big paneled rumpus room in the basement. That's where the meeting took place. We were the seventh couple to arrive and soon after us the Maxwells the Bruces and the Thomasons came in. Folding chairs were set out and Cindy Wesley had done her usual great trays of canapés and such and there was a lot of liquor, self-service at the bar. Jerry stood up in front of everybody and grinned and said I guess you've all been wondering why I called you together this evening. He held up his copy of the newspaper. From where I was sitting I could make out only one headline clearly it was 10 HURT AS GUNMEN SHOOT WAY INTO AND OUT OF BANK but that was enough to enable me to recognize it as *the* newspaper.

Jerry said did all of you get a copy of this paper today?

Everybody nodded.

You know Jerry said that this paper gives us some extraordinary opportunities to improve our situation in life. I mean if we can accept it as the real December 1 edition and not some kind of fantastic hoax then I don't need to tell you what sort of benefits we can get from it, right?

Sure Bob Thomason said but what makes anybody think it isn't a hoax? I mean next week's newspaper who could believe that?

Jerry looked at Mike Nesbit. Mike teaches at Columbia Law and is more of an intellectual than most of us.

Mike said well of course the obvious conclusion is that somebody's playing a joke on us. But have you looked at the newspaper closely? Every one of those stories has been written in a perfectly legitimate way. There aren't any details that ring false. It isn't like one of those papers where the headlines have been cooked up but the body of the text is an old edition. So we have to consider the probabilities. Which sounds more fantastic? That someone would take the trouble of composing an entire fictional edition of the *Times* setting it in type printing it and having it delivered or that through some sort of fluke of the fourth dimension we've been allowed a peek at next week's newspaper? Personally I don't find either notion easy to believe but I can accept fourth-dimensional hocus-pocus more readily than I can the idea of a hoax. For one thing unless you've had a team the size of the *Times'* own staff working on this newspaper it would take months and months to prepare it and there's no way that anybody could have begun work on the paper more than a few days in advance because there are things in it that nobody could have possibly known as recently as a week ago. Like the Phase Two stuff and the fighting between India and Pakistan.

But how could we get next week's newspaper Bob Thomason still wanted to know?

I can't answer that said Mike Nesbit. I can only reply that I am willing to accept it as genuine. A miracle if you like.

So am I, said Tim McDermott and a few others said the same.

We can make a pile of money out of this thing said Dave Bruce.

Everybody began to smile in a strange strained way. Obviously everybody had looked at the stock market stuff and the racetrack stuff and had come to the same conclusions.

Jerry said there's one important thing we ought to find out first. Has anybody here spoken about this newspaper to anybody who isn't currently in this room?

People said nope and uh-uh and not me.

Good said Jerry. I propose we keep it that way. We don't notify the *Times* and we don't tell Walter Cronkite and we don't even let our brother-in-law on Dogwood Lane know, right? We just put our newspapers away in a safe place and quietly do whatever we want to do about the information we've got. Okay? Let's put that to a vote. All in favor of stamping this newspaper top secret raise your right hand.

Twenty-two hands went up.

Good said Jerry. That includes the kids you realize. If you let the kids know anything they'll want to bring the paper to school for show and tell for Christ's sake. So cool it you hear?

Sid Fischer said are we going to work together on exploiting this thing or do we each act independently?

Independently said Dave Bruce.

Right independently said Bud Maxwell.

It went all around the room that way. The only one who wanted some sort of committee system was Charlie Harris. Charlie has bad luck in the stock market and I guess he was afraid to take any risks even with a sure thing like next week's paper. Jerry called for a vote and it came out ten to one in favor of individual enterprise. Of course if anybody wants to team up with anybody else I said there's nothing stopping anybody.

As we started to adjourn for refreshments Jerry said remember you only have a week to make use of what you've been handed. By the first of December this is going to be just another newspaper and a million other people will have copies of it. So move fast while you've got an advantage.

[3]

The trouble is when they give you only next week's paper you don't ordinarily have a chance to make a big killing in the market. I mean stocks don't generally go up 50% or 80% in just a few trading sessions. The really broad swings take weeks or months to develop. Still and all I figured I could make out all right with the data I had. For one thing there evidently was going to be a pretty healthy rally over the next few days. According to the afternoon edition of the *Post* that I brought home with me the market had been off seven on the 22nd, closing with the Dow at 803.15, the lowest all year. But the December 1 *Times* mentioned "a stunning two-day advance" and the average finished at 831.34 on the 30th. Not bad. Then too I could work on margin and other kinds of leverage to boost my return. We're going to make a pile out of this I told my wife.

If you can trust that newspaper she said.

I told her not to worry. When we got home from Jerry's I spread out the *Post* and the *Times* in the den and started hunting for stocks that moved up at least 10% between Nov 22 and Nov 30. This is the chart I made up:

Stock	Nov 22 *close*	Nov 30 *high*
Levitz Furniture	89½	103¾
Bausch & Lomb	133⅜	149
Natomas	45¼	57
Disney	99⅞	116¾
EG&G	19¼	23¾

Spread your risk Bill I told myself. Don't put all your eggs in one basket. Even if the newspaper was phony I couldn't get hurt too badly if I bought all five. So at 9:30 the next morning I phoned my broker and told him I wanted to do some buying in the margin account at the opening. He said don't be in a hurry Bill the market's in lousy shape. Look at yesterday there were 201 new lows this market's going to be under 750 by Christmas. You can see from this that he's an unusual kind of broker since most of them will never try to discourage you from placing an order that'll bring them a commission. But I said no I'm playing a hunch I want to go all out on this and I put in buys on Levitz Bausch Natomas Disney and EG&G. I used the margin right up to the hilt and then some. Okay I told myself if this works out the way you hope it will you've just bought yourself a vacation in Europe and a new Chrysler and a mink for the wife and a lot of other goodies. And if not? If not you just lost yourself a hell of a lot of money Billy boy.

[4]

Also I made some use out of the sports pages.

At the office I looked around for bets on the Knicks vs. the SuperSonics next Tuesday at the Garden. A couple of guys wondered why I was interested in action so far ahead but I didn't bother to answer and finally I got Eddie Martin to take the Knicks by 11 points. Also I got Marty Felks to take Milwaukee by 8 over the Warriors that same night. Felks thinks Abdul-Jabbar is the best center the game ever had and he'll always bet the Bucks but my paper had it that the Warriors would cop it, 106-103. At lunch with the boys from Leclair & Anderson I put down $250 with Butch Hunter on St. Louis over the Giants on Sunday. Next I stopped off at the friendly neighborhood Off Track Betting office and entered a few wagers on the races at Aqueduct. My handy guide to the future told me that the Double paid $54.20 and the third Exacta paid $62.20, so I spread a little cash on each. Too bad there were no $2500 payoffs that day but you can't be picky about your miracles can you?

[5]

Tuesday night when I got home I had a drink and asked my wife what's new and she said everybody on the block had been talking about the newspaper all day and some of the girls had been placing bets and phoning their brokers. A lot of the women here play the market and even the horses though my wife is not like that, she leaves the male stuff strictly to me.

What stocks were they buying I asked?

Well she didn't know the names. But a little while later Joni Bruce called up for a recipe and my wife asked her about the market and Joni said she had bought Winnebago Xerox and Transamerica. I was relieved at that because I figured it might look really suspicious if everybody on Redbud Crescent suddenly phoned in orders the same day for Levitz Bausch Disney Natomas and EG&G. On the other hand what was I worrying about nobody would draw any conclusions and if anybody did we could always say we had organized a neighborhood investment club. In any case I don't think there's any law against people making stock market decisions on the basis of a peek at next week's newspaper. Still and all who needs publicity and I was glad we were all buying different stocks.

I got the paper out after dinner to check out Joni's stocks. Sure enough Winnebago moved up from $33\frac{1}{8}$ to $38\frac{1}{8}$, Xerox from $105\frac{3}{4}$ to $111\frac{7}{8}$, and Transamerica from $14\frac{7}{8}$ to $17\frac{5}{8}$. I thought it was dumb of Joni to bother with Xerox getting only a 6% rise since it's the percentages where you pay off but Winnebago was up better than 10% and Transamerica close to 20%. I wished I had noticed Transamerica at least although no sense being greedy, my own choices would make out all right.

Something about the paper puzzled me. The print looked a little blurry in places and on some pages I could hardly read the words. I didn't remember any blurry pages. Also the paper it's printed on seemed a different color, darker gray, older-looking. I compared it with the newspaper that came this morning and the December 1 issue was definitely darker. A paper shouldn't get old-looking that fast, not in two days.

I wonder if something's happening to the paper I said to my wife.

What do you mean?

Like it's deteriorating or anyway starting to change.

Anything can happen said my wife. It's like a dream you know and in dreams things change all the time without warning.

[6]

Wed Nov 24. I guess we just have to sweat this thing out so far the market in general isn't doing much one way or the other. This afternoon's *Post* gives the closing prices there was a rally in the morning but it all faded by the close and the Dow is down to 798.63. However my own five stocks all have had decent upward moves Tues and Wed so maybe I shouldn't worry. I have four points profit in Bausch already two in Natomas five in Levitz two in Disney three-quarters in EG&G and even though that's a long way from the quotations in the Dec 1 newspaper it's better than having losses, also there's still that "stunning two-day advance" due at the end of the month. Maybe I'm going to make out all right. Winnebago Transamerica and Xerox are also up a little bit. Market's closed tomorrow on account of Thanksgiving.

[7]

Thanksgiving Day. We went to the Nesbits in the afternoon. It used to be that people spent Thanksgiving with their own kin their aunts uncles grandparents cousins et cetera but you can't do that out here in a new suburb where everybody comes from someplace else far away so we eat the turkey with neighbors instead. The Nesbits invited the Fischers the Harrises the Thomasons and us with all the kids of course too. A big noisy gathering. The Fischers came very late so late that we were worried and thinking of sending someone over to find out what was the matter. It was practically time for the turkey when they showed up and Edith Fischer's eyes were red and puffy from crying.

My God my God she said I just found out my older sister is dead.

We started to ask the usual meaningless consoling questions like was she a sick woman and where did she live and what did she die of? And Edith sobbed and said I don't mean she's dead yet I mean she's going to die next Tuesday.

Next Tuesday Tammy Nesbit asked? What do you mean I don't understand how you can know that now. And then she thought a moment and she did understand and so did all the rest of us. Oh Tammy said the newspaper.

The newspaper yes Edith said. Sobbing harder.

Edith was reading the death notices Sid Fischer explained God knows why she was bothering to look at them just curiosity I guess and all of a sudden she lets out this terrible cry and says she sees her sister's name. Sudden passing, a heart attack.

Her heart is weak Edith told us. She's had two or three bad attacks this year.

Lois Thomason went to Edith and put her arms around her the way Lois does so well and said there there Edith it's a terrible shock to you naturally but you know it must have been inevitable sooner or later and at least the poor woman isn't suffering any more.

But don't you see Edith cried she's still alive right now maybe if I phone and say go to the hospital right away they can save her? They might put her under intensive care and get ready for the attack before it even comes. Only I can't say that can I? Because what can I tell her? That I read about her death in next week's newspaper? She'll think I'm crazy and she'll laugh and she won't pay any attention to me. Or maybe she'll get very upset and drop dead right on the spot all on account of me. What can I do oh God what can I do?

You could say it was a premonition my wife suggested. A very vivid dream that had the ring of truth to you. If your sister puts any faith at all in things like that maybe she'll decide it can't hurt to see her doctor and then—

No Mike Nesbit broke in you mustn't do any such thing Edith. Because they can't save her. No way. They *didn't* save her when the time came.

The time hasn't come yet said Edith.

So far as we're concerned said Mike the time has already come because we have the newspapers that describe the events of Nov 30 in the past tense. So we know your sister is going to die and to all intents and purposes is already dead. It's absolutely certain because it's in the newspaper and if we accept the newspaper as authentic then it's a record of actual events beyond any hope of changing.

But my sister Edith said.

Your sister's name is already on the roll of the dead. If you interfere now it'll only bring unnecessary aggravation to her family and it won't change a thing.

How do you know it won't Mike?

The future mustn't be changed Mike said. For us the events of that one day in the future are as permanent as any event in the past. We don't dare play around with changing the future not when it's already signed sealed and delivered in that newspaper. For all we know the future's like a house of cards. If we pull one card out say your sister's life we might bring the whole house tumbling down. You've got to accept the decree of fate Edith. You've got to. Otherwise there's no telling what might happen.

My sister Edith said. My sister's going to die and you won't let me do anything to save her.

[8]

Edith carrying on like that put a damper on the whole Thanksgiving celebration. After a while she pulled herself together more or less but she couldn't help behaving like a woman in mourning and it was hard for us to be very jolly and thankful with her there choking back the sobs. The Fischers left right after dinner and we all hugged Edith and told her how sorry we were. Soon afterward the Thomasons and the Harrises left too.

Mike looked at my wife and me and said I hope you aren't going to run off also.

No I said not yet there's no hurry is there?

We sat around some while longer. Mike talked about Edith and her sister. The sister can't be saved he kept saying. And it might be very dangerous for everybody if Edith tries to interfere with fate.

To get the subject away from Edith we started talking about the stock market. Mike said he had bought Natomas Transamerica and Electronic Data Systems which he said was due to rise from 36¾ on Nov 22 to 47 by the 30th. I told him I had bought Natomas too and I told him my other stocks and pretty soon he had his copy of the December 1 paper out so we could check some of the quotations. Looking over his shoulder I observed that the print was even blurrier than it had seemed to me Tuesday night which was the last occasion I had examined my paper and also the pages seemed very gray and rough.

What do you think is going on I said? The paper definitely seems to be deteriorating.

It's entropic creep he said.

Entropic creep?

Entropy you know is the natural tendency of everything in the universe to come apart at the seams as time goes along. These newspapers must be subject to unusually strong entropic strains because of their anomalous position out of their proper place in time. I've been noticing how the print is getting harder to read and I wouldn't be surprised if it became completely illegible in another couple of days.

We hunted up the prices of my stocks in his paper and the first one we saw was Bausch & Lomb hitting a high of $149\frac{3}{4}$ on November 30.

Wait a second I said I'm sure the high is supposed to be 149 even.

Mike thought it might be an effect of the general blurriness but no it was still quite clear on that page of stock market quotations and it said $149\frac{3}{4}$. I looked up Natomas and the high that was listed was $56\frac{7}{8}$. I said I'm positive it's 57. And so on with several other stocks. The figures didn't jibe with what I remembered. We had a friendly little discussion about that and then it became not so friendly as Mike implied my memory was faulty and in the end I jogged down the street to my place and got my own copy of the paper. We spread them both out side by side and compared the quotes. Sure enough the two were different. Hardly any quote in his paper matched those in mine, all of them off an eighth here, a quarter there. What was even worse the figures didn't quite match the ones I had noted down on the first day. My paper now gave the Bausch high for November 30 as $149\frac{1}{2}$ and Natomas as $56\frac{1}{2}$ and Disney as 117. Levitz 104, EG&G $23\frac{5}{8}$. Everything seemed to be sliding around.

It's a bad case of entropic creep Mike said.

I wonder if the newspapers were ever identical to each other I said. We should have compared them on the first day. Now we'll never know whether we all had the same starting point.

Let's check out the other pages Bill.

We compared things. The front page headlines were all the same but there were little differences in the writing. The classified ads had a lot of rearrangements. Some of the death notices were different. All in all the papers were similar but not anything like identical.

How can this be happening I asked? How can words on a printed page be different one day from another?

How can a newspaper from the future get delivered in the first place Mike asked?

[9]

We phoned some of the others and asked about stock prices. Just trying to check something out we explained. Charlie Harris said Natomas was quoted at 56 and Jerry Wesley said it was 57¼ and Bob Thomason found that the whole stock market page was too blurry to read although he thought the Natomas quote was 57½. And so on. Everybody's paper slightly different.

Entropic creep. It's hitting hard.

What can we trust? What's real?

[10]

Saturday afternoon Bob Thomason came over very agitated. He had his newspaper under his arm. He showed it to me and said look at this Bill how can it be? The pages were practically falling apart and they were completely blank. You could make out little dirty traces where there once had been words but that was all. The paper looked about a million years old.

I got mine out of the closet. It was in bad shape but not that bad. The print was faint and murky yet I could still make some things out clearly. Natomas 56¼. Levitz Furniture 103½. Disney 117¼. New numbers all the time.

Meanwhile out in the real world the market has been rallying for a couple of days right on schedule and all my stocks are going up. I may go crazy but it looks at least like I'm not going to take a financial beating.

[11]

Monday night Nov 29. One week since this whole thing started. Everybody's newspaper is falling apart. I can read patches of print on two or three pages of mine and the rest is pretty well shot. Dave Bruce says his paper is completely blank the way Bob's was on Saturday. Mike's is in better condition but it won't last long. They're all getting eaten up by entropy. The market rallied strongly again this afternoon. Yesterday the Giants got beaten by St. Louis and at lunch today I collected my winnings from Butch Hunter. Yesterday also Sid and Edith Fischer left suddenly for a vacation in Florida. That's where Edith's sister lives, the one who's supposed to die tomorrow.

[12]

I can't help wondering whether Edith did something about her sister after all despite the things Mike said to her Thanksgiving.

[13]

So now it's Tuesday night November 30 and I'm home with the *Post* and the closing stock prices. Unfortunately I can't compare them with the figures in my copy of tomorrow's *Times* because I don't have the paper any more it turned completely to dust and so did everybody else's but I still have the notes I took the first night when I was planning my market action. And I'm happy to say everything worked out perfectly despite the effects of entropic creep. The Dow Industrials closed at 831.34 today which is just what my record says. And look at this list of highs for the day where my broker sold me out on the nose:

Levitz Furniture	103¾
Bausch & Lomb	149
Natomas	57
Disney	116¾
EG&G	23¾

So whatever this week has cost me in nervous aggravation it's more than made up in profits.

Tomorrow is December 1 finally and it's going to be funny to see that newspaper again. With the headlines about Nixon going to China and the people wounded in the bank robbery and the currency negotiations in Rome. Like an old friend coming home.

[14]

I suppose everything has to balance out. This morning before breakfast I went outside as usual to get the paper and it was sitting there in the bushes but it wasn't the paper for Wednesday December 1 although this is in fact Wednesday December 1. What the newsboy gave me this morning was the paper for Monday November 22 which I never actually received the day of the first mixup.

That in itself wouldn't be so bad. But this paper is full of stuff I don't remember from last Monday. As though somebody has reached into last week and switched everything around, making up a bunch of weird events. Even though I didn't get to see the *Times* that day I'm sure I would have heard about the assassination of the Governor of Missouri. And the earthquake in Peru that killed ten thousand people. And Mayor Lindsay resigning to become Nixon's new Secretary of State. Especially about Mayor Lindsay resigning to become Nixon's new Secretary of State. This paper *has* to be a joke.

But what about the one we got last week? How about those stock prices and the sports results?

When I get into the city this morning I'm going to stop off first thing at the New York Public Library and check the file copy of the November 22 *Times*. I want to see if the library's copy is anything like the one I just got.

What kind of newspaper am I going to get tomorrow?

[15]

Don't think I'm going to get to work at all today. Went out after breakfast to get the car and drive to the station and the car wasn't there nothing was there just gray everything gray no lawn no shrubs no trees none of the other houses in sight just gray like a thick fog swallowing everything up at ground level. Stood there on the front step afraid to go into that gray. Went back into the house woke up my wife told her. What does it mean Bill she asked what does it mean why is it all gray? I don't know I said. Let's turn on the radio. But there was no sound out of the radio nothing on the TV not even a test pattern the phone line dead too everything dead and I don't know what's happening or where we are I don't understand any of this except that this must be a very bad case of entropic creep. All of time must have looped back on itself in some crazy way and I don't know anything I don't understand a thing.

Edith what have you done to us?

I don't want to live here any more I want to cancel my newspaper subscription I want to sell my house I want to get away from here back into the real world but how how I don't know it's all gray gray gray everything gray nothing out there just a lot of gray.

12

IN ENTROPY'S JAWS

Static crackles from the hazy golden cloud of airborne loudspeakers drifting just below the ceiling of the spaceliner cabin. A hiss: communications filters are opening. An impending announcement from the bridge, no doubt. Then the captain's bland, mechanical voice: "We are approaching the Panama Canal. All passengers into their bottles until the all-clear after insertion. When we come out the far side, we'll be traveling at eighty lights toward the Perseus relay booster. Thank you." In John Skein's cabin the warning globe begins to flash, dousing him with red, yellow, green light, going up and down the visible spectrum, giving him some infra- and ultra- too. Not everybody who books passage on this liner necessarily has human sensory equipment. The signal will not go out until Skein is safely in his bottle. Go on, it tells him. Get in. Get in. Panama Canal coming up.

Obediently he rises and moves across the narrow cabin toward the tapering dull-skinned steel container, two and a half meters high, that will protect him against the dimensional stresses of canal insertion. He is a tall, angular man with thin lips, a strong chin, glossy black hair that clings close to his high-vaulted skull. His skin is deeply tanned but his eyes are those of one who has been in winter for some time. This is the fiftieth year of his second go-round. He is traveling alone toward a world of the Abbondanza system, perhaps the last leg on a journey that has occupied him for several years.

The passenger bottle swings open on its gaudy rhodium-jacketed hinge when its sensors, picking up Skein's mass and thermal output, tell it that its protectee is within entry range. He gets in. It closes and seals, wrapping him in a seamless magnetic field. "Please be seated," the bottle tells him softly. "Place your arms through the stasis loops and your feet in the security platens. When you have done this the pressor fields will automatically be activated and you will be fully insulated against injury during the coming period of turbulence." Skein, who has had plenty of experience with faster-than-light travel, has anticipated the instructions and is already in stasis. The bottle closes. "Do you wish music?" it asks him. "A book? A vision spool? Conversation?"

"Nothing, thanks," Skein says, and waits.

He understands waiting very well by this time. Once he was an impatient man, but this is a thin season in his life, and it has been teaching him the arts of stoic acceptance. He will sit here with the Buddha's own complacency until the ship is through the canal. Silent, alone, self-sufficient. If only there will be no fugues this time. Or, at least—he is negotiating the terms of his torment with his demons—at least let them not be flashforwards. If he must break loose again from the matrix of time, he prefers to be cast only into his yesterdays, never into his tomorrows.

"We are almost into the canal now," the bottle tells him pleasantly.

"It's all right. You don't need to look after me. Just let me know when it's safe to come out."

He closes his eyes. Trying to envision the ship: a fragile glimmering purple needle squirting through clinging blackness, plunging toward the celestial vortex just ahead, the maelstrom of clashing forces, the soup of contravariant tensors. The Panama Canal, so-called. Through which the liner will shortly rush, acquiring during its passage such a garland of borrowed power that it will rip itself free of the standard fourspace; it will emerge on the far side of the canal into a strange, tranquil pocket of the universe where the speed of light is the downside limiting velocity, and no one knows where the upper limit lies.

Alarms sound in the corridor, heavy, resonant: clang, clang, clang. The dislocation is beginning. Skein is braced. What does it look like out there? Folds of glowing black velvet, furry swatches of the disrupted continuum, wrapping themselves around the ship? Titanic lightnings hammering on the hull? Laughing centaurs flashing across the twisted heavens? Despondent masks, fixed in tragic grimaces, dangling between the blurred stars? Streaks of orange, green, crimson: sick rainbows, limp, askew? In we go. *Clang, clang, clang.* The next phase of the voyage now begins. He thinks of his destination, holding an image of it rigidly in mind. The picture is vivid, though this is a world he has visited only in spells of temporal fugue. Too often; he has been there again and again in these moments of disorientation in time. The colors are wrong on that world. Purple sand. Blue-leaved trees. Too much manganese? Too little copper? He will forgive it its colors if it will grant him his answers. And then. Skein feels the familiar ugly throbbing at the base of his neck, as if the tip of his spine is swelling like a balloon. He curses. He tries to resist. As he feared, not even the bottle can wholly protect him against these stresses. Outside the ship the universe is being wrenched apart; some of that slips in here and throws him into a private epilepsy of the time-line. Space-time is breaking up for him. He will go into fugue. He clings, fighting, knowing it is futile. The currents of time buffet him, knocking him a short distance into the future, then a reciprocal distance into the past, as if he is a bubble of insect spittle glued loosely to a dry reed. He cannot hold on much longer. Let it not be flashforward, he prays, wondering who it is to whom he prays. Let it not be flashforward. And he loses his grip. And shatters. And is swept in shards across time.

Of course, if x *is before* y *then it remains eternally before* y, *and nothing in the passage of time can change this. But the peculiar position of the "now" can be easily expressed simply because our language has tenses. The future* will be, *the present* is, *and the past* was; *the light will be red, it is now yellow, and it was green. But do we, in these terms, really describe the "processional" character of time? We sometimes say that an event* is future, *then it is present, and finally it is past; and by this means we seem to dispense with tenses, yet we portray the passage of time. But this is really not the case; for all that we have done is to translate our tenses into the words "then" and "finally," and into the order in which we state our clauses. If we were to omit these words or their equivalents, and mix up the clauses, our sentences would no longer be meaningful. To say that the future, the present, and the past* are *in some sense* is *to dodge the problem of time by resorting to the tenseless language of logic and mathematics. In*

such an atemporal *language it would be meaningful to say that*
Socrates is mortal because all men are mortal and Socrates is a man,
even though Socrates has been dead many centuries. But if we cannot
describe time either by a language containing tenses or by a tenseless
language, how shall *we symbolize it?*

He feels the curious doubleness of self, the sense of having been here
before, and knows it is flashback. Some comfort in that. He is a
passenger in his own skull, looking out through the eyes of John Skein
on an event that he has already experienced, and which he now is
powerless to alter.

His office. All its gilded magnificence. A crystal dome at the summit
of Kenyatta Tower. With the amplifiers on he can see as far as
Serengeti in one direction, Mombasa in another. Count the fleas on an
elephant in Tsavo Park. A wall of light on the east-southeast face of the
dome, housing his data-access units. No one can stare at that wall more
than thirty seconds without suffering intensely from a surfeit of
information. Except Skein; he drains nourishment from it, hour after
hour.

As he slides into the soul of that earlier Skein he takes a brief joy in
the sight of his office, like Aeneas relishing a vision of unfallen Troy,
like Adam looking back into Eden. How good it was. That broad sweet
desk with its subtle components dedicated to his service. The gentle
psychosensitive carpet, so useful and so beautiful. The undulating
ribbon-sculpture gliding in and out of the dome's skin, undergoing
molecular displacement each time and forever exhibiting the newest of
its infinity of possible patterns. A rich man's office; he was unabashed in
his pursuit of elegance. He had earned the right to luxury through the
intelligent use of his innate skills. Returning now to that lost dome of
wonders, he quickly seizes his moment of satisfaction, aware that
shortly some souring scene of subtraction will be replayed for him, one
of the stages in the darkening and withering of his life. But which one?

"Send in Coustakis," he hears himself say, and his words give him the
answer. That one. He will again watch his own destruction. Surely there
is no further need to subject him to this particular re-enactment. He has
been through it at least seven times; he is losing count. An endless
spiraling track of torment.

Coustakis is bald, blue-eyed, sharp-nosed, with the desperate look of a man who is near the end of his first go-round and is not yet sure that he will be granted a second. Skein guesses that he is about seventy. The man is unlikable: he dresses coarsely, moves in aggressive blurting little strides, and shows in every gesture and glance that he seethes with envy of the opulence with which Skein surrounds himself. Skein feels no need to like his clients, though. Only to respect. And Coustakis is brilliant; he commands respect.

Skein says, "My staff and I have studied your proposal in great detail. It's a cunning scheme."

"You'll help me?"

"There are risks for me," Skein points out. "Nissenson has a powerful ego. So do you. I could get hurt. The whole concept of synergy involves risk for the Communicator. My fees are calculated accordingly."

"Nobody expects a Communicator to be cheap," Coustakis mutters.

"I'm not. But I think you'll be able to afford me. The question is whether I can afford you."

"You're very cryptic, Mr. Skein. Like all oracles."

Skein smiles. "I'm not an oracle, I'm afraid. Merely a conduit through whom connections are made. I can't foresee the future."

"You can evaluate probabilities."

"Only concerning my own welfare. And I'm capable of arriving at an incorrect evaluation."

Coustakis fidgets. "Will you help me or won't you?"

"The fee," Skein says, "is half a million down, plus an equity position of fifteen percent in the corporation you'll establish with the contacts I provide."

Coustakis gnaws at his lower lip. "So much?"

"Bear in mind that I've got to split my fee with Nissenson. Consultants like him aren't cheap."

"Even so. Ten percent."

"Excuse me, Mr. Coustakis. I really thought we were past the point of negotiation in this transaction. It's going to be a busy day for me, and so—" Skein passes his hand over a black rectangle on his desk and a section of the floor silently opens, uncovering the drop shaft access. He nods toward it. The carpet reveals the colors of Coustakis' mental processes: black for anger, green for greed, red for anxiety, yellow for fear, blue for temptation, all mixed together in the hashed pattern betraying the calculations now going on in his mind. Coustakis will yield. Nevertheless Skein proceeds with the charade of standing, gesturing toward the exit, trying to usher his visitor out. "All right," Coustakis says explosively, "fifteen percent!"

Skein instructs his desk to extrude a contract cube. He says, "Place your hand here, please," and as Coustakis touches the cube he presses his own palm against its opposite face. At once the cube's sleek crystalline surface darkens and roughens as the double sensory output bombards it. Skein says, "Repeat after me. I, Nicholas Coustakis, whose handprint and vibration pattern are being imprinted in this contract as I speak—"

"I, Nicholas Coustakis, whose handprint and vibration pattern are being imprinted in this contract as I speak—"

"—do knowingly and willingly assign to John Skein Enterprises, as payment for professional services to be rendered, an equity interest in Coustakis Transport Ltd. or any successor corporation amounting to—"

"—do knowingly and willingly assign—"

They drone on in turns through a description of Coustakis' corporation and the irrevocable nature of Skein's part ownership in it. Then Skein files the contract cube and says, "If you'll phone your bank and put your thumb on the cash part of the transaction, I'll make contact with Nissenson and you can get started."

"Half a million?"

"Half a million."

"You know I don't have that kind of money."

"Let's not waste time, Mr. Coustakis. You have assets. Pledge them as collateral. Credit is easily obtained."

Scowling, Coustakis applies for the loan, gets it, transfers the funds to Skein's account. The process takes eight minutes; Skein uses the time to review Coustakis' ego profile. It displeases Skein to have to exert such sordid economic pressures; but the service he offers does, after all, expose him to dangers, and he must cushion the risk by high guarantees, in case some mishap should put him out of business.

"Now we can proceed," Skein says, when the transaction is done.

Coustakis has almost invented a system for the economical instantaneous transportation of matter. It will not, unfortunately, ever be useful for living things, since the process involves the destruction of the material being shipped and its virtually simultaneous reconstitution elsewhere. The fragile entity that is the soul cannot withstand the withering blast of Coustakis' transmitter's electron beam. But there is tremendous potential in the freight business; the Coustakis transmitter will be able to send cabbages to Mars, computers to Pluto, and, given the proper linkage facilities, it should be able to reach the inhabited extrasolar planets.

However, Coustakis has not yet perfected his system. For five years he has been stymied by one impassable problem: keeping the beam tight enough between transmitter and receiver. Beam-spread has led to chaos in his experiments; marginal straying results in the loss of transmitted information, so that that which is being sent invariably arrives incomplete. Coustakis has depleted his resources in the unsuccessful search for a solution, and thus has been forced to the desperate and costly step of calling in a Communicator.

For a price, Skein will place him in contact with someone who can solve his problem. Skein has a network of consultants on several worlds, experts in technology and finance and philology and nearly everything else. Using his own mind as the focal nexus, Skein will open telepathic communion between Coustakis and a consultant.

"Get Nissenson into a receptive state," he orders his desk.

Coustakis, blinking rapidly, obviously uneasy, says, "First let me get it clear. This man will see everything that's in my mind? He'll get access to my secrets?"

"No. No. I filter the communion with great care. Nothing will pass from your mind to his except the nature of the problem you want him to tackle. Nothing will come back from his mind to yours except the answer."

"And if he doesn't have the answer?"

"He will."

Skein gives no refunds in the event of failure, but he has never had a failure. He does not accept jobs that he feels will be inherently impossible to handle. Either Nissenson will see the solution Coustakis has been overlooking, or else he will make some suggestion that will nudge Coustakis toward finding the solution himself. The telepathic communion is the vital element. Mere talking would never get anywhere. Coustakis and Nissenson could stare at blueprints together for months, pound computers side by side for years, debate the difficulty with each other for decades, and still they might not hit on the answer. But the communion creates a synergy of minds that is more than a doubling of the available brainpower. A union of perceptions, a heightening, that always produces that mystic flash of insight, that leap of the intellect.

"And if he goes into the transmission business for himself afterward?" Coustakis asks.

"He's bonded," Skein says curtly. "No chance of it. Let's go, now. Up and together."

The desk reports that Nissenson, half the world away in São Paulo, is ready. Skein's power does not vary with distance. Quickly he throws Coustakis into the receptive condition, and swings around to face the brilliant lights of his data-access units. Those sparkling, shifting little blazes kindle his gift, jabbing at the electrical rhythms of his brain until he is lifted into the energy level that permits the opening of a communion. As he starts to go up, the other Skein who is watching, the time-displaced prisoner behind his forehead, tries frenziedly to prevent him from entering the fatal linkage. *Don't. Don't. You'll overload. They're too strong for you.* Easier to halt a planet in its orbit, though. The course of the past is frozen; all this has already happened; the Skein who cries out in silent anguish is merely an observer, necessarily passive, here to view the maiming of his earlier self.

Skein reaches forth one tendril of his mind and engages Nissenson. With another tendril he snares Coustakis. Steadily, now, he draws the two tendrils together.

There is no way to predict the intensity of the forces that will shortly course through his brain. He has done what he could, checking the ego profiles of his client and the consultant, but that really tells him little. What Coustakis and Nissenson may be as individuals hardly matters; it is what they may become in communion that he must fear. Synergistic intensities are unpredictable. He has lived for a lifetime and a half with the possibility of a burnout.

The tendrils meet.

Skein the observer winces and tries to armor himself against the shock. But there is no way to deflect it. Out of Coustakis' mind flows a description of the matter transmitter and a clear statement of the beam-spread problem; Skein shoves it along to Nissenson, who begins to work on a solution. But when their minds join it is immediately evident that their combined strength will be more than Skein can control. This time the synergy will destroy him. But he cannot disengage; he has no mental circuitbreaker. He is caught, trapped, impaled. The entity that is Coustakis/Nissenson will not let go of him, for that would mean its own destruction. A wave of mental energy goes rippling and dancing along the vector of communion from Coustakis to Nissenson and goes bouncing back, pulsating and gaining strength, from Nissenson to Coustakis. A fiery oscillation is set up. Skein sees what is happening; he has become the amplifier of his own doom. The torrent of energy continues to gather power each time it reverberates from Coustakis to Nissenson, from Nissenson to Coustakis. Powerless, Skein watches the energy-pumping effect building up a mighty charge. The discharge is bound to come soon, and he will be the one who must receive it. How long? How long? The juggernaut fills the corridors of his mind. He ceases to know which end of the circuit is Nissenson, which is Coustakis; he perceives only two shining walls of mental power, between which he is stretched ever thinner, a twanging wire of ego, heating up, heating up, glowing now, emitting a searing blast of heat, particles of identity streaming away from him like so many liberated ions—

Then he lies numb and dazed on the floor of his office, grinding his face into the psychosensitive carpet, while Coustakis barks over and over, "Skein? Skein? Skein? Skein?"

Like any other chronometric device, our inner clocks are subject to their own peculiar disorders and, in spite of the substantial concordance between private and public time, discrepancies may occur as the result of sheer inattention. Mach noted that if a doctor focuses his

attention on the patient's blood, it may seem to him to squirt out
before the lancet enters the skin and, for similar reasons, the feebler of
two stimuli presented simultaneously is usually perceived later. . . .
Normal life requires the capacity to recall experiences in a sequence
corresponding, roughly at least, to the order in which they actually
occurred. It requires in addition that our potential recollections should
be reasonably accessible to consciousness. These potential recollec-
tions mean not only a perpetuation within us of representations of the
past, but also a ceaseless interplay between such representations and
the uninterrupted input of present information from the external
world. Just as our past may be at the service of our present, so the
present may be remotely controlled by our past: in the words of
Shelley, "Swift as a Thought by the snake Memory stung."

"Skein? Skein? Skein? Skein?"

His bottle is open and they are helping him out. His cabin is full of
intruders. Skein recognizes the captain's robot, the medic, and a couple
of passengers, the little swarthy man from Pingalore and the woman
from Globe Fifteen. The cabin door is open and more people are
coming in. The medic makes a cuff-shooting gesture and a blinding
haze of metallic white particles wraps itself about Skein's head. The
little tingling prickling sensations spur him to wakefulness. "You didn't
respond when the bottle told you it was all right," the medic explains.
"We're through the canal."

"Was it a good passage? Fine. Fine. I must have dozed."

"If you'd like to come to the infirmary—a routine check, only—put
you through the diagnostat—"

"No. No. Will you all please go? I assure you, I'm quite all right."

Reluctantly, clucking over him, they finally leave. Skein gulps cold
water until his head is clear. He plants himself flatfooted in midcabin,
trying to pick up some sensation of forward motion. The ship now is
traveling at something like fifteen million miles a second. How long is
fifteen million miles? How long is a second? From Rome to Naples it
was a morning's drive on the autostrada. From Tel Aviv to Jerusalem
was the time between twilight and darkness. San Francisco to San
Diego spanned lunch to dinner by superpod. As I slide my right foot

two inches forward we traverse fifteen million miles. From where to where? And why? He has not seen Earth in twenty-six months. At the end of this voyage his remaining funds will be exhausted. Perhaps he will have to make his home in the Abbondanza system; he has no return ticket. But of course he can travel to his heart's discontent within his own skull, whipping from point to point along the time-line in the grip of the fugues.

He goes quickly from his cabin to the recreation lounge.

The ship is a second-class vessel, neither lavish nor seedy. It carries about twenty passengers, most of them, like him, bound outward on one-way journeys. He has not talked directly to any of them, but he has done considerable eavesdropping in the lounge, and by now can tag each one of them with the proper dull biography. The wife bravely joining her pioneer husband, whom she has not seen for half a decade. The remittance man under orders to place ten thousand light-years, at the very least, between himself and his parents. The glittery-eyed entrepreneur, a Phoenician merchant sixty centuries after his proper era, off to carve an empire as a middleman's middleman. The tourists. The bureaucrat. The colonel. Among this collection Skein stands out in sharp relief; he is the only one who has not made an effort to know and be known, and the mystery of his reserve tantalizes them.

He carries the fact of his crackup with him like some wrinkled dangling yellowed wen. When his eyes meet those of any of the others he says silently, You see my deformity? I am my own survivor. I have been destroyed and lived to look back on it. Once I was a man of wealth and power, and look at me now. But I ask for no pity. Is that understood?

Hunching at the bar, Skein pushes the node for filtered rum. His drink arrives, and with it comes the remittance man, handsome, young, insinuating. Giving Skein a confidential wink, as if to say, *I know. You're on the run, too.*

"From Earth, are you?" he says to Skein.

"Formerly."

"I'm Pid Rocklin."

"John Skein."

"What were you doing there?"

"On Earth?" Skein shrugs. "A Communicator. I retired four years ago."

"Oh." Rocklin summons a drink. "That's good work, if you have the gift."

"I had the gift," Skein says. The unstressed past tense is as far into self-pity as he will go. He drinks and pushes for another one. A great gleaming screen over the bar shows the look of space: empty, here beyond the Panama Canal, although yesterday a million suns blazed on that ebony rectangle. Skein imagines he can hear the whoosh of hydrogen molecules scraping past the hull at eighty lights. He sees them as blobs of brightness millions of miles long, going *zip!* and *zip!* and *zip!* as the ship spurts along. Abruptly a purple nimbus envelops him and he drops into a flashforward fugue so quickly there is not even time for the usual futile resistance. "Hey, what's the matter?" Pid Rocklin says, reaching for him. "Are you all—" and Skein loses the universe.

He is on the world that he takes to be Abbondanza VI, and his familiar companion, the skull-faced man, stands beside him at the edge of an oily orange sea. They appear to be having the debate about time once again. The skull-faced man must be at least a hundred twenty years old; his skin lies against his bones with, seemingly, no flesh at all under it, and his face is all nostrils and burning eyes. Bony sockets, sharp shelves for cheekbones, a bald dome of a skull. The neck no more than wrist-thick, rising out of shriveled shoulders. Saying, "Won't you ever come to see that causality is merely an illusion, Skein? The notion that there's a consecutive series of events is nothing but a fraud. We impose form on our lives, we talk of time's arrow, we say that there's a flow from A through G and Q to Z, we make believe everything is nicely linear. But it isn't, Skein. It isn't."

"So you keep telling me."

"I feel an obligation to awaken your mind to the truth. G can come before A, and Z before both of them. Most of us don't like to perceive it that way, so we arrange things in what seems like a more logical pattern, just as a novelist will put the motive before the murder and the murder before the arrest. But the universe isn't a novel. We can't make nature imitate art. It's all random, Skein, random, random! Look there. You see what's drifting on the sea?"

On the orange waves tosses the bloated corpse of a shaggy blue beast. Upturned saucery eyes, drooping snout, thick limbs. Why is it not waterlogged by now? What keeps it afloat?

The skull-faced man says, "Time is an ocean, and events come drifting to us as randomly as dead animals on the waves. We filter them. We screen out what doesn't make sense and admit them to our consciousness in what seems to be the right sequence." He laughs. "The grand delusion! The past is nothing but a series of films slipping unpredictably into the future. And vice versa."

"I won't accept that," Skein says stubbornly. "It's a demonic, chaotic, nihilistic theory. It's idiocy. Are we graybeards before we're children? Do we die before we're born? Do trees devolve into seeds? Deny linearity all you like. I won't go along."

"You can say that after all you've experienced?"

Skein shakes his head. "I'll go on saying it. What I've been going through is a mental illness. Maybe I'm deranged, but the universe isn't."

"Contrary. You've only recently become sane and started to see things as they really are," the skull-faced man insists. "The trouble is that you don't want to admit the evidence you've begun to perceive. Your filters are down, Skein! You've shaken free of the illusion of linearity! Now's your chance to show your resilience. Learn to live with the real reality. Stop this silly business of imposing an artificial order on the flow of time. Why *should* effect follow cause? Why *shouldn't* the seed follow the tree? Why must you persist in holding tight to a useless, outworn, contemptible system of false evaluations of experience when you've managed to break free of the—"

"Stop it! Stop it! Stop it! Stop it!"

"—right, Skein?"

"What happened?"

"You started to fall off your stool," Pid Rocklin says. "You turned absolutely white. I thought you were having some kind of a stroke."

"How long was I unconscious?"

"Oh, three, four seconds, I suppose. I grabbed you and propped you up, and your eyes opened. Can I help you to your cabin? Or maybe you ought to go to the infirmary."

"Excuse me," Skein says hoarsely, and leaves the lounge.

When the hallucinations began, not long after the Coustakis overload, he assumed at first that they were memory disturbances produced by the fearful jolt he had absorbed. Quite clearly most of them invoked scenes of his past, which he would relive, during the moments of fugue, with an intensity so brilliant that he felt he had actually been thrust back into time. He did not merely recollect, but rather he experienced the past anew, following a script from which he could not deviate as he spoke and felt and reacted. Such strange excursions into memory could be easily enough explained: his brain had been damaged, and it was heaving old segments of experience into view in some kind of attempt to clear itself of debris and heal the wounds. But while the flashbacks were comprehensible, the flashforwards were not, and he did not recognize them at all for what they actually were. Those scenes of himself wandering alien worlds, those phantom conversations with people he had never met, those views of spaceliner cabins and transit booths and unfamiliar hotels and passenger terminals, seemed merely to be fantasies, random fictions of his injured brain. Even when he started to notice that there was a consistent pattern to these feverish glimpses of the unknown, he still did not catch on. It appeared as though he was seeing himself performing a sort of quest, or perhaps a pilgrimage; the slices of unexperienced experience that he was permitted to see began to fit into a coherent structure of travel and seeking. And certain scenes and conversations recurred, yes, sometimes several times the same day, the script always the same, so that he began to learn a few of the scenes word for word. Despite the solid texture of these episodes, he persisted in thinking of them as mere brief flickering segments of nightmare. He could not imagine why the injury to his brain was causing him to have these waking dreams of long space voyages and unknown planets, so vivid and so momentarily real, but they seemed no more frightening to him than the equally vivid flashbacks.

Only after a while, when many months had passed since the Coustakis incident, did the truth strike him. One day he found himself living through an episode that he considered to be one of his fantasies. It was a minor thing, one that he had experienced, in whole or in part, seven or eight times. What he had seen, in fitful bursts of uninvited delusion, was himself in a public garden on some hot spring morning, standing before an immense baroque building while a grotesque group of non-human tourists filed past him in a weird creaking, clanking procession of inhalator suits and breather-wheels and ion-disperser masks. That was all. Then it happened that a harrowing legal snarl brought him to a city in North Carolina about fourteen months after the overload, and, after having put in his appearance at the courthouse, he set out on a long walk through the grimy, decayed metropolis, and came, as if by an enchantment, to a huge metal gate behind which he could see a dark sweep of lavish forest, oaks and rhododendrons and magnolias, laid out in an elegant formal manner. It was, according to a sign posted by the gate, the estate of a nineteenth-century millionaire, now open to all and preserved in its ancient state despite the encroachments of the city on its borders. Skein bought a ticket and went in, on foot, hiking for what seemed like miles through cool leafy glades, until abruptly the path curved and he emerged into the bright sunlight and saw before him the great gray bulk of a colossal mansion, hundreds of rooms topped by parapets and spires, with a massive portico from which vast columns of stairs descended. In wonder he moved toward it, for this was the building of his frequent fantasy, and as he approached he beheld the red and green and purple figures crossing the portico, those coiled and gnarled and looping shapes he had seen before, the eerie horde of alien travelers here to take in the wonders of Earth. Heads without eyes, eyes without heads, multiplicities of limbs and absences of limbs, bodies like tumors and tumors like bodies, all the universe's imagination on display in these agglomerated life-forms, so strange and yet not at all strange to him. But this time it was no fantasy. It fit smoothly into the sequence of the events of the day, rather than dropping, dreamlike, intrusive, into that sequence. Nor did it fade after a few moments; the scene remained sharp, never leaving him to plunge back into "real" life. This was reality itself, and he had experienced it before.

Twice more in the next few weeks things like that happened to him, until at last he was ready to admit the truth to himself about his fugues, that he was experiencing flashforwards as well as flashbacks, that he was being subjected to glimpses of his own future.

T'ang, the high king of the Shang, asked Hsia Chi saying, "In the beginning, were there already individual things?" Hsia Chi replied, "If there were no things then, how could there be any now? If later generations should pretend that there had been no things in our time, would they be right?" T'ang said, "Have things then no before and no after?" To which Hsia Chi replied, "The ends and the origins of things have no limit from which they began. The origin of one thing may be considered the end of another; the end of one may be considered the origin of the next. Who can distinguish accurately between these cycles? What lies beyond all things, and before all events, we cannot know."

They reach and enter the Perseus relay booster, which is a whirling celestial anomaly structurally similar to the Panama Canal but not nearly so potent, and it kicks the ship's velocity to just above a hundred lights. That is the voyage's final acceleration; the ship will maintain this rate for two and a half days, until it clocks in at Scylla, the main deceleration station for this part of the galaxy, where it will be seized by a spongy web of forces twenty light-minutes in diameter and slowed to sublight velocities for the entry into the Abbondanza system.

Skein spends nearly all of this period in his cabin, rarely eating and sleeping very little. He reads almost constantly, obsessively dredging from the ship's extensive library a wide and capricious assortment of books. Rilke. Kafka. Eddington, *The Nature of the Physical World.* Lowry, *Hear Us O Lord From Heaven Thy Dwelling Place.* Elias. Razhuminin. Dickey. Pound. Fraisse, *The Psychology of Time.* Greene, *Dream and Delusion.* Poe. Shakespeare. Marlowe. Tourneur. *The Waste Land. Ulysses. Heart of Darkness.* Bury, *The Idea of Progress.*

Jung. Büchner. Pirandello. *The Magic Mountain.* Ellis, *The Rack.*
Cervantes. Blenheim. Fierst. Keats. Nietzsche. His mind swims with
images and bits of verse, with floating sequences of dialogue, with
unscaffolded dialectics. He dips into each work briefly, magpielike,
seeking bright scraps. The words form a scaly impasto on the inner
surface of his skull. He finds that this heavy verbal overdose helps, to
some slight extent, to fight off the fugues; his mind is weighted,
perhaps, bound by this leaden clutter of borrowed genius to the moving
line of the present, and during his debauch of reading he finds himself
shifting off that line less frequently than in the recent past. His mind
whirls. *Man is a rope stretched between the animal and the Superman
—A rope over an abyss.* My patience are exhausted. *See, see where
Christ's blood streams in the firmament! One drop would save my soul.*
I had not thought death had undone so many. These fragments I have
shored against my ruins. *Hoogspanning. Levensgevaar. Peligro de
Muerte. Electricidad. Danger.* Give me my spear. *Old father, old
artificer, stand me now and ever in good stead.* You like this garden?
Why is it yours? We evict those who destroy! *And then went down to
the ship, set keel to breakers, forth on the godly sea.* There is no
"official" theory of time, defined in creeds or universally agreed upon
among Christians. Christianity is not concerned with the purely
scientific aspects of the subject nor, within wide limits, with its
philosophical analysis, except insofar as it is committed to a fundamen-
tally realist view and could not admit, as some Eastern philosophies
have done, that temporal existence is mere illusion. *A shudder in the
loins engenders there the broken wall, the burning roof and tower and
Agamemnon dead.* Stately, plump Buck Mulligan came from the
stairhead, bearing a bowl of lather on which a mirror and a razor lay
crossed. *In what distant deeps or skies burnt the fire of thine eyes? On
what wings dare he aspire? What the hand dare seize the fire?* These
fragments I have shored against my ruins. Hieronymo's mad againe.
*Then felt I like some watcher of the skies when a new planet swims
into his ken.* It has also lately been postulated that the physical concept
of information is identical with a phenomenon of reversal of entropy.
The psychologist must add a few remarks here: It does not seem
convincing to me that information is *eo ipso* identical with a *pouvoir*

d'organisation which undoes entropy. *Datta. Dayadhvam. Damyata. Shantih shantih shantih*

Nevertheless, once the ship is past Scylla and slowing toward the Abbondanza planets, the periods of fugue become frequent once again, so that he lives entrapped, shuttling between the flashing shadows of yesterday and tomorrow.

After the Coustakis overload he tried to go on in the old way, as best he could. He gave Coustakis a refund without even being asked, for he had been of no service, nor could he ever be. Instantaneous transportation of matter would have to wait. But Skein took other clients. He could still make the communion, after a fashion, and when the nature of the task was sufficiently low-level he could even deliver a decent synergetic response.

Often his work was unsatisfactory, however. Contacts would break at awkward moments, or, conversely, his filter mechanism would weaken and he would allow the entire contents of his client's mind to flow into that of his consultant. The results of such disasters were chaotic, involving him in heavy medical expenses and sometimes in damage suits. He was forced to place his fees on a contingency basis: no synergy, no pay. About half the time he earned nothing for his output of energy. Meanwhile his overhead remained the same as always: the domed office, the network of consultants, the research staff, and the rest. His effort to remain in business was eating rapidly into the bank accounts he had set aside against just such a time of storm.

They could find no organic injury to his brain. Of course, so little was known about a Communicator's gift that it was impossible to determine much by medical analysis. If they could not locate the center from which a Communicator powered his communions, how could they detect the place where he had been hurt? The medical archives were of no value; there had been eleven previous cases of overload, but each instance was physiologically unique. They told him he would eventually heal, and sent him away. Sometimes the doctors gave him silly therapies: counting exercises, rhythmic blinkings, hopping on his left leg and then his right, as if he had had a stroke. But he had not had a stroke.

For a time he was able to maintain his business on the momentum of his reputation. Then, as word got around that he had been hurt and was no longer any good, clients stopped coming. Even the contingency basis for fees failed to attract them. Within six months he found that he was lucky to find a client a week. He reduced his rates, and that seemed only to make things worse, so he raised them to something not far below what they had been at the time of the overload. For a while the pace of business increased, as if people were getting the impression that Skein had recovered. He gave such spotty service, though. Blurred and wavering communions, unanticipated positive feedbacks, filtering problems, information deficiencies, redundancy surpluses—"You take your mind in your hands when you go to Skein," they were saying now.

The fugues added to his professional difficulties.

He never knew when he would snap into hallucination. It might happen during a communion, and often did. Once he dropped back to the moment of the Coustakis-Nissenson hookup and treated a terrified client to a replay of his overload. Once, although he did not understand at the time what was happening, he underwent a flashforward and carried the client with him to a scarlet jungle on a formaldehyde world, and when Skein slipped back to reality the client remained in the scarlet jungle. There was a damage suit over that one, too.

Temporal dislocation plagued him into making poor guesses. He took on clients whom he could not possibly serve, and wasted his time on them. He turned away people whom he might have been able to help to his own profit. Since he was no longer anchored firmly to his time-line, but drifted in random oscillations of twenty years or more in either direction, he forfeited the keen sense of perspective on which he had previously founded his professional judgments. He grew haggard and lean, also. He passed through a tempest of spiritual doubts that amounted to total submission and then total rejection of faith within the course of four months. He changed lawyers almost weekly. He liquidated assets with invariably catastrophic timing to pay his cascading bills.

A year and a half after the overload, he formally renounced his registration and closed his office. It took six months more to settle the remaining damage suits. Then, with what was left of his money, he bought a spaceliner ticket and set out to search for a world with purple sand and blue-leaved trees, where, unless his fugues had played him false, he might be able to arrange for the repair of his broken mind.

Now the ship has returned to the conventional four-space and dawdles planetward at something rather less than half the speed of light. Across the screens there spreads a necklace of stars; space is crowded here. The captain will point out Abbondanza to anyone who asks: a lemon-colored sun, bigger than that of Earth, surrounded by a dozen bright planetary pips. The passengers are excited. They buzz, twitter, speculate, anticipate. No one is silent except Skein. He is aware of many love affairs; he has had to reject several offers just in the past three days. He has given up reading and is trying to purge his mind of all he has stuffed into it. The fugues have grown worse. He has to write notes to himself, saying things like *You are a passenger aboard a ship heading for Abbondanza VI, and will be landing in a few days,* so that he does not forget which of his three entangled time-lines is the true one.

Suddenly he is with Nilla on the island in the Gulf of Mexico, getting aboard the little excursion boat. Time stands still here; it could almost be the twentieth century. The frayed, sagging cords of the rigging. The lumpy engine inefficiently converted from internal combustion to turbines. The mustachioed Mexican bandits who will be their guides today. Nilla, nervously coiling her long blonde hair, saying, "Will I get seasick, John? The boat rides right in the water, doesn't it? It won't even hover a little bit?"

"Terribly archaic," Skein says. "That's why we're here."

The captain gestures them aboard. Juan, Francisco, Sebastián. Brothers. *Los hermanos.* Yards of white teeth glistening below the drooping mustaches. With a terrible roar the boat moves away from the dock. Soon the little town of crumbling pastel buildings is out of sight and they are heading jaggedly eastward along the coast, green shore-ward water on their left, the blue depths on the right. The morning sun coming up hard. "Could I sunbathe?" Nilla asks. Unsure of herself; he has never seen her this way, so hesitant, so abashed. Mexico has robbed her of her New York assurance. "Go ahead," Skein says. "Why not?"

She drops her robe. Underneath she wears only a waist-strap; her heavy breasts look white and vulnerable in the tropic glare, and the small nipples are a faded pink. Skein sprays her with protective sealant and she sprawls out on the deck. *Los hermanos* stare hungrily and talk to each other in low rumbling tones. Not Spanish. Mayan, perhaps? The natives have never learned to adopt the tourists' casual nudity here. Nilla, obviously still uneasy, rolls over and lies face down. Her broad smooth back glistens.

Juan and Francisco yell. Skein follows their pointing fingers. Porpoises! A dozen of them, frisking around the bow, keeping just ahead of the boat, leaping high and slicing down into the blue water. Nilla gives a little cry of joy and rushes to the side to get a closer look. Throwing her arm self-consciously across her bare breasts. "You don't need to do that," Skein murmurs. She keeps herself covered. "How lovely they are," she says softly. Sebastián comes up beside them. "*Amigos,*" he says. "They are. My friends." The cavorting porpoises eventually disappear. The boat bucks bouncily onward, keeping close to the island's beautiful empty palmy shore. Later they anchor, and he and Nilla swim masked, spying on the coral gardens. When they haul themselves on deck again it is almost noon. The sun is terrible. "Lunch?" Francisco asks. "We make you good lunch now?" Nilla laughs. She is no longer hiding her body. "I'm starved!" she cries.

"We make you good lunch," Francisco says, grinning, and he and Juan go over the side. In the shallow water they are clearly visible near the white sand of the bottom. They have spear-guns; they hold their breaths and prowl. Too late Skein realizes what they are doing. Francisco hauls a fluttering spiny lobster out from behind a rock. Juan impales a huge pale crab. He grabs three conchs also, surfaces, dumps his prey on the deck. Francisco arrives with the lobster. Juan, below again, spears a second lobster. The animals are not dead; they crawl sadly in circles on the deck as they dry. Appalled, Skein turns to Sebastián and says, "Tell them to stop. We're not that hungry." Sebastián, preparing some kind of salad, smiles and shrugs. Francisco has brought up another crab, bigger than the first. "Enough," Skein says. "*Basta! Basta!*" Juan, dripping, tosses down three more conchs. "You pay us good," he says. "We give you good lunch." Skein shakes his head. The deck is becoming a slaughterhouse for ocean life. Sebastián now energetically splits conch shells, extracts the meat, drops it into a vast bowl to marinate in a yellow-green fluid. *"Basta!"* Skein yells. Is that the right word in Spanish? He knows it's right in Italian. *Los hermanos* look amused. The sea is full of life, they seem to be telling him. We give you good lunch. Suddenly Francisco erupts from the water, bearing something immense. A turtle! Forty, fifty pounds! The joke has gone too far. "No," Skein says. "Listen, I have to forbid this. Those turtles are almost extinct. Do you understand that? *Muerto. Perdido. Desaparecido.* I won't eat a turtle. Throw it back. Throw it back." Francisco smiles. He shakes his head. Deftly he binds the turtle's flippers with rope. Juan says, "Not for lunch, *señor*. For us. For to sell. *Mucho dinero."* Skein can do nothing. Francisco and Sebastián have begun to hack up the crabs and lobsters. Juan slices peppers into the bowl where the conchs are marinating. Pieces of dead animals litter the deck. "Oh, I'm *starving*," Nilla says. Her waist-strap is off too, now. The turtle watches the whole scene, beady-eyed. Skein shudders. Auschwitz, he thinks. Buchenwald. For the animals it's Buchenwald every day.

Purple sand, blue-leaved trees. An orange sea gleaming not far to the west under a lemon sun. "It isn't much farther," the skull-faced man says. "You can make it. Step by step by step is how."

"I'm winded," Skein says. "Those hills—"

"I'm twice your age, and I'm doing fine."

"You're in better shape. I've been cooped up on spaceships for months and months."

"Just a short way on," says the skull-faced man. "About a hundred meters from the shore."

Skein struggles on. The heat is frightful. He has trouble getting a footing in the shifting sand. Twice he trips over black vines whose fleshy runners form a mat a few centimeters under the surface; loops of the vines stick up here and there. He even suffers a brief fugue, a seven-second flashback to a day in Jerusalem. Somewhere at the core of his mind he is amused by that: a flashback within a flashforward. Encapsulated concentric hallucinations. When he comes out of it, he finds himself getting to his feet and brushing sand from his clothing. Ten steps onward the skull-faced man halts him and says, "There it is. Look there, in the pit."

Skein sees a funnel-shaped crater right in front of him, perhaps five meters in diameter at ground level and dwindling to about half that width at its bottom, some six or seven meters down. The pit strikes him as a series of perfect circles making up a truncated cone. Its sides are smooth and firm, almost glazed, and the sand has a brown tinge. In the pit, resting peacefully on the flat floor, is something that looks like a golden amoeba the size of a large cat. A row of round blue-black eyes crosses the hump of its back. From the perimeter of its body comes a soft green radiance.

"Go down to it," the skull-faced man says. "The force of its power falls off with the cube of the distance; from up here you can't feel it. Go down. Let it take you over. Fuse with it. Make communion, Skein, make communion!"

"And will it heal me? So that I'll function as I did before the trouble started?"

"If you let it heal you, it will. That's what it wants to do. It's a completely benign organism. It thrives on repairing broken souls. Let it into your head; let it find the damaged place. You can trust it. Go down."

Skein trembles on the edge of the pit. The creature below flows and eddies, becoming first long and narrow, then high and squat, then resuming its basically circular form. Its color deepens almost to scarlet, and its radiance shifts toward yellow. As if preening and stretching itself. It seems to be waiting for him. It seems eager. This is what he has sought so long, going from planet to wearying planet. The skull-faced man, the purple sand, the pit, the creature. Skein slips his sandals off. *What have I to lose?* He sits for a moment on the pit's rim; then he shimmies down, sliding part of the way, and lands softly, close beside the being that awaits him. And immediately feels its power.

He enters the huge desolate cavern that is the cathedral of Haghia Sophia. A few Turkish guides lounge hopefully against the vast marble pillars. Tourists shuffle about, reading to each other from cheap plastic guidebooks. A shaft of light enters from some improbable aperture and splinters against the Moslem pulpit. It seems to Skein that he hears the tolling of bells and feels incense prickling at his nostrils. But how can that be? No Christian rites have been performed here in a thousand years. A Turk looms before him. "Show you the mosyics?" he says. *Mosyics.* "Help you understand this marvelous building? A dollar. No? Maybe change money? A good rate. Dollars, marks, Eurocredits, what? You speak English? Show you the mosyics?" The Turk fades. The bells grow louder. A row of bowed priests in white silk robes files past the altar, chanting in—what? Greek? The ceiling is encrusted with gems. Gold plate gleams everywhere. Skein senses the terrible complexity of the cathedral, teeming now with life, a whole universe engulfed in this gloom, a thousand chapels packed with worshippers, long lines waiting to urinate in the crypts, a marketplace in the balcony, jeweled necklaces changing hands with low murmurs of negotiation, babies being born behind the alabaster sarcophagi, the bells tolling, dukes nodding to one another, clouds of incense swirling toward the dome, the figures in the mosaics alive, making the sign of the Cross, smiling, blowing kisses, the pillars moving now, becoming fat-middled as they bend from side to side, the entire colossal structure shifting and flowing and melting. And a ballet of Turks. "Show you the mosyics?" "Change money?" "Postcards? Souvenir of Istanbul?" A plump, pink American face: "You're John Skein, aren't you? The Communicator? We worked together on the big fusion-chamber merger in '53." Skein shakes his head. "It must be that you are mistaken," he says, speaking in Italian. "I am not he. Pardon. Pardon." And joins the line of chanting priests.

Purple sand, blue-leaved trees. An orange sea under a lemon sun. Looking out from the top deck of the terminal, an hour after landing, Skein sees a row of towering hotels rising along the nearby beach. At once he feels the wrongness: there should be no hotels. The right planet has no such towers; therefore this is another of the wrong ones.

He suffers from complete disorientation as he attempts to place himself in sequence. *Where am I?* Aboard a liner heading toward Abbondanza VI. *What do I see?* A world I have previously visited. *Which one?* The one with the hotels. The third out of seven, isn't it?

He has seen this planet before, in flashforwards. Long before he left Earth to begin his quest he glimpsed those hotels, that beach. Now he views it in flashback. That perplexes him. He must try to see himself as a moving point traveling through time, viewing the scenery now from this perspective, now from that.

He watches his earlier self at the terminal. Once it was his future self. How confusing, how needlessly muddling! "I'm looking for an old Earthman," he says. "He must be a hundred, hundred twenty years old. A face like a skull—no flesh at all, really. A brittle man. No? Well, can you tell me, does this planet have a life-form about this big, a kind of blob of golden jelly, that lives in pits down by the seashore, and—No? No? Ask someone else, you say? Of course. And perhaps a hotel room? As long as I've come all this way."

He is getting tired of finding the wrong planets. What folly this is, squandering his last savings on a quest for a world seen in a dream! He would have expected planets with purple sand and blue-leaved trees to be uncommon, but no, in an infinite universe one can find a dozen of everything, and now he has wasted almost half his money and close to a year, visiting two planets and this one and not finding what he seeks.

He goes to the hotel they arrange for him.

The beach is packed with sunbathers, most of them from Earth. Skein walks among them. "Look," he wants to say, "I have this trouble with my brain, an old injury, and it gives me these visions of myself in the past and future, and one of the visions I see is a place where there's a skull-faced man who takes me to a kind of amoeba in a pit that can heal me, do you follow? And it's a planet with purple sand and blue-leaved trees, just like this one, and I figure if I keep going long enough I'm bound to find it and the skull-face and the amoeba, do you follow me? And maybe this is the planet after all, only I'm in the wrong part of it. What should I do? What hope do you think I really have?" This is the third world. He knows that he must visit a number of wrong ones before he finds the right one. But how many? How many? And when will he know that he has the right one?

Standing silent on the beach, he feels confusion come over him, and drops into fugue, and is hurled to another world. Purple sand, blue-leaved trees. A fat, friendly Pingalorian consul. "A skull-faced

man? No, I can't say I know of any." Which world is this, Skein
wonders? One that I have already visited, or one that I have not yet
come to? The manifold layers of illusion dazzle him. Past and future
and present lie like a knot around his throat. Shifting planes of reality;
intersecting films of event. Purple sand, blue-leaved trees. Which planet
is this? Which one? Which one? He is back on the crowded beach. A
lemon sun. An orange sea. He is back in his cabin on the spaceliner. He
sees a note in his own handwriting: *You are a passenger aboard a ship
heading for Abbondanza VI, and will be landing in a few days.* So
everything was a vision. Flashback? Flashforward? He is no longer able
to tell. He is baffled by these identical worlds. Purple sand. Blue-leaved
trees. He wishes he knew how to cry.

Instead of a client and a consultant for today's communion, Skein has a
client and a client. A man and a woman, Michaels and Miss
Schumpeter. The communion is of an unusually intimate kind.
Michaels has been married six times, and several of the marriages
apparently have been dissolved under bitter circumstances. Miss
Schumpeter, a woman of some wealth, loves Michaels but doesn't
entirely trust him; she wants a peep into his mind before she'll put her
thumb to the marital cube. Skein will oblige. The fee has already been
credited to his account. Let me not to the marriage of true minds admit
impediments. If she does not like what she finds in her beloved's soul,
there may not be any marriage, but Skein will have been paid.
     A tendril of his mind goes to Michaels, now. A tendril to Miss
Schumpeter. Skein opens his filters. "Now you'll meet for the first
time," he tells them. Michaels flows to her. Miss Schumpeter flows to
him. Skein is merely the conduit. Through him pass the ambitions,
betrayals, failures, vanities, deteriorations, disputes, treacheries, lusts,
generosities, shames, and follies of these two human beings. If he
wishes, he can examine the most private sins of Miss Schumpeter and
the darkest yearnings of her future husband. But he does not care. He
sees such things every day. He takes no pleasure in spying on the
psyches of these two. Would a surgeon grow excited over the sight of
Miss Schumpeter's Fallopian tubes or Michaels' pancreas? Skein is

merely doing his job. He is no voyeur, simply a Communicator. He looks upon himself as a public utility.

When he severs the contact, Miss Schumpeter and Michaels both are weeping.

"I love you!" she wails.

"Get away from me!" he mutters.

Purple sand. Blue-leaved trees. Oily orange sea.

The skull-faced man says, "Won't you ever come to see that causality is merely an illusion, Skein? The notion that there's a consecutive series of events is nothing but a fraud. We impose form on our lives, we talk of time's arrow, we say that there's a flow from A through G and Q to Z, we make believe everything is nicely linear. But it isn't, Skein. It isn't."

"So you keep telling me."

"I feel an obligation to awaken your mind to the truth. G can come before A, and Z before both of them. Most of us don't like to perceive it that way, so we arrange things in what seems like a more logical pattern, just as a novelist will put the motive before the murder and the murder before the arrest. But the universe isn't a novel. We can't make nature imitate art. It's all random, Skein, random, random!"

"Half a million?"

"Half a million."

"You know I don't have that kind of money."

"Let's not waste time, Mr. Coustakis. You have assets. Pledge them as collateral. Credit is easily obtained." Skein waits for the inventor to clear his loan. "Now we can proceed," he says, and tells his desk, "Get Nissenson into a receptive state."

Coustakis says, "First let me get it clear. This man will see everything that's in my mind? He'll get access to my secrets?"

"No. No. I filter the communion with great care. Nothing will pass from your mind to his except the nature of the problem you want him to tackle. Nothing will come back from his mind to yours except the answer."

"And if he doesn't have the answer?"

"He will."

"And if he goes into the transmission business for himself afterward?"

"He's bonded," Skein says curtly. "No chance of it. Let's go, now. Up and together."

"Skein? Skein? Skein? Skein?"

The wind is rising. The sand, blown aloft, stains the sky gray. Skein clambers from the pit and lies by its rim, breathing hard. The skull-faced man helps him get up.

Skein has seen this series of images hundreds of times.

"How do you feel?" the skull-faced man asks.

"Strange. Good. My head seems so clear!"

"You had communion down there?"

"Oh, yes. Yes."

"And?"

"I think I'm healed," Skein says in wonder. "My strength is back. Before, you know, I felt cut down to the bone, a minimum version of myself. And now. And now." He lets a tendril of consciousness slip forth. It meets the mind of the skull-faced man. Skein is aware of a glassy interface; he can touch the other mind, but he cannot enter it. "Are you a Communicator too?" Skein asks, awed.

"In a sense. I feel you touching me. You're better, aren't you?"

"Much. Much. Much."

"As I told you. Now you have your second chance, Skein. Your gift has been restored. Courtesy of our friend in the pit. They love being helpful."

"Skein? Skein? Skein? Skein?"

We conceive of time either as flowing or as enduring. The problem is how to reconcile these concepts. From a purely formalistic point of view there exists no difficulty, as these properties can be reconciled by means of the concept of a duratio successiva. *Every unit of time measure has this characteristic of a flowing permanence: an hour streams by while it lasts and so long as it lasts. Its flowing is thus identical with its duration. Time, from this point of view, is transitory; but its passing away lasts.*

In the early months of his affliction he experienced a great many scenes of flashforward while in fugue. He saw himself outside the nineteenth-century mansion, he saw himself in a dozen lawyers' offices, he saw himself in hotels, terminals, spaceliners, he saw himself discussing the nature of time with the skull-faced man, he saw himself trembling on the edge of the pit, he saw himself emerging healed, he saw himself wandering from world to world, looking for the right one with purple sand and blue-leaved trees. As time unfolded most of these flashforwards duly entered the flow of the present; he *did* come to the mansion, he *did* go to those hotels and terminals, he *did* wander those useless worlds. Now, as he approaches Abbondanza VI, he goes through a great many flashbacks and a relatively few flashforwards, and the flashforwards seem to be limited to a fairly narrow span of time, covering his landing on Abbondanza VI, his first meeting with the skull-faced man, his journey to the pit, and his emergence, healed, from the amoeba's lair. Never anything beyond that final scene. He wonders if time is going to run out for him on Abbondanza VI.

The ship lands on Abbondanza VI half a day ahead of schedule. There are the usual decontamination procedures to endure, and while they are going on Skein rests in his cabin, counting minutes to liberty. He is curiously confident that this will be the world on which he finds the skull-faced man and the benign amoeba. Of course, he has felt that way before, looking out from other spaceliners at other planets of the proper coloration, and he has been wrong. But the intensity of his confidence is something new. He is sure that the end of his quest lies here.

"Debarkation beginning now," the loudspeakers say.

He joins the line of outgoing passengers. The others smile, embrace, whisper; they have found friends or even mates on this voyage. He remains apart. No one says goodbye to him. He emerges into a brightly lit terminal, a great cube of glass that looks like all the other terminals scattered across the thousands of worlds that man has reached. He could be in Chicago or Johannesburg or Beirut: the scene is one of porters, reservations clerks, customs officials, hotel agents, taxi drivers, guides. A blight of sameness spreading across the universe. Stumbling through the customs gate, Skein finds himself set upon. Does he want a taxi, a hotel room, a woman, a man, a guide, a homestead plot, a servant, a ticket to Abbondanza VII, a private car, an interpreter, a bank, a telephone? The hubbub jolts Skein into three consecutive ten-second fugues, all flashbacks; he sees a rainy day in Tierra del Fuego, he conducts a communion to help a maker of sky-spectacles perfect the plot of his latest extravaganza, and he puts his palm to a cube in order to dictate contract terms to Nicholas Coustakis. Then Coustakis fades, the terminal reappears, and Skein realizes that someone has seized him by the left arm just above the elbow. Bony fingers dig painfully into his flesh. It is the skull-faced man. "Come with me," he says. "I'll take you where you want to go."

"This isn't just another flashforward, is it?" Skein asks, as he has watched himself ask so many times in the past. "I mean, you're really here to get me."

The skull-faced man says, as Skein has heard him say so many times in the past, "No, this time it's no flashforward. I'm really here to get you."

"Thank God. Thank God. Thank God."

"Follow along this way. You have your passport handy?"

The familiar words. Skein is prepared to discover he is merely in fugue, and expects to drop back into frustrating reality at any moment. But no. The scene does not waver. It holds firm. It holds. At last he has caught up with this particular scene, overtaking it and enclosing it, pearl-like, in the folds of the present. He is on the way out of the terminal. The skull-faced man helps him through the formalities. How withered he is! How fiery the eyes, how gaunt the face! Those frightening orbits of bone jutting through the skin of the forehead. That parched cheek. Skein listens for a dry rattle of ribs. One sturdy punch and there would be nothing left but a cloud of white dust, slowly settling.

"I know your difficulty," the skull-faced man says. "You've been caught in entropy's jaws. You're being devoured. The injury to your mind—it's tipped you into a situation you aren't able to handle. You *could* handle it, if you'd only learn to adapt to the nature of the perceptions you're getting now. But you won't do that, will you? And you want to be healed. Well, you can be healed here, all right. More or less healed. I'll take you to the place."

"What do you mean, I could handle it, if I'd only learn to adapt?"

"Your injury has liberated you. It's shown you the truth about time. But you refuse to see it."

"What truth?" Skein asks flatly.

"You still try to think that time flows neatly from alpha to omega, from yesterday through today to tomorrow," the skull-faced man says, as they walk slowly through the terminal. "But it doesn't. The idea of the forward flow of time is a deception we impose on ourselves in childhood. An abstraction, agreed upon by common convention, to make it easier for us to cope with phenomena. The truth is that events are random, that chronological flow is only our joint hallucination, that if time can be said to flow at all, it flows in all 'directions' at once. Therefore—"

"Wait," Skein says. "How do you explain the laws of thermodynamics? Entropy increases; available energy constantly diminishes; the universe heads toward ultimate stasis."

"Does it?"

"The second law of thermodynamics—"

"Is an abstraction," the skull-faced man says, "which unfortunately fails to correspond with the situation in the true universe. It isn't a divine law. It's a mathematical hypothesis developed by men who weren't able to perceive the real situation. They did their best to account for the data within a framework they could understand. Their laws are formulations of probability, based on conditions that hold within closed systems, and given the right closed system the second law is useful and illuminating. But in the universe as a whole it simply isn't true. There *is* no arrow of time. Entropy does *not* necessarily increase. Natural processes *can* be reversible. Causes do *not* invariably precede effects. In fact, the concepts of cause and effect are empty. There are neither causes nor effects, but only events, spontaneously generated, which we arrange in our minds in comprehensible patterns of sequence."

"No," Skein mutters. "This is insanity!"

"There are no patterns. Everything is random."

"No."

"Why not admit it? Your brain has been injured; what was destroyed was the center of temporal perception, the node that humans use to impose this unreal order on events. Your time filter has burned out. The past and the future are as accessible to you as the present, Skein: you can go where you like, you can watch events drifting past as they really do. Only you haven't been able to break up your old habits of thought. You still try to impose the conventional entropic order on things, even though you lack the mechanism to do it, now, and the conflict between what you perceive and what you think you perceive is driving you crazy. Eh?"

"How do you know so much about me?"

The skull-faced man chuckles. "I was injured in the same way as you. I was cut free from the time-line long ago, through the kind of overload you suffered. And I've had years to come to terms with the new reality. I was as terrified as you were, at first. But now I understand. I move about freely. I know things, Skein." A rasping laugh. "You need rest, though. A room, a bed. Time to think things over. Come. There's no rush now. You're on the right planet; you'll be all right soon."

Further, the association of entropy increase with time's arrow is in no sense circular; rather, it both tells us something about what will happen to natural systems in time, and about what the time order must be for a series of states of a system. Thus, we may often establish a time order among a set of events by use of the time-entropy association, free from any reference to clocks and magnitudes of time intervals from the present. In actual judgments of before-after we frequently do this on the basis of our experience (even though without any explicit knowledge of the law of entropy increase): we know, for example, that for iron in air the state of pure metal must have been before that of a rusted surface, or that the clothes will be dry after, not before, they have hung in the hot sun.

A tense, humid night of thunder and temporal storms. Lying alone in his oversized hotel room, five kilometers from the purple shore, Skein suffers fiercely from fugue.

"Listen, I have to forbid this. Those turtles are almost extinct. Do you understand that? *Muerto. Perdido. Desaparecido.* I won't eat a turtle. Throw it back. Throw it back."

"I'm happy to say your second go-round has been approved, Mr. Skein. Not that there was ever any doubt. A long and happy new life to you, sir."

"Go down to it. The force of its power falls off with the cube of the distance; from up here you can't feel it. Go down. Let it take you over. Fuse with it. Make communion, Skein, make communion!"

"Show you the mosyics? Help you understand this marvelous building? A dollar. No? Maybe change money? A good rate."

"First let me get it clear. This man will see everything that's in my mind? He'll get access to my secrets?"

"I love you."
   "Get away from me!"

"Won't you ever come to see that causality is merely an illusion, Skein? The notion that there's a consecutive series of events is nothing but a fraud. We impose form on our lives, we talk of time's arrow, we say that there's a flow from A through G and Q to Z, we make believe everything is nicely linear. But it isn't, Skein. It isn't."

Breakfast on a leafy veranda. Morning light out of the west, making the trees glow with an ultramarine glitter. The skull-faced man joins him. Skein secretly searches the parched face. Is everything an illusion? Perhaps *he* is an illusion.
   They walk toward the sea. Well before noon they reach the shore. The skull-faced man points to the south, and they follow the coast; it is often a difficult hike, for in places the sand is washed out and they must detour inland, scrambling over quartzy cliffs. The monstrous old man is indefatigable. When they pause to rest, squatting on a timeless purple

strand made smooth by the recent tide, the debate about time resumes, and Skein hears words that have been echoing in his skull for four years and more. It is as though everything up till now has been a rehearsal for a play, and now at last he has taken the stage.

"Won't you ever come to see that causality is merely an illusion, Skein?"

"I feel an obligation to awaken your mind to the truth."

"Time is an ocean, and events come drifting to us as randomly as dead animals on the waves."

Skein offers all the proper cues.

"I won't accept that! It's a demonic, chaotic, nihilistic theory."

"You can say that after all you've experienced?"

"I'll go on saying it. What I've been going through is a mental illness. Maybe I'm deranged, but the universe isn't."

"Contrary. You've only recently become sane and started to see things as they really are. The trouble is that you don't want to admit the evidence you've begun to perceive. Your filters are down, Skein! You've shaken free of the illusion of linearity! Now's your chance to show your resilience. Learn to live with the real reality. Stop this silly business of imposing an artificial order on the flow of time. Why *should* effect follow cause? Why *shouldn't* the seed follow the tree? Why must you persist in holding tight to a useless, outworn, contemptible system of false evaluations of experience when you've managed to break free of the—"

"Stop it! Stop it! Stop it! Stop it!"

By early afternoon they are many kilometers from the hotel, still keeping as close to the shore as they can. The terrain is uneven and divided, with rugged fingers of rock running almost to the water's edge, and Skein finds the journey even more exhausting than it had seemed in his visions of it. Several times he stops, panting, and has to be urged to go on.

"It isn't much farther," the skull-faced man says. "You can make it. Step by step is how."

"I'm winded. Those hills—"

"I'm twice your age, and I'm doing fine."

"You're in better shape. I've been cooped up on spaceships for months and months."

"Just a short way on," says the skull-faced man. "About a hundred meters from the shore."

Skein struggles on. The heat is frightful. He trips in the sand; he is blinded by sweat; he has a momentary flashback fugue. "There it is," the skull-faced man says, finally. "Look there, in the pit."

Skein beholds the conical crater. He sees the golden amoeba.

"Go down to it," the skull-faced man says. "The force of its power falls off with the cube of the distance; from up here you can't feel it. Go down. Let it take you over. Fuse with it. Make communion, Skein, make communion!"

"And will it heal me? So that I'll function as I did before the trouble started?"

"If you let it heal you, it will. That's what it wants to do. It's a completely benign organism. It thrives on repairing broken souls. Let it into your head; let it find the damaged place. You can trust it. Go down."

Skein trembles on the edge of the pit. The creature below flows and eddies, becoming first long and narrow, then high and squat, then resuming its basically circular form. Its color deepens almost to scarlet, and its radiance shifts toward yellow. As if preening and stretching itself. It seems to be waiting for him. It seems eager. This is what he has sought so long, going from planet to wearying planet. The skull-faced man, the purple sand, the pit, the creature. Skein slips his sandals off. *What have I to lose?* He sits for a moment on the pit's rim; then he shimmies down, sliding part of the way, and lands softly, close beside the being that awaits him. And immediately feels its power. Something brushes against his brain. The sensation reminds him of the training sessions of his first go-round, when the instructors were showing him how to develop his gift. The fingers probing his consciousness. Go on, enter, he tells them. I'm open. I'm open. And he finds himself in contact with the being of the pit. Wordless. A two-way flow of unintelligible images is the only communion; shapes drift from and into his mind. The universe blurs. He is no longer sure where the center of his ego lies. He has thought of his brain as a sphere with himself at its center, but now it seems extended, elliptical, and an ellipse has no center, only a pair of foci, here and here, one focus in his own skull and one—where?—within that fleshy amoeba. And suddenly he is looking at himself through the amoeba's eyes. The large biped with the bony body. How strange, how grotesque! Yet it suffers. Yet it must be helped. It is injured. It is broken. We go to it with all our love. We will heal. And Skein feels something flowing over the bare folds and fissures of his brain. But he can no longer remember whether he is the human or the alien, the bony one or the boneless. Their identities have mingled. He goes through fugues by the scores, seeing yesterdays and tomorrows, and everything is formless and without content; he is unable to recognize himself or to understand the words being spoken. It does not matter. All is random. All is illusion. Release the knot of pain you clutch within you. Accept. Accept. Accept. Accept.

He accepts.

He releases.

He merges.

He casts away the shreds of ego, the constricting exoskeleton of self, and placidly permits the necessary adjustments to be made.

The possibility, however, of genuine thermodynamic entropy decrease for an isolated system—no matter how rare—does raise an objection to the definition of time's direction in terms of entropy. If a large, isolated system did by chance go through an entropy decrease as one state evolved from another, we would have to say that time "went backward" if our definition of time's arrow were basically in terms of entropy increase. But with an ultimate definition of the forward direction of time in terms of the actual occurrence of states, and measured time intervals from the present, we can readily accommodate the entropy decrease; it would become merely a rare anomaly in the physical processes of the natural world.

The wind is rising. The sand, blown aloft, stains the sky gray. Skein clambers from the pit and lies by its rim, breathing hard. The skull-faced man helps him get up.

Skein has seen this series of images hundreds of times.

"How do you feel?" the skull-faced man asks.

"Strange. Good. My head seems clear!"

"You had communion down there?"

"Oh, yes. Yes."

"And?"

"I think I'm healed," Skein says in wonder. "My strength is back. Before, you know, I felt cut down to the bone, a minimum version of myself. And now. And now." He lets a tendril of consciousness slip forth. It meets the mind of the skull-faced man. Skein is aware of a glassy interface; he can touch the other mind, but he cannot enter it. "Are you a Communicator too?" Skein asks, awed.

"In a sense. I feel you touching me. You're better, aren't you?"

"Much. Much. Much."

"As I told you. Now you have your second chance, Skein. Your gift has been restored. Courtesy of our friend in the pit. They love being helpful."

"What shall I do now? Where shall I go?"

"Anything. Anywhere. Anywhen. You're free to move along the time-line as you please. In a state of controlled, directed fugue, so to speak. After all, if time is random, if there is no rigid sequence of events—"

"Yes."

"Then why not choose the sequence that appeals to you? Why stick to the set of abstractions your former self has handed you? You're a free man, Skein. Go. Enjoy. Undo your past. Edit it. Improve on it. It isn't your past, any more than this is your present. It's all one, Skein, all *one*. Pick the segment you prefer."

He tests the truth of the skull-faced man's words. Cautiously Skein steps three minutes into the past and sees himself struggling up out of the pit. He slides four minutes into the future and sees the skull-faced man, alone, trudging northward along the shore. Everything flows. All is fluidity. He is free. He is free.

"You see, Skein?"

"Now I do," Skein says. He is out of entropy's jaws. He is time's master, which is to say he is his own master. He can move at will. He can defy the imaginary forces of determinism. Suddenly he realizes what he must do now. He will assert his free will; he will challenge entropy on its home ground. Skein smiles. He cuts free of the time-line and floats easily into what others would call the past.

"Get Nissenson into a receptive state," he orders his desk.

Coustakis, blinking rapidly, obviously uneasy, says, "First let me get it clear. This man will see everything that's in my mind? He'll get access to my secrets?"

"No. No. I filter the communion with great care. Nothing will pass from your mind to his except the nature of the problem you want him to tackle. Nothing will come back from his mind to yours except the answer."

"And if he doesn't have the answer?"

"He will."

"And if he goes into the transmission business for himself afterward?" Coustakis asks.

"He's bonded," Skein says curtly. "No chance of it. Let's go, now. Up and together."

The desk reports that Nissenson, half the world away in São Paulo, is ready. Quickly Skein throws Coustakis into the receptive condition, and swings around to face the brilliant lights of his data-access units. Here is the moment when he can halt the transaction. Turn again, Skein. Face Coustakis, smile sadly, inform him that the communion will be impossible. Give him back his money, send him off to break some other Communicator's mind. And live on, whole and happy, ever after. It was at this point, visiting this scene endlessly in his fugues, that Skein silently and hopelessly cried out to himself to stop. Now it is within his power, for this is no fugue, no illusion of time-shift. He has shifted. He is here, carrying with him the knowledge of all that is to come, and he is the only Skein on the scene, the operative Skein. Get up, now. Refuse the contract.

He does not. Thus he defies entropy. Thus he breaks the chain.

He peers into the sparkling, shifting little blazes until they kindle his gift, jabbing at the electrical rhythms of his brain until he is lifted into the energy level that permits the opening of a communion. He starts to go up. He reaches forth one tendril of his mind and engages Nissenson. With another tendril he snares Coustakis. Steadily, now, he draws the two tendrils together. He is aware of the risks, but believes he can surmount them.

The tendrils meet.

Out of Coustakis' mind flows a description of the matter transmitter and a clear statement of the beam-spread problem; Skein shoves it along to Nissenson, who begins to work on a solution. The combined strength of the two minds is great, but Skein deftly lets the excess charge bleed away, and maintains the communion with no particular effort, holding Coustakis and Nissenson together while they deal with their technical matters. Skein pays little attention as their excited minds rush toward answers. *If you. Yes, and then. But if. I see, yes. I could. And. However, maybe I should. I like that. It leads to. Of course. The inevitable result. Is it feasible, though? I think so. You might have to. I could. Yes. I could. I could.*

"I thank you a million times," Coustakis says to Skein. "It was all so simple, once we saw how we ought to look at it. I don't begrudge your fee at all. Not at all."

Coustakis leaves, glowing with delight. Skein, relieved, tells his desk, "I'm going to allow myself a three-day holiday. Fix the schedule to move everybody up accordingly."

He smiles. He strides across his office, turning up the amplifiers, treating himself to the magnificent view. The nightmare undone. The past revised. The burnout avoided. All it took was confidence. Enlightenment. A proper understanding of the processes involved.

He feels the sudden swooping sensations of incipient temporal fugue. Before he can intervene to regain control, he swings off into darkness and arrives instantaneously on a planet of purple sand and blue-leaved trees. Orange waves lap at the shore. He stands a few meters from a deep conical pit. Peering into it, he sees an amoebalike creature lying beside a human figure; strands of the alien's jellylike substance are wound around the man's body. He recognizes the man to be John Skein. The communion in the pit ends; the man begins to clamber from the pit. The wind is rising. The sand, blown aloft, stains the sky gray. Patiently he watches his younger self struggling up from the pit. Now he understands. The circuit is closed; the knot is tied; the identity loop is complete. He is destined to spend many years on Abbondanza VI, growing ancient and withered. He is the skull-faced man.

Skein reaches the rim of the pit and lies there, breathing hard. He helps Skein get up.

"How do you feel?" he asks.

13

THE WIND AND
THE RAIN

The planet cleanses itself. That is the important thing to remember, at moments when we become too pleased with ourselves. The healing process is a natural and inevitable one. The action of the wind and the rain, the ebbing and flowing of the tides, the vigorous rivers flushing out the choked and stinking lakes—these are all natural rhythms, all healthy manifestations of universal harmony. Of course, we are here too. We do our best to hurry the process along. But we are only auxiliaries, and we know it. We must not exaggerate the value of our work. False pride is worse than a sin: it is a foolishness. We do not deceive ourselves into thinking we are important. If we were not here at all, the planet would repair itself anyway within 20 to 50 million years. It is estimated that our presence cuts that time down by somewhat more than half.

The uncontrolled release of methane into the atmosphere was one of the most serious problems. Methane is a colorless, odorless gas, sometimes known as "swamp gas." Its components are carbon and hydrogen. Much of the atmosphere of Jupiter and Saturn consists of methane. (Jupiter and Saturn have never been habitable by human beings.) A small amount of methane was always normally present in the atmosphere of Earth. However, the growth of human population produced a consequent increase in the supply of methane. Much of the methane released into the atmosphere came from swamps and coal mines. A great deal of it came from Asian rice-fields fertilized with human or animal waste; methane is a byproduct of the digestive process.

The surplus methane escaped into the lower stratosphere, from 10 to 30 miles above the surface of the planet, where a layer of ozone molecules once existed. Ozone, formed of three oxygen atoms, absorbs the harmful ultraviolet radiation that the sun emits. By reacting with free oxygen atoms in the stratosphere, the intrusive methane reduced the quantity available for ozone formation. Moreover, methane reactions in the stratosphere yielded water vapor that further depleted the ozone. This methane-induced exhaustion of the ozone content of the stratosphere permitted the unchecked ultraviolet bombardment of the Earth, with a consequent rise in the incidence of skin cancer.

A major contributor to the methane increase was the flatulence of domesticated cattle. According to the U.S. Department of Agriculture, domesticated ruminants in the late twentieth century were generating more than 85 million tons of methane a year. Yet nothing was done to check the activities of these dangerous creatures. Are you amused by the idea of a world destroyed by herds of farting cows? It must not have been amusing to the people of the late twentieth century. However, the extinction of domesticated ruminants shortly helped to reduce the impact of this process.

Today we must inject colored fluids into a major river. Edith, Bruce, Paul, Elaine, Oliver, Ronald, and I have been assigned to this task. Most members of the team believe the river is the Mississippi, although there is some evidence that it may be the Nile. Oliver, Bruce, and Edith believe it is more likely to be the Nile than the Mississippi, but they defer to the opinion of the majority. The river is wide and deep and its color is black in some places and dark green in others. The fluids are computer-mixed on the east bank of the river in a large factory erected by a previous reclamation team. We supervise their passage into the river. First we inject the red fluid, then the blue, then the yellow; they have different densities and form parallel stripes running for many hundreds of kilometers in the water. We are not certain whether these fluids are active healing agents—that is, substances which dissolve the solid pollutants lining the riverbed—or merely serve as markers permitting further chemical analysis of the river by the orbiting satellite system. It is not necessary for us to understand what we are doing, so long as we follow instructions explicitly. Elaine jokes about going swimming. Bruce says, "How absurd. This river is famous for deadly fish that will strip the flesh from your bones." We all laugh at that. *Fish?* Here? What fish could be as deadly as the river itself? This water would consume our flesh if we entered it, and probably dissolve our bones as well. I scribbled a poem yesterday and dropped it in, and the paper vanished instantly.

In the evenings we walk along the beach and have philosophical discussions. The sunsets on this coast are embellished by rich tones of purple, green, crimson, and yellow. Sometimes we cheer when a particularly beautiful combination of atmospheric gases transforms the sunlight. Our mood is always optimistic and gay. We are never depressed by the things we find on this planet. Even devastation can be an art-form, can it not? Perhaps it is one of the greatest of all art-forms, since an art of destruction *consumes* its medium, it *devours* its own epistemological foundations, and in this sublimely nullifying doubling-back upon its origins it far exceeds in moral complexity those forms which are merely productive. That is, I place a higher value on transformative art than on generative art. Is my meaning clear? In any event, since art ennobles and exalts the spirits of those who perceive it, we are exalted and ennobled by the conditions on Earth. We envy those who collaborated to create those extraordinary conditions. We know ourselves to be small-souled folk of a minor latter-day epoch; we lack the dynamic grandeur of energy that enabled our ancestors to commit such depredations. This world is a symphony. Naturally you might argue that to restore a planet takes more energy than to destroy it, but you would be wrong. Nevertheless, though our daily tasks leave us weary and drained, we also feel stimulated and excited, because by restoring this world, the mother-world of mankind, we are in a sense participating in the original splendid process of its destruction. I mean in the sense that the resolution of a dissonant chord participates in the dissonance of that chord.

Now we have come to Tokyo, the capital of the island empire of Japan. See how small the skeletons of the citizens are? That is one way we have of identifying this place as Japan. The Japanese are known to have been people of small stature. Edward's ancestors were Japanese. He is of small stature. (Edith says his skin should be yellow as well. His skin is just like ours. Why is his skin not yellow?) "See?" Edward cries. "There is Mount Fuji!" It is an extraordinarily beautiful mountain, mantled in white snow. On its slopes one of our archaeological teams is at work, tunneling under the snow to collect samples from the twentieth-century strata of chemical residues, dust, and ashes. "Once there were over 75,000 industrial smokestacks around Tokyo," says Edward proudly, "from which were released hundreds of tons of sulfur, nitrous oxides, ammonia, and carbon gases every day. We should not forget that this city had more than 1,500,000 automobiles as well." Many of the automobiles are still visible, but they are very fragile, worn to threads by the action of the atmosphere. When we touch them they collapse in puffs of gray smoke. Edward, who has studied his heritage well, tells us, "It was not uncommon for the density of carbon monoxide in the air here to exceed the permissible levels by factors of 250% on mild summer days. Owing to atmospheric conditions, Mount Fuji was visible only one day of every nine. Yet no one showed dismay." He conjures up for us a picture of his small, industrious yellow ancestors toiling cheerfully and unremittingly in their poisonous environment. The Japanese, he insists, were able to maintain and even increase their gross national product at a time when other nationalities had already begun to lose ground in the global economic struggle because of diminished population owing to unfavorable ecological factors. And so on and so on. After a time we grow bored with Edward's incessant boasting. "Stop boasting," Oliver tells him, "or we will expose you to the atmosphere." We have much dreary work to do here. Paul and I guide the huge trenching machines; Oliver and Ronald follow, planting seeds. Almost immediately, strange angular shrubs spring up. They have shiny bluish leaves and long crooked branches. One of them seized Elaine by the throat yesterday and might have hurt her seriously had Bruce not uprooted it. We were not upset. This is merely one phase in the long, slow process of repair. There will be many such incidents. Some day cherry trees will blossom in this place.

This is the poem that the river ate:

DESTRUCTION

I. *Nouns.* Destruction, desolation, wreck, wreckage, ruin, ruination, rack and ruin, smash, smashup, demolition, demolishment, ravagement, havoc, ravage, dilapidation, decimation, blight, breakdown, consumption, dissolution, obliteration, overthrow, spoilage; mutilation, disintegration, undoing, pulverization; sabotage, vandalism; annulment, damnation, extinguishment, extinction, invalidation, nullification, shatterment, shipwreck; annihilation, disannulment, discreation, extermination, extirpation, obliteration, perdition, subversion.

II. *Verbs.* Destroy, wreck, ruin, ruinate, smash, demolish, raze, ravage, gut, dilapidate, decimate, blast, blight, break down, consume, dissolve, overthrow; mutilate, disintegrate, unmake, pulverize; sabotage, vandalize; annul, blast, blight, damn, dash, extinguish, invalidate, nullify, quell, quench, scuttle, shatter, shipwreck, torpedo, smash, spoil, undo, void; annihilate, devour, disannul, discreate, exterminate, obliterate, extirpate, subvert; corrode, erode, sap, undermine, waste, waste away, whittle away (*or* down); eat away, canker, gnaw; wear away, abrade, batter, excoriate, rust.

III. *Adjectives.* Destructive, ruinous, vandalistic, baneful, cutthroat, fell, lethiferous, pernicious, slaughterous, predatory, sinistrous, nihilistic; corrosive, erosive, cankerous, caustic, abrasive.

"I validate," says Ethel.
"I unravage," says Oliver.
"I integrate," says Paul.
"I devandalize," says Elaine.
"I unshatter," says Bruce.
"I unscuttle," says Edward.
"I discorrode," says Ronald.
"I undesolate," says Edith.
"I create," say I.
We reconstitute. We renew. We repair. We reclaim. We refurbish. We restore. We renovate. We rebuild. We reproduce. We redeem.

We reintegrate. We replace. We reconstruct. We retrieve. We revivify. We resurrect. We fix, overhaul, mend, put in repair, retouch, tinker, cobble, patch, darn, staunch, calk, splice. We celebrate our successes by energetic and lusty singing. Some of us copulate.

Here is an outstanding example of the dark humor of the ancients. At a place called Richland, Washington, there was an installation that manufactured plutonium for use in nuclear weapons. This was done in the name of "national security," that is, to enhance and strengthen the safety of the United States of America and render its inhabitants carefree and hopeful. In a relatively short span of time these activities produced approximately 55 million gallons of concentrated radioactive waste. This material was so intensely hot that it would boil spontaneously for decades, and would retain a virulently toxic character for many thousands of years. The presence of so much dangerous waste posed a severe environmental threat to a large area of the United States. How, then, to dispose of this waste? An appropriately comic solution was devised. The plutonium installation was situated in a seismically unstable area located along the earthquake belt that rings the Pacific Ocean. A storage site was chosen nearby, directly above a fault line that had produced a violent earthquake half a century earlier. Here 140 steel and concrete tanks were constructed just below the surface of the ground and some 240 feet above the water table of the Columbia River, from which a densely populated region derived its water supply. Into these tanks the boiling radioactive wastes were poured: a magnificent gift to future generations. Within a few years the true subtlety of the jest became apparent when the first small leaks were detected in the tanks. Some observers predicted that no more than 10 to 20 years would pass before the great heat caused the seams of the tanks to burst, releasing radioactive gases into the atmosphere or permitting radioactive fluids to escape into the river. The designers of the tanks maintained, though, that they were sturdy enough to last at least a century. It will be noted that this was something less than 1% of the known half-life of the materials placed in the tanks. Because of discontinuities in the records, we are unable to determine which estimate was more nearly correct. It should be possible for our decontamination squads to enter the affected regions in 800 to 1300 years. This episode arouses tremendous admiration in me. How much gusto, how much robust wit, those old ones must have had!

We are granted a holiday so we may go to the mountains of Uruguay to visit the site of one of the last human settlements, perhaps the very last. It was discovered by a reclamation team several hundred years ago and has been set aside, in its original state, as a museum for the tourists who one day will wish to view the mother-world. One enters through a lengthy tunnel of glossy pink brick. A series of airlocks prevents the outside air from penetrating. The village itself, nestling between two craggy spires, is shielded by a clear shining dome. Automatic controls maintain its temperature at a constant mild level. There were a thousand inhabitants. We can view them in the spacious plazas, in the taverns, and in places of recreation. Family groups remain together, often with their pets. A few carry umbrellas. Everyone is in an unusually fine state of preservation. Many of them are smiling. It is not yet known why these people perished. Some died in the act of speaking, and scholars have devoted much effort, so far without success, to the task of determining and translating the last words still frozen on their lips. We are not allowed to touch anyone, but we may enter their homes and inspect their possessions and toilet furnishings. I am moved almost to tears, as are several of the others. "Perhaps these are our very ancestors," Ronald exclaims. But Bruce declares scornfully, "You say ridiculous things. Our ancestors must have escaped from here long before the time these people lived." Just outside the settlement I find a tiny glistening bone, possibly the shinbone of a child, possibly part of a dog's tail. "May I keep it?" I ask our leader. But he compels me to donate it to the museum.

The archives yield much that is fascinating. For example, this fine example of ironic distance in ecological management. In the ocean off a place named California were tremendous forests of a giant seaweed called kelp, housing a vast and intricate community of maritime creatures. Sea urchins lived on the ocean floor, 100 feet down, amid the holdfasts that anchored the kelp. Furry aquatic mammals known as sea otters fed on the urchins. The Earth people removed the otters because they had some use for their fur. Later, the kelp began to die. Forests many square miles in diameter vanished. This had serious commercial consequences, for the kelp was valuable and so were many of the animal forms that lived in it. Investigation of the ocean floor showed a great increase in sea urchins. Not only had their natural enemies, the otters, been removed, but the urchins were taking nourishment from the immense quantities of organic matter in the sewage discharges dumped into the ocean by the Earth people. Millions of urchins were nibbling at the holdfasts of the kelp, uprooting the huge plants and killing them. When an oil tanker accidentally released its cargo into the sea, many urchins were killed and the kelp began to re-establish itself. But this proved to be an impractical means of controlling the urchins. Encouraging the otters to return was suggested, but there was not a sufficient supply of living otters. The kelp foresters of California solved their problem by dumping quicklime into the sea from barges. This was fatal to the urchins; once they were dead, healthy kelp plants were brought from other parts of the sea and embedded to become the nucleus of a new forest. After a while the urchins returned and began to eat the kelp again. More quicklime was dumped. The urchins died and new kelp was planted. Later, it was discovered that the quicklime was having harmful effects on the ocean floor itself, and other chemicals were dumped to counteract those effects. All of this required great ingenuity and a considerable outlay of energy and resources. Edward thinks there was something very Japanese about these maneuvers. Ethel points out that the kelp trouble would never have happened if the Earth people had not originally removed the otters. How naive Ethel is! She has no understanding of the principles of irony. Poetry bewilders her also. Edward refuses to sleep with Ethel now.

In the final centuries of their era the people of Earth succeeded in paving the surface of their planet almost entirely with a skin of concrete and metal. We must pry much of this up so that the planet may start to breathe again. It would be easy and efficient to use explosives or acids, but we are not overly concerned with ease and efficiency; besides there is great concern that explosives or acids may do further ecological harm here. Therefore we employ large machines that insert prongs in the great cracks that have developed in the concrete. Once we have lifted the paved slabs they usually crumble quickly. Clouds of concrete dust blow freely through the streets of these cities, covering the stumps of the buildings with a fine, pure coating of grayish-white powder. The effect is delicate and refreshing. Paul suggested yesterday that we may be doing ecological harm by setting free this dust. I became frightened at the idea and reported him to the leader of our team. Paul will be transferred to another group.

Toward the end here they all wore breathing-suits, similar to ours but even more comprehensive. We find these suits lying around everywhere like the discarded shells of giant insects. The most advanced models were complete individual housing units. Apparently it was not necessary to leave one's suit except to perform such vital functions as sexual intercourse and childbirth. We understand that the reluctance of the Earth people to leave their suits even for those functions, near the close, immensely hastened the decrease in population.

Our philosophical discussions. God created this planet. We all agree on that, in a manner of speaking, ignoring for the moment definitions of such concepts as "God" and "created." Why did He go to so much trouble to bring Earth into being, if it was His intention merely to have it rendered uninhabitable? Did He create mankind especially for this purpose, or did they exercise free will in doing what they did here? Was mankind God's way of taking vengeance against His own creation? Why would He want to take vengeance against his own creation? Perhaps it is a mistake to approach the destruction of Earth from the moral or ethical standpoint. I think we must see it in purely esthetic terms, i.e., a self-contained artistic achievement, like a *fouetté en tournant* or an *entrechat-dix*, performed for its own sake and requiring no explanations. Only in this way can we understand how the Earth people were able to collaborate so joyfully in their own asphyxiation.

My tour of duty is almost over. It has been an overwhelming experience; I will never be the same. I must express my gratitude for this opportunity to have seen Earth almost as its people knew it. Its rusted streams, its corroded meadows, its purpled skies, its bluish puddles. The debris, the barren hillsides, the blazing rivers. Soon, thanks to the dedicated work of reclamation teams such as ours, these superficial but beautiful emblems of death will have disappeared. This will be just another world for tourists, of sentimental curiosity but no unique value to the sensibility. How dull that will be: a green and pleasant Earth once more, why, why? The universe has enough habitable planets; at present it has only one Earth. Has all our labor here been an error, then? I sometimes do think it was misguided of us to have undertaken this project. But on the other hand I remind myself of our fundamental irrelevance. The healing process is a natural and inevitable one. With us or without us, the planet cleanses itself. The wind, the rain, the tides. We merely help things along.

A rumor reaches us that a colony of live Earthmen has been found on the Tibetan plateau. We travel there to see if this is true. Hovering above a vast red empty plain, we see large dark figures moving slowly about. Are these Earthmen, inside breathing suits of a strange design? We descend. Members of other reclamation teams are already on hand. They have surrounded one of the large creatures. It travels in a wobbly circle, uttering indistinct cries and grunts. Then it comes to a halt, confronting us blankly as if defying us to embrace it. We tip it over; it moves its massive limbs dumbly but is unable to arise. After a brief conference we decide to dissect it. The outer plates lift easily. Inside we find nothing but gears and coils of gleaming wire. The limbs no longer move, although things click and hum within it for quite some time. We are favorably impressed by the durability and resilience of these machines. Perhaps in the distant future such entities will wholly replace the softer and more fragile life-forms on all worlds, as they seem to have done on Earth.

The wind. The rain. The tides. All sadnesses flow to the sea.